SAHM I Am

D0957317

To my best friend and husband, Jason, for your
unconditional love and unwavering belief in me,

To my daughters, Jessamyn and Catrin,
for giving me the blessings of mommyhood,

And to my brother, Timothy,
for laughing at my stories of domestic bliss
and encouraging me to write them in a book.

Meredith Efken
SAHM I Am

Steeple
Hill
Café

Published by Steeple Hill Books™

STEEPLE HILL BOOKS

ISBN 0-373-78551-8

SAHM I AM

Copyright © 2005 by Meredith Efken

Photo credit: Ron Sammons

This edition published by arrangement with Steeple Hill Books.

® and TM are trademarks of Steeple Hill Books, used under license.
Trademarks indicated with ® are registered in the United States Patent
and Trademark Office, the Canadian Trade Marks Office and in other
countries.

www.SteepleHill.com

Printed in U.S.A.

Acknowledgments

My own mommy stories alone could never have filled an entire book. I am especially grateful to the following moms whose humorous anecdotes and life experiences inspired or helped me create many of the events in my book: Joan Hall, Daisy Witherell Déry, Nicole Small, Allison Wilson, Kathy Fuller, Vickie McDonough, Barbara Curtis, Tina Pinson, Megan DiMaria, Tricia Nguyen and Amy Kampfer.

A young mom like me finds it difficult to travel around the country to find out what autumn is like in Washington, or how to "talk Texan," so I rely on my many Internet friends to help me research their local settings. Anything I got right is due to their help, and anything I got wrong is my own fault. A big thank-you to these friends who shared with me what life is like in their corners of the U.S.: Linda Baldwin, Wanda Brunstetter, Sunni Jeffers, Lynette Sowell, Mary DeMuth, Eileen Key, Staci Stallings, Marion Bullock, Karen Witemeyer, Donna Gilbert, DiAnn Mills and Kathleen Y'Barbo.

I could not have brought life to the fictional SAHM I Am e-mail loop without having experienced the joys and trials of belonging to several e-mail communities. The loop for members of American Christian Fiction Writers is an excellent example of the support, encouragement and friendship available through the Internet, and I thank God for the privilege of being part of their fellowship.

Writing a book can be a lonely experience, but thanks to a support network of authors, agents, editors and friends, I've found my heart gladdened and my writing skills sharpened. A special thank-you to Ron Sammons of A Finer Choice, LLC, for making my author photo look so nice. He's been a friend to my family for many years, and it was a privilege to have him involved with my book in this way. I so appreciate those who have read my manuscript, in whole or part, or who have helped me with other aspects of writing this book: Camy Tang, Kristin Billerbeck, Mary Griffith and Brandilyn Collins. In addition, the following people have my deepest respect and appreciation for the contributions they've made in my life and my career:

Deb Raney—fellow author who has given me encouragement, advice and a great education about the behind-the-scenes life of an author. When I first started writing, I begged God to give me a mentor, and in Deb, He supplied more than that. He gave me a special friend.

Andrea Boeshaar—part coach, part cheerleader and 100% wonderful agent who believes in me even when I doubt myself, and whose hard work and commitment to my books helped me turn my dream of becoming an author into reality.

Randy Ingermanson—another dear friend and fellow author who read my manuscript in draft form and gave me a great critique. In addition to sharing my book with his daughters (who decided to give Rosalyn's "Father's Homecoming" ideas a test-drive, resulting in much hilarity in the Ingermanson household), he always looks for a chance to encourage me, promote my book, make me laugh and help me become a better writer. His generosity and friendship is such a blessing.

Stephenie McBride—my best friend and former college roommate. It's not often that a writer is blessed with a friend who is also an avid reader and an expert in the book's subject matter, but I am so blessed. Steph read my book in manuscript form and also helped me with several areas of research. I'm grateful for her feedback and for sharing her experiences with me and for being a sister of my heart for so many years.

Krista Stroever—my editor at Steeple Hill, who was willing to take a chance on my crazy book, nontraditional format, unique subject matter and all. I've learned a lot working with her, and I'm a better writer because of it.

From:	VIM <vivalaveronica@marcelloportraits.com>
To:	Rosalyn Ebberly <prov31woman@home.com>
Subject:	**Home from Italy**

Hey Honey Sis!

Just little ol' me, letting all y'all know we're home from Italy. Great to be back on our native TEXAS soil. Frank and I were so disappointed you couldn't make it to the wedding, though we understand it was short notice, bless your heart. Mama and Daddy said it was the most beautiful wedding in the world. I thought that was a tad insensitive considering your wedding was pretty, too, but I do believe mine was the day of my dreams—designer gown, gorgeous Italian husband, sunset on the beach, all my friends. And dear Patricia gave me a promotion and a raise as a wedding gift. You'd have had to scrape me off the floor I was so surprised! I'll be headed back to work tomorrow with a ring on my finger and the title of senior public relations manager for the biggest marketing firm in Houston!

I wish you could see how great Ashley, Courtney and Stanley took to their new Nana and Papa. Mama and Daddy were fussing over them so much, you'd never know they already have three grandchildren. How ARE y'all's sweet little kiddos, anyway? I can't hardly wait for them to meet my stepchildren. My darlings and me just love each other to pieces already—the poor dears needed a mother. Frank and them treat me like I'm some hero, bless their hearts. And Mama said if there was a mother-of-the-year award, I deserved it, taking on a 9-, 6-, and 4-year-old, and me only 30 years old! I said, "Well, Rosalyn just turned 32, and she has 3 kids." Mama laughed and said, "True, but she doesn't have any career or social life, so what else could she do but have children?"

I'm attaching pictures of the wedding and our Italian honeymoon. Frank took all the Italy pictures, and he's already griping about the wedding photos. But he's such an artist about his photography, I didn't expect nothing else. So there ya go. Enjoy!

Ciao,

Mrs. Veronica Marcello, WIFE of Francesco Marcello (doesn't that sound beautiful?)

From:	Rosalyn Ebberly <prov31woman@home.com>
To:	SAHM I Am <sahmiam@loophole.com>
Subject:	**[SAHM I Am] TOTW August 2:** **Positive Self-image**

Blessed Mothers,

I hope you are having a FABULOUS day at home with your precious little ones. I know I am. It's a sunny, beautiful morning here in Hibiscus, WA. Jefferson, my five-year-old, just gave me a bouquet of flowers he picked from our garden. He gave me a kiss and said, "Daddy gives you flowers so I wanted to, too." Isn't that just the sweetest thing?

Our Topic of the Week is all about how to have a healthy self-image without being self-centered. Some ways I do that are:

1) Make a list of all the nice things people say about me. (This took a while since there were many things to write.)

2) Make a list of all the things I'm good at.

3) Make a list of my best accomplishments.

4) Make a list of things I need to improve. (Fortunately, this was relatively short.)

5) Write out all the verses in the Bible that talk about how much God loves me. (I whipped this one out during my quiet time this morning. It only took two hours, leaving me with enough time to go jogging before my children woke up and DH had to leave for work.)

As you can see, I'm into lists. What about you ladies? What can you do to promote a positive self-image?

As always, humbled to be serving you as,

Rosalyn Ebberly

SAHM I AM Loop Moderator

"She looks well to the ways of her household, and does not eat the bread of idleness."

Proverbs 31:27 (NASB)

From:	Zelia Muzuwa <zeemuzu@vivacious.com>
To:	SAHM I Am <sahmiam@loophole.com>
Subject:	**[SAHM I AM] Are worms poisonous?**

'cause Griffith just ate one.

Z

From:	The Millards <jstcea4jesus@familymail.net>
To:	SAHM I Am <sahmiam@loophole.com>
Subject:	**Re: [SAHM I AM] Are worms poisonous?**

Zelia,

No, he'll be fine. Tyler ate a lizard when he was 2, and he's managed to survive to the ripe old age of 8. Don't worry.

Speaking of Tyler, you all have to cheer for his soccer team tomorrow night. Go PIKES!!!

Jocelyn

From:	Zelia Muzuwa <zeemuzu@vivacious.com>
To:	SAHM I Am <sahmiam@loophole.com>
Subject:	**Re: [SAHM I AM] Are worms poisonous?**

That's a relief. Of course, I should be more worried about whether or not Seamus will live to see his 7th birthday. Turns out, he talked little brother into swallowing the worm. Threatened to cut the head off Griffith's Big Bird if he didn't chow down. When Tristan got home, Seamus had to confess it all to daddy.

So Tristan puts on his James Earl Jones voice, all low and rumbly with that Zimbabwean/English accent (oooh, gives me tingles just thinking about it) and looks WAYYYY down at Seamus, whose little brown body is now trembling in boxer pj's. "Seamus," he says, "did you force your brother to eat a worm?"

Seamus has the nerve to squeak out that he did not FORCE Griffith to eat the worm, he merely SUGGESTED that it might be the only way to save Big Bird. So Tristan says, "Son, you will go TO your room, and I will dee-al with you in a moment." I tell you, even I shivered at that. No one is as good at sounding ominous and foreboding as my husband!

Daddy's little girl, Cosette, knows no fear. She marches over to him, looks up with those huge brown eyes and says, "Daddy, be careful with Seamus. He's still in his formative years."

Tristan remains granite-faced. He taps Cosette's nose and says, "Yes, little one, and so he shall be formed, while there's still time for it." I just LOVE how he talks!

The short of it is that Seamus will not be able to go with us to the children's museum tomorrow, but instead has to stay with Molly—a friend of mine who has a five-year-old girl, Allison, who loves to play "getting married" and makes Seamus be the groom every time we visit. A worse punishment couldn't be found!

So, to quote the Bard, "All's well that ends well" and "Come, come, you froward and unable worms!"

Z

From:	Connie Lawson <clmo5@home.com>
To:	SAHM I Am <sahmiam@loophole.com>
Subject:	[SAHM I AM] Topic of the Week/Reminder

Hi Girls,

Loop Mom Connie here. I just wanted to send a friendly reminder to put OT for "Off Topic" in the subject heading of e-mails not pertaining to the weekly topic. We have over three hundred moms on this loop, and including OT in the subject helps us sort through the e-mails we aren't interested in. Not that I'm not interested in all the little details of your lives, like worms and soccer games, but we really need to focus.

TTFN,

Connie Lawson

SAHM I AM Loop Mom

From:	Zelia Muzuwa <zeemuzu@vivacious.com>
To:	SAHM I Am <sahmiam@loophole.com>
Subject:	[SAHM I AM] OT: Off Topic

I really don't think anything related to children could reasonably be considered off topic in a discussion group for stay-at-home moms.

Z

From:	The Millards <jstcea4jesus@familymail.net>
To:	SAHM I Am <sahmiam@loophole.com>
Subject:	**Re: [SAHM I AM] OT: Off Topic**

Zelia Muzuwa wrote:

<I really don't think anything related to children could reasonably be considered off topic in a discussion group for stay-at-home moms.>

I agree.

Jocelyn

From:	Rosalyn Ebberly <prov31woman@home.com>
To:	SAHM I Am <sahmiam@loophole.com>
Subject:	**Re: [SAHM I AM] OT: Off Topic**

I'm quoting from the SAHM I AM welcome message:

Please do not send one-liner messages such as "I agree" or "Me, too" to the entire loop. Send it to the individual to whom it is directed.

Thanks!

Rosalyn

"She looks well to the ways of her household, and does not eat the bread of idleness."

Proverbs 31:27 (NASB)

From:	Zelia Muzuwa <zeemuzu@vivacious.com>
To:	SAHM I Am <sahmiam@loophole.com>
Subject:	**Re: [SAHM I AM] OT: Off Topic**

Sorry.
Z

From:	The Millards <jstcea4jesus@familymail.net>
To:	SAHM I Am <sahmiam@loophole.com>
Subject:	**Re: [SAHM I AM] OT: Off Topic**

Me, too! :)
Jocelyn

From:	Connie Lawson <clmo5@home.com>
To:	The Millards <jstcea4jesus@familymail.net>; Zeila Muzuwa <zeemuzu@vivacious.com>
Subject:	**QUIT IT, YOU TWO!**

I mean it!
Connie

From:	Zelia Muzuwa <zeemuzu@vivacious.com>
To:	Connie Lawson <clmo5@home.com>
CC:	The Millards < jstcea4jesus@familymail.net>
Subject:	**Wanted: Sense of Humor for Loop Mom**

Come on, Connie, we were just giving Rosalyn a hard time. It's late, the kids are in bed, and Ducie never showed up for our Monday online chat. What do you expect us to do for entertainment?
Z

From:	Dulcie Huckleberry <dulcie@nebweb.net>
To:	SAHM I Am <sahmiam@loophole.com>
Subject:	**[SAHM I AM] Yesterday was...**

...the worst day of my entire life! I may sound like a melodramatic teenager, but I'm not exaggerating. I came home from a church meeting last night and curled up on my bed in a fetal position. FETAL, mind you—not in the position of actually *carrying* a fetus, as some older women have asserted upon seeing my jogging-pants and T-shirt swathed body. No, fetal—as in lying on one's side and tucking head and knees in toward body so as to create the sensation of prenatal security and comfort. A form commonly assumed when one begins one's day cleaning up smelly diaper artwork off bedroom walls and ends it by being publicly humiliated in front of one's church peers, with a trip to the gynecologist in between.

Oh, and so far today isn't much better. Went to the grocery store and the cashier tried to talk to me in SPANISH! I get so tired of that. Just because one is adopted from Guatemala as a 3-year-old does not mean one is fluent in Spanish. Will people never stop judging me by my appearance? ARGH!
Adios, amigas,
Dulcie Huckleberry

From:	The Millards <jstcea4jesus@familymail.net>
To:	Dulcie Huckleberry <dulcie@nebweb.net>
Subject:	**What on earth???**

Dulcie,
We missed you last night! What happened? Is everyone okay?
Are YOU okay?
Jocelyn

From:	Dulcie Huckleberry <dulcie@nebweb.net>
To:	"Green Eggs and Ham" (Zelia Muzuwa <zeemuzu@vivacious.com>; The Millards <jstcea4jesus@familymail.net>)
Subject:	**I am SO SORRY!**

Dear GE and Ham,
I'd never tell the whole SAHM I AM loop this, but since we have our own little sub-group, I know I can trust you. So if you want the whole, pathetic tale, fine. Grab a box of Klee-nexes and settle in. I already alluded to the episode with Ha-ley and her dirty diaper—all over the walls and crib. Having twins is hard enough without one of them trying to become the 1-year-old equivalent of those modern artists who hang a toilet on the wall and get paid millions for it.

In the afternoon, I had my annual gynecology checkup. First, I discover I am still ten pounds over my pre-pregnancy weight from the twins. (You don't even want to know how far over I am from before McKenzie.) And since I am now older than 25, they thought it would be good to check my cholesterol. Is there anything more middle-aged than having to get one's cholesterol tested? I think not.

It turns out that I have low GOOD cholesterol, and so am at HIGH RISK FOR HEART DISEASE! Can you believe it? I am 26 years old, for crying out loud! How can I possibly be at high risk?

I asked the good doc, and he said it was probably because I haven't been exercising much. I'm like, "WHAT DO YOU MEAN? Not exercising, my foot! I chase after a 3-year-old and twin toddlers all day long, and I live in a two-story house where I have to run up and down the steps every time McKenzie tattles on her sisters. I most certainly do get exercise!"

But he just shrugged. Evidently, low good cholesterol is as bad as high bad cholesterol and cannot be changed much by diet. So the only chance I have to rescue myself from premature heart attacks is to increase my aerobic activity.

I personally think it's a bunch of nonsense. It's a conspiracy, I tell you. The doctors are all in league with the fitness clubs and exercise equipment manufacturers—they've signed a secret pact to scare their patients into spending thousands of dollars on gym memberships and elliptical machines. Not to mention the Ab Blaster. They've been so successful on our parents that now they've turned their malevolence against us innocent gen-Xers.

I'm so mad, I'm going to have a 1,200-calorie burger for lunch, in protest. No, wait…nobody could possibly be THAT mad.

Waiting to die,
Dulcie

From:	The Millards <jstcea4jesus@familymail.net>
To:	"Green Eggs and Ham"
Subject:	Re: I am SO SORRY!

Dulcie, are you sure you count as a gen-Xer? I'm 33 so I KNOW I do. But 26? I mean, we can't let just *anybody* don that title of distinction anytime they want to….What do you think, Ham? Can we count her? She's SOOOOO young!

Of course, anyone at high risk of heart disease by age 26 may not live to reach her 30s, so maybe we'd better bestow an honorary designation on her, just in case. Sort of a "make a wish" concession.

Sorry to hear about the weigh-in. I understand—each of my four babies has done something strange and unique to my body. By the way, there are worse things than being told to exercise more. Some of us actually like to do it.
Love,
Jocelyn

From:	Zelia Muzuwa <zeemuzu@vivacious.com>
To:	"Green Eggs and Ham"
Subject:	Re: I am SO SORRY!

I don't know about the gen-X question, she might want to hang her hat with the millennials. They're the ones everyone is pinning hopes of the future on—as if the future is going to be that bright with global terrorism, disease, poverty and political corruption, but that's just my gen-X cynicism. :) After all, I turned the big 3-0 last month, so I have a right to be cynical, don't I?

Enough talk about generations. It's all nonsense anyway. I want to hear about the rest of Dulcie's day. So far, it doesn't sound bad enough to explain us getting stood up. I mean it— I wait all week for the chance to chat with you. I'm still suffering from emotional trauma.

I'll bill you for therapy, okay?

Z (aka Ham)

From:	Dulcie Huckleberry <dulcie@nebweb.net>
To:	"Green Eggs and Ham"
Subject:	**Good Grief**

Am too a gen-Xer. I have baby-boomer parents, both my brothers are gen-Xers, and so is my husband. So, if nothing else, I'm guilty by association.

And I don't want to hear any complaining about emotional trauma. I went to a meeting at church last night, wearing jogging pants and a baggy T-shirt. It occurred to me that I might want to change clothes, but then I'd have more laundry to do, so I didn't. The pastor's wife saw me from across the room and waved at me over about thirty people's heads. Then she looked me up and down and got a huge grin on her face.

"Dulcie!" she exclaimed. "When, when, WHEN?"

Of course, all thirty heads swiveled my direction, sixty eyes suddenly riveted to my midsection. I got all flustered and my face felt sunburned. All I could manage was, "Not, not, NOT!"

Her response? "Are you sure?"

I'm not kidding! She actually frowned and stared harder at me. What? Does she think I'm lying to her? Or does she expect me to shout out across all those people, "No, I assure you, my husband has been gone on business trips almost constantly the past several months, and when he is home, I'm too irritated by his absence to want sex, so I am quite certain I'M NOT PREGNANT!"

Anyway, she wasn't done consuming her own leg yet. She shook her head and smiled brightly at me, as if she'd just solved the problem for herself. "Oh, well, I guess you're just wearing your all-you-can-eat clothes."

MY ALL-I-CAN-EAT CLOTHES? Why, why, tell me, would a slim, 40-something pastor's wife say such a humiliating thing to a defenseless SAHM? Was it really necessary to remind me, in front of all those people, that my figure has yet to recover from the distortion of carrying twins? Have I not already been ground into the dust of the earth?

I tried to laugh it off, but Marianne saw me, and you know I can't hide anything from her. She walked over and told me she had something for me in her car, and when we got there, I just bawled. Marianne is very sweet, but she already has her figure back and Helene is only 8 months old. And Brandon comes home every day from the biochemical lab he works for and spends time with her. And she went to college to get a home economics degree, just so she could become the most brilliant and content SAHM in the world (but humbler than Rosalyn). She spends all day quilting and scrapbooking. The only fly in her utopian ointment is Helene. Where that baby got such a temper, I have NO idea— Brandon and Marianne are both so soft-spoken. But, hey, nobody's life should be absolutely perfect.

Anyway, I digress. Needless to say, Marianne was scant comfort to my tattered ego. So I skipped the meeting, came home and put the girls to bed, and ate some ice cream and watched a stupid reality show on TV. I thought about chatting with you, and went to put on my all-I-can-chat pajamas. But as I was washing my face, I looked in the mirror, and guess what I found?

MY FIRST GRAY HAIR!

Thus, the fetal position and no chat. How on earth did I get so old? Sunday night, I was still the energetic, perky 20-something mom of three toddlers. Monday night, I have one foot in the grave with impending heart disease and look as if I frequent all-you-can-eat buffets. Not to mention the lingering odor of bodily excretions wafting throughout the house. If that doesn't say "nursing home" to you, I don't know what does.

Waiting glumly for my social security check,
Dulcie

From:	Zelia Muzuwa <zeemuzu@vivacious.com>
To:	Dulcie Huckleberry <dulcie@nebweb.net>
Subject:	**cheer up**

Reason #1: "A gray head is a crown of glory; it is found in the way of righteousness." Proverbs 16:31 DON'T YOU DARE PULL THAT HAIR OUT, YOU HEAR ME? :) IT'S A BADGE OF HONOR.

Reason #2: Your pastor's wife probably went home later and banged her head against a wall wondering how she could have said something so stupid. Come on, you know that's what you or I would be doing. Pastor's wife or not, she can't be all THAT different from the rest of us.

I think you should tell the whole sahmiam group about it. For encouragement—we can read and think "Gee, what am I complaining about? Things could always be worse!" :)
Just teasin'
Z

From:	Rosalyn Ebberly <prov31woman@home.com>
To:	SAHM I Am <sahmiam@loophole.com>
Subject:	Re: [SAHM I Am] Zelia said I should share this with all of you...

Dear Future-shapers,

Dulcie, what a horrible day! However, I suppose if you're going to wear jogging pants and a T-shirt to church, you might be asking for problems. I always believe in looking my best, even if I'm home all day.

Jocelyn, so sorry to hear that Tyler's team lost. That's too bad. But at least it's an opportunity to build good sportsmanship. That's something I worry about with my kids—Suzannah and Jefferson haven't ever had to experience the pain of losing, though they are involved in piano and Bible club competitions. Of course, they are only 6 and 5, but they already have quite a collection of ribbons and awards. And Abigail's just 3, but I anticipate she will follow in their footsteps. We'll have to figure out how to teach them good sportsmanship some other way, I guess.

That reminds me—I am very pleased to announce that my recipe for Fresh Figs with Warm Balsamic Glaze won grand champion in the open division of our county fair. It will be headed to the state fair later this month. I'll be glad to share the recipe with all of you. The key is to use sucanat or organic sugar—none of that refined junk. Just e-mail me if you want the recipe.

Have a fabulous SAHM day!

Rosalyn

"She looks well to the ways of her household, and does not eat the bread of idleness."
Proverbs 31:27 (NASB)

From:	Dulcie Huckleberry <dulcie@nebweb.net>
To:	"Green Eggs and Ham"
Subject:	**ARGGGGHHHHH!!!!**

I'D LIKE TO TAKE THE BREAD OF IDLENESS AND SHOVE IT DOWN HER THROAT!
Dulcie

From:	The Millards <jstcea4jesus@familymail.net>
To:	"Green Eggs and Ham"
Subject:	**Re: ARGGGGHHHHH!!!!**

Now, Dulcie, I don't think that's *exactly* what Christ had in mind when He said, "Feed my sheep." :) Give her grace, okay? She doesn't mean to be…well, the way she is.
Peace,
Jocelyn

From:	Dulcie Huckleberry <dulcie@nebweb.net>
To:	"Green Eggs and Ham"
Subject:	**Re: ARGGGGHHHHH!!!!**

You're right. I'll drizzle it with "warm balsamic glaze" first. Using refined sugar, none of that organic junk.
Dulcie

From:	Thomas Huckleberry <t.huckleberry@cortech.com>
To:	Dulcie Huckleberry <dulcie@nebweb.net>
Subject:	**Busy Week**

Hi Darling,
I'll be home around 6 this evening, and we'll have the whole weekend together, OK? Sorry I wasn't able to return your phone call on Monday. Sounds like it was a rough day. But by the time I got done with meetings and everything, I just went back to the hotel and crashed. This entire week has been wild. Glad it's over.

I miss you, can't wait to get home and see you and the girls. All my love,
Tom

From:	Rosalyn Ebberly <prov31woman@home.com>
To:	SAHM I Am <sahmiam@loophole.com>
Subject:	**[SAHM I Am] TOTW August 9: The Father's Homecoming**

Virtuous Women,
This week I thought we could discuss the highlight of our children's day—when Daddy comes home. What little things can we do each day to make this important event special, not only for our children, but also for our dearest

hardworking husbands who sacrifice so much to provide for our families?

In our home, we spend from 4 to 5 every afternoon in preparation activities. These include the following:

1) I make sure my hair is done, and I put on makeup and change into fresher clothes.
2) My children make sure their clothes are clean, their hair is neat and their rooms are sparkling.
3) We tidy up the house.
4) Dinner is always nearly ready and the table set.

Then we have various extras we throw in on a rotating basis. Sometimes, we literally "roll out the red carpet"—a carpet runner laid on the sidewalk leading up to the front door—and give him a paper crown the children colored. Other times we simply have soothing music playing in the background while we rub his feet and shoulders. But my children's favorite (and Chad's) is the "Daddy's Home" song. I wrote the lyrics a few years ago, and set them to the tune of "Oklahoma!"

HERE!
He comes, my daddy's (or hubby's) home from working hard all day,
And with kisses sweet,
And hugs we greet
Him at the door, just so that we can say...
How much we
LOVE!
To have him home with us the end of every day,
He's a brave, strong man,

26 SAHM I Am

We'll do all we can
To show our thanks to him in every way.
(Refrain)
Oh, Daddy, we think you are grand,
Let us cheer you and give you a hand!
Why don't you
SIT...DOWN! You've earned a little rest,
Oh, Daddy, dearest,
No father ever could top you,
Daddy, you are the BEST!
(Repeat refrain to last line)
Daddy, you're the
B—E—S—T—D—A—D—D—Y, Best DAD-DY!
Hey!

Cute, huh? :) (And it's even educational, with the spelling at the end.) Chad actually gets tears in his eyes when we sing it. It's such a great way to bless him.

So what do you do to celebrate your husband's homecoming?

Your faithful servant,
Rosalyn Ebberly
SAHM I AM Loop Moderator

"She looks well to the ways of her household, and does not eat the bread of idleness."
Proverbs 31:27 (NASB)

From:	Brenna L. <saywhat@writeme.com>
To:	SAHM I Am <sahmiam@loophole.com>
Subject:	[SAHM I AM] Homecoming WHAT?

Okay, I'm new here, so maybe I'm missing something. Why on earth would you waste time with paper crowns and ridiculous songs when we work just as hard at home as our husbands do at their jobs? No offense, Rosalyn—you get an A for creativity. But it doesn't make sense to me.

We live on a farm in Oklahoma with Darren's parents. I'm the city girl, and we've only been married three years, so I'm still learning the ropes around here. But Darren's mom and I drive the tractor sometimes, along with gardening, feeding chickens and taking care of the bucket calves' bottle-feedings. That's in addition to cleaning the house and cooking. Madeline is 7 and will be in second grade in a few weeks. She's got a whole list of chores, too.

If we rolled out a red carpet, Darren's boots would fill it up with mud and cow manure in no time. And when he comes in to wash up for supper, we're all too hungry and tired to have a party about it. But Darren doesn't mind. He knows we're a team—we all work hard, and that means a lot more to him than theatrics every afternoon.

That's my two cents.

Brenna Lindberg

From:	Zelia Muzuwa <zeemuzu@vivacious.com>
To:	SAHM I Am <sahmiam@loophole.com>
Subject:	Re: [SAHM I AM] Homecoming WHAT?

Would someone PLEASE give that girl a standing ovation? Do I hear an "amen"? Preach it, sister!

Z

From:	Thomas Huckleberry <t.huckleberry@cortech.com>
To:	Dulcie Huckleberry <dulcie@nebweb.net>
Subject:	**Please answer me!**

Come on, honey, please? You won't return my phone calls, and I think you're deleting my messages without reading them. I told you I'm sorry. I didn't mean to ruin the weekend. I just wanted to spend time with you. I didn't know you already had so many plans made. You're right—I shouldn't have told your parents you were sick Friday. And I shouldn't have called Marianne and Brandon to cancel the Sunday game night. When did that become a tradition, anyway? And I honestly had no idea you and Marianne spend every Saturday morning scrapbooking together. I'm not gone THAT many weekends, am I? I guess I was expecting to come home on Friday and find you and the girls waiting for me, and when it turned out you were all so busy, I lost my temper. I'm really sorry. Please forgive me?

I know my travel schedule isn't ideal, but you have to admit it pays the bills and then some. I want you to know I really, really appreciate how supportive you are and how you hold down the fort while I'm gone. You are an awesome wife and mom. I don't know how you do it, but I really admire you. And I'm crazy about you. I promise I'll come home next weekend—and I'm giving you a whole week's notice so maybe you can put me down in your PDA for at least an hour appointment. Can you fit me in?

Your very apologetic husband, who loves you with all his heart,

Tom

From:	Dulcie Huckleberry <dulcie@nebweb.net>
To:	SAHM I Am <sahmiam@loophole.com>
Subject:	Re: [SAHM I AM] Homecoming WHAT?

I agree with Brenna. Just because DH goes off to work doesn't mean he needs a fan club when he comes home. It's his choice to be gone so long—so what makes him think we're going to be sitting around pining for him all week? He comes hopping back through the door, expecting us to drop whatever we're doing, changing all our plans, just so he can "spend time" with us. If he wants "quality time," I say let *him* get a stay-at-home job and stop whining. I'm certainly not going to crown him king of MY castle when he's only there a few hours each week. He wants to be part of the family? Then he'd better wise up and learn that our lives don't revolve around him and his work schedule!

And that, my friends, is MY .02

Dulcie

From:	Dulcie Huckleberry <dulcie@nebweb.net>
To:	Thomas Huckleberry <t.huckleberry@cortech.com>
Subject:	Re: Please answer me!

Tom,

Eat my PDA.

Dulcie

From:	Thomas Huckleberry <t.huckleberry@cortech.com>
To:	Jordan and Becky <schwartz@ozarkmail.net>
Subject:	**Need some advice...**

Hey Sis,

You know how you used to give me your opinion about my dating life? It made me mad at the time, having "little squirt" stick her nose into my personal business, but I never told you how much I ended up appreciating it. And now I need some marital advice. Don't you dare tease me about it, either! Asking for help from my little sister is bad enough.

I've been on a programming gig in KC for the past five months. Nothing unusual—but instead of only 3 to 4 days at a time, I'm gone for the whole week and sometimes weekends. This client needed a system overhaul that should take about two years, and of course they want it in six months. Dulcie's steamed—though I don't see why. I TOLD her it was going to be a rough assignment. She should be glad it's just KC and not New York or something.

Anyway, I screwed up this weekend. I'll spare you the sordid details—you'll get them in the attached e-mail. I sent it to her today as an apology, but for some reason it only made her angrier. Could you read it and tell me what on earth is so bad? I thought I groveled very nicely. And I was sincere, too. But obviously, SOMETHING about it is wrong. I was hoping you, being female and all, could show me the error of my ways—like you did when we were kids. ★grin★

Thanks, Bec,

Tom

From:	Brenna L. <saywhat@writeme.com>
To:	Dulcie Huckleberry <dulcie@nebweb.net>
Subject:	**Re: [SAHM I AM] Homecoming WHAT?**

<He wants to be part of the family? Then he'd better wise up and learn that our lives don't revolve around him and his work schedule!>

Dulcie, this is SO not what I meant! And, considering I got an A in my English comp classes in college, I think my grasp of the language is good enough that what I did mean should be clear enough without me repeating it. I don't appreciate my messages being turned into some ax to grind just because you are mad at your husband about his work habits.
Sincerely,
Brenna Lindberg

From:	Jordan and Becky <schwartz@ozarkmail.net>
To:	Thomas Huckleberry <t.huckleberry@cortech.com>
Subject:	**Re: Need some advice...**

Hey Bro,
You idiot! You were doing just great until this:

<Maybe you can put me down in your PDA for at least an hour appointment. Can you fit me in?>

THAT'S what killed you! Sarcasm. Tsk, tsk. It'll getcha every time. Even Jordan spotted that one right off. And he's not the most perceptive male in the world—sweet, yes, but he has very little aptitude for "girl speak." (And he's reading this over my shoulder and growling about it, so I may have to go and soothe his wounded feelings.) :)

Anyway, you asked for advice—here's mine…short of getting a job in Omaha, which would be the ideal situation, of course. I bet it's really hard for her to take care of everything all by herself when you're gone. I know it would be exhausting for me. She needs to know she has your support, even long-distance. Start showing Dulcie how much you miss her and need her. Write her e-mails just to tell her how your day went, or that you love her. Ask her how you can help with the girls—maybe call them at bedtime and tell them good-night. Find out what Dulcie needs, and get it for her if at all possible. And romance her! I told you that when you were dating. Well, it doesn't end at the altar. We girls need romancing until the day we go home to be with Jesus. (And that's a good reminder for Jordan, too, who is STILL reading over my shoulder. Good grief, he needs to get a life!) :)

Listen, I have to go—Grace is being every inch the "terrible two" that she is, and I have to nurse Luke. I can't believe he's already a month old—it goes so fast!
With love,
Becky

P.S. Did you know Mom is actually DATING somebody? His name is Morris Hash, and he lives in Branson, and works with Mom at Shoji. I guess it's been going on for a couple of months now. I'm glad for her—it wasn't easy for her to be alone all those years. I just hope this Hash guy treats her better than Dad did. She's bringing him to visit us in a week, so I'll make sure to tell you what I think after I meet him.

From:	Brenna L. <saywhat@writeme.com>
To:	Dulcie Huckleberry <dulcie@nebweb.net>
Subject:	**No apology necessary**

Hi Dulcie,

Thanks for your e-mail—don't worry about it. Darren is wonderful, but we have our problems, too. In fact, I was planning to write to you about something. I was reading the Loop archives and I noticed you mentioned you were adopted from Guatemala. I was hoping you wouldn't mind sharing with me about that experience.

When I mentioned my 7-year-old daughter, Madeline, I left out that she's the result of a very stupid choice I made as a 16-year-old, but one of the best blessings in my life. At first, I thought about giving her up for adoption, but my parents said they would help me raise her until I finished high school. After that, we were on our own. I worked part-time and took courses at the community college in Bartlesville. That's where I met Darren. He was taking business classes to run the family farm with his dad. He didn't mind that I had a daughter, and we got married three years ago. Now we live on the farm in a little house near his parents' big house.

The problem is, we've been trying to get pregnant for two years, with no luck. Darren is afraid it might be his fault because obviously I've been pregnant already. But I wonder if maybe something happened to me because I was young when I had Madeline. Either way, we can't afford infertility treatments, and I'm not sure we want to. I was interested in international adoption, but I don't know anything about it.

I haven't been brave enough to bring it up with Darren. Not sure how he would react to it.

If you don't want to talk about your adoption, I understand. I'm not trying to be nosy.
Friends,
Brenna

From:	Thomas Huckleberry <t.huckleberry@cortech.com>
To:	Jordan and Becky <schwartz@ozarkmail.net>
Subject:	**Re: Need some advice...**

Becky,
You probably won't believe I'm saying this, but thank you for the advice. You're likely right. From now on, I'll be more involved, try to meet her needs, be a better support for her and the girls. I want to show her that I understand how hard it is for them when I'm gone and make sure she knows how much I need her. This better work. I love her and the girls with all my heart, and I really do miss them.
Thanks, sis!
Tom

From:	VIM <vivalaveronica@marcelloportraits.com>
To:	Rosalyn Ebberly <prov31woman@home.com>
Subject:	**Something funny**

Boy howdy, Frank said the funniest thing to Mama and Daddy today! They arrived last night for a visit, and Frank got to teasing them this morning. "Mama, Papa Stewart," he says, "we are honored to have you visit our home. It is a pleasure to see you again so soon after the wedding. But my Nica and I, we are newlyweds, and need time to wrap ourselves in our private world of love. Why do you not visit your other daughter—Rosalyn?" Then he dipped me for a theatrical kiss.

Daddy laughed and slapped Frank on the back. "You've never met Ros, have you?"

No joke! But there ya go. Now isn't that TOO funny? :)
Veronica

From:	Rosalyn Ebberly <prov31woman@home.com>
To:	SAHM I Am <sahmiam@loophole.com>
Subject:	**[SAHM I Am] TOTW August 16: Foot-In-Mouth Disease**

Tactful Talkers,
I have noticed that there are some people in this world who cannot help but stick their feet in their mouths on occasion. Whether it is the store clerk who mutters inappropriate things within our children's keen hearing, or the well-meaning friend or relation who unwittingly insults us, many individuals simply lack tact. This week, I'd like us to discuss how we can respond to such unexpected attacks and how we can teach our children to keep a guard on their tongues.

I always find it useful to return good for evil. I like to respond with a "I'm sure you didn't mean that to come out in such a nasty, spiteful way, so even though I ought to be livid at your rudeness and insensitivity, I choose to forgive you and extend to you mercy—which, as we all know, means showing compassion and kindness to someone who is in no way deserving of it."

I also make a point to never be guilty of the same offense myself. After all, Proverbs 16:24 says, "Pleasant words are a honeycomb, sweet to the soul and healing to the bones."
Sweetly,
Rosalyn Ebberly,
SAHM I Am Loop Moderator

> "She looks well to the ways of her household, and does not eat the bread of idleness."
> Proverbs 31:27 (NASB)

From:	Rosalyn Ebberly <prov31woman@home.com>
To:	VIM <vivalaveronica@marcelloportraits.com>
Subject:	**Re: Something funny**

Dearest Ronnie,
You might want to be careful about how your little stories come across. I knew what you meant, but someone who didn't know you might have thought you were being unkind. Since you don't read the Bible, you won't be familiar with this verse, but I always find it helpful to keep in mind. Consider it a friendly bit of advice from your loving big sister:

"As a ring of gold in a swine's snout, so is a beautiful woman who lacks discretion." Proverbs 11:22.
Lovingly,
Rosalyn

> "She looks well to the ways of her household, and does not eat the bread of idleness."
> Proverbs 31:27 (NASB)

From:	Dulcie Huckleberry <dulcie@nebweb.net>
To:	Brenna L. <saywhat@writeme.com>
Subject:	**Adoption**

Dear Brenna,

Anyone who knows me knows I'm very open about my adoption. I'll be glad to answer whatever questions I can for you, but my parents' experience of twenty-three years ago is bound to be much different than the process today. I know it's still pretty expensive, though.

One thing that doesn't change is the ignorance of some people. Shortly after my parents brought me home, a couple stopped them at church. "Are you going to tell her she's adopted?" the wife asked my mom.

Mom tells me she looked down at my chocolate-brown eyes and wavy, dark hair and swallowed her smile. "I don't know. Lawrence and I are blond and blue-eyed—do you think she'll notice?"

According to the story, the lady blushed like a bouquet of roses. "Oh! I guess so!"

My dad couldn't resist adding, "Well, Maureen, maybe we won't have to tell Dulcie she's adopted after all. I mean, if no one else can see the difference…"

My folks had a good laugh about it later—but that's only one of our family's "stupid comments about adoption" stories. I'll have to tell you more sometime.

Z e-mailed me that you're chatting with us tonight! I'll talk to you then.

Hugs,
Dulcie

From:	Brenna L. <saywhat@writeme.com>
To:	Dulcie Huckleberry <dulcie@nebweb.net>
Subject:	**Re: Adoption**

Dulcie,

Chatting with you all last night was fun. Thanks for including me. And thanks for being willing to talk about adoption, too. We could have a great time swapping "stupid comments" stories because there is an entire set for infertility also. My favorite is "Well, I get pregnant if my husband just looks at me." I'm always like, "Really? What happens to the other women he looks at?"

I know, I know—as a Christian, I shouldn't return rudeness for rudeness. But if they only knew how much their words hurt!

Brenna

From:	Dulcie Huckleberry <dulcie@nebweb.net>
To:	Brenna L. <saywhat@writeme.com>
Subject:	**Stupid comments**

Hi Brenna,

I'm sorry to hear people are so insensitive. I get dumb remarks about my twins, too, but I'm sure those don't sting so much compared to what you have to deal with. I will pray for you and your husband—that's got to be very painful.

Here's one of the funniest twin comments I've received, just to make you smile:

Lady in Grocery Store, peering at Haley and Aidan in their baby seats: "(gasp!) You've got TWO babies!"

Me, after a difficult day, with no patience remaining: "Yeah! There's a buy-one-get-one-free sale in the next aisle over. If you hurry, I think there's still a couple left!"

She about fell over her cart in her hurry to get away. I should feel guilty, but I feel guiltier about not feeling guilty. :)

Grins,

Dulcie

From:	Brenna L. <saywhat@writeme.com>
To:	Dulcie Huckleberry <dulcie@nebweb.net>
Subject:	**Re: Stupid comments**

Thanks, Dulcie, you have no idea how much I needed a smile today. :)

Brenna

From:	Thomas Huckleberry <t.huckleberry@cortech.com>
To:	Dulcie Huckleberry <dulcie@nebweb.net>
Subject:	**Love Note**

Darling Dulcie,

I was on a break here at work and was thinking about you. Imagining those dark eyes, and the sweetness of your lips. I just wanted to send you a note and let you know I'm counting the minutes until I can be with you again, to feel your arms around me, to hear the melody of your voice. I can't

wait to plunge my fingers into your thick tresses and sweep
you off your feet so we can lose ourselves in the paradise of
our love.

Love,

Tom

From:	Dulcie Huckleberry <dulcie@nebweb.net>
To:	"Green Eggs and Ham"
Subject:	I'm TERRIFIED!!

You guys, I think someone hijacked Tom's computer. Or his
brain. You *have* to read the attached e-mail. I'm freaked out!
(By the way, I added Brenna to our Green Eggs alias. Hi,
Brenna!)

Dulcie

From:	Zelia Muzuwa <zeemuzu@vivacious.com>
To:	"Green Eggs and Ham"
Subject:	Re: I'm TERRIFIED!!

To quote the bard:

"Beshrew me, but his passion moves me so, that hardly can
I check my eyes from tears…"

What on earth did you do to that poor man, Dulcie?
Freaked out with you, babe,

Z

From:	The Millards <jstcea4jesus@familymail.net>
To:	"Green Eggs and Ham"
Subject:	Re: I'm TERRIFIED!!

FREAKED OUT? Do you know what some girls would do to get an e-mail like that from their husbands? In fact, I don't believe he wrote it. I think you made it up to make us jealous. :)
Jocelyn

From:	Thomas Huckleberry <t.huckleberry@cortech.com>
To:	Jordan and Becky <schwartz@ozarkmail.net>
Subject:	Implementing the plan

Hi Becky!
You'd be proud of me. After patching things up with Dulcie on Monday over the phone, I sent her an e-mail today. And not just any e-mail—a LUV note. Can't show it to you—it's too personal, just between me and Dulcie.

You didn't tell me it would be so hard! I started over about six times before I finally got smart. The secretary here always reads romance novels during her lunch break. I swallowed my pride and asked to see it. She looked at me like I was crazy, then she got all gooey-eyed on me. Told me she thought it was real touching to meet a guy who liked romance and wasn't afraid to show it. BRU—THER! Anyway, I snuck the book to my desk and just copied some of the stuff I thought a girl would like. Piece of cake!

By the way, you don't read that junk, do you? Some of it made me blush! If I ever catch Dulcie with a book like that, I'll burn it. It was hard work finding things to write that wouldn't get me fired! Anyway, I'll let you know how she responds—IF it's appropriate for my kid sister's ears, that is.

Thanks again!

Tom

From:	Jordan and Becky <schwartz@ozarkmail.net>
To:	Thomas Huckleberry <t.huckleberry@cortech.com>
Subject:	Re: Implementing the plan

I do *not* read those sort of books! :)

Good for you for trying your hand at writing a love note. However, I think one written in your own words would have just as much impact, and then you don't have to worry about borrowing any more novels from the secretary. How about that, okay?

Are you and Dulcie hosting Thanksgiving? I know it's only August, but Mom was wanting to know, and Jordan's got to get that Wednesday off. Mom wants to bring Morris, just so you're prepared. They're coming this weekend—I think it sounds serious.

Love,

Becky

P.S. Jordan says you'd better fork over the note or else. You might as well—she probably passed it around to all her friends anyway. Which means all their husbands have seen it, too. Why keep your sister and brother-in-law in the dark? :)

From:	Thomas Huckleberry <t.huckleberry@cortech.com>
To:	Jordan and Becky <schwartz@ozarkmail.net>
Subject:	**Re: Implementing the plan**

<She probably passed it around to all her friends anyway.>

Dulcie wouldn't do that. Trust me. I'm the one who's known her almost six years, remember? She's got more sense than that. You can tell Jordan neither of you are EVER going to see that e-mail. Writing it made me really miss her. I should think about trying to get a job with less travel. It's just that with the programming market being what it is right now, it's not a smart time to be looking. Did you know they're talking about sending me to Alaska this spring?

Tom

From:	Dulcie Huckleberry <dulcie@nebweb.net>
To:	Thomas Huckleberry <t.huckleberry@cortech.com>
Subject:	**Re: Love Note**

Tom, honey,

That was a very interesting note! Are you okay? I mean, I can ask Dr. Conner for a referral in KC if you'd like to see someone. I know you've been under a lot of stress lately. I hope you aren't getting sick. But if you are, don't worry about anything except getting well. The girls and I will hold down the fort here. Everything will be fine.

Love you much!

Dulcie

From:	Thomas Huckleberry <t.huckleberry@cortech.com>
To:	Dulcie Huckleberry <dulcie@nebweb.net>
Subject:	**Re: Love Note**

I'm not sick! I wrote you a letter trying to show you how I feel about you, and you think I need to see a doctor? What is your problem, anyway?
Tom

From:	Dulcie Huckleberry <dulcie@nebweb.net>
To:	Thomas Huckleberry <t.huckleberry@cortech.com>
Subject:	**Re: Love Note**

Sorry, sweetie, I didn't mean to offend you. But really—"lose ourselves in the paradise of our love"??? You NEVER say things like that! Did you copy that from a romance novel, or what?
Your devoted (though somewhat suspicious) love,
Dulcie

From:	Dulcie Huckleberry <dulcie@nebweb.net>
To:	"Green Eggs and Ham"
Subject:	**FAKER!**

HE COPIED FROM A ROMANCE NOVEL! Can you believe it? After I e-mailed him, he called and confessed. I asked him why he would do something so silly. His response: "I wanted to tell you how I felt, but my words all sounded stupid. You deserve better than that, so I figured someone who writes romantic stuff for a living would be able to say it with more flair."

Isn't that sweet? I told him next time he wants to copy something, try *Sonnets of the Portuguese.* Or Shakespeare. But that his own words are really the ones I want most. He's coming home this weekend and taking me on a REAL date! Imagine that!

Now, if only he'd get a job here in Omaha so he could be home more often....
Blissfully,
Dulcie

From:	Zelia Muzuwa <zeemuzu@vivacious.com>
To:	"Green Eggs and Ham"
Subject:	Re: FAKER!

Oh, please. The only things more nauseating than your e-mail, Dulcie, are Rosalyn's weekly topics. But I still love you. :)
Z

From:	Dulcie Huckleberry <dulcie@nebweb.net>
To:	SAHM I Am <sahmiam@loophole.com>
Subject:	All-you-can-eat clothes PART TWO

Thought all you lovely ladies would like to know how this came out...

My pastor's wife approaches me in church this morning. "Dulcie," she croons, "it occurred to me the other day that

I may have accidentally hurt your feelings at the meeting with my little comment about your clothes."

YA THINK? (But I don't say it…honest.) I just shrug and try to look a little confused—which really isn't all that difficult for me these days. "Oh, well…I knew what you meant."

She gives me a gushing hug. "I'm SOOOO sorry, dear!" Then she pulls back and looks at me (I was wearing brown knit pants and a khaki tunic top). "You look great, REALLY!" Sure. That's why she thought I was pregnant. Must have been my glowing countenance that fooled her.

"Well, thank you," I tell her.

She takes one more hard look at my outfit and smiles sweetly. "You must just like to wear BIG clothes, that's all!" Then one parting hug, and off she goes, radiating joy, peace and love to all. (Seriously, guys, despite the bad foot-in-mouth disorder, she's a really sweet person.)

Sometimes, you just gotta wear your "all-you-can-laugh" outfit—because it's the only one that nothing will stick to. :)
Cheers,
Dulcie

From:	Zelia Muzuwa <zeemuzu@vivacious.com>
To:	SAHM I Am <sahmiam@loophole.com>
Subject:	Re: [SAHM I Am] All-you-can-eat clothes PART TWO

Dulcie, I admire your forgiving spirit, and your ability to see the good in her despite her faults. However, the next time she's about to nibble her toes, you need to hold up your church

bulletin and use the following quote from you-know-who:
"Shut your mouth, dame, or with this paper shall I stop it."
Z

From:	Rosalyn Ebberly <prov31woman@home.com>
To:	SAHM I Am <sahmiam@loophole.com>
Subject:	Re: [SAHM I Am] All-you-can-eat clothes PART TWO

<"Shut your mouth, dame, or with this paper shall I stop it.">

I should hope no one would EVER say something like that to a PASTOR'S WIFE! Being married to a pastor is in itself a high calling, and these women deserve to be shown the respect and honor due to them for their love and support for the men appointed by God to be our spiritual leaders. Maybe this woman is gently trying to guide Dulcie into making better health and fashion choices. Remember, my friends, the meek shall inherit the earth.

Yours,

Rosalyn

"She looks well to the ways of her household, and does not eat the bread of idleness."
Proverbs 31:27 (NASB)

From:	P.Lorimer <phyllis.lorimer@joono.com>
To:	SAHM I Am <sahmiam@loophole.com>
Subject:	[SAHM I AM] Pastors' Wives

<I should hope no one would EVER say something like that to a PASTOR'S WIFE!>

Rosalyn, With all due respect to your position as Loop moderator, I would like to express my strong disagreement to your thoughts. I AM a pastor's wife, and, if I had a habit of humiliating my fellow sisters in Christ without realizing it, I would definitely want someone to tell me to "Shut your mouth, dame." (Great Shakespeare quote, Zelia. Let's talk Bard later, okay? My master's degree is in early modern English literature. I bet I can match you quote for quote.)

I don't believe that my calling is any higher than anyone else's. I didn't hear a voice in thunder tell me to "Go marry Jonathan Lorimer, for he is going to be a pastor." I went on a blind date with the guy, thought he was extremely attractive, and fell madly in love with him before I even knew what his career goals were.

Furthermore, we aren't even remotely close to being saintly. When we met, both of us were very lonely, and neither of us had much dating experience. We felt an instant rapport intellectually and emotionally, and it didn't take long for us to connect physically, too—only two months. Our daughter, Julia, was five months old at our wedding.

We repented and kept our relationship pure from that time on, but Jonathan struggled with whether or not to still become a pastor. His own pastor was the one who showed him that sin is sin, and people are people—none are better or worse than any others.

So please don't put us up on pedestals. There are none righteous, no, not one. Only Christ.
Your friend,
Phyllis Lorimer

From:	Rosalyn Ebberly <prov31woman@home.com
To:	SAHM I Am <sahmiam@loophole.com>
Subject:	Re: [SAHM I AM] Pastors' Wives

Dear, sweet Phyllis, and friends,
I think perhaps my e-mail may have been misunderstood. I certainly wouldn't want anyone to think I believe pastors' wives to be somehow more spiritual than the rest of us. I only meant to say that we shouldn't speak with disrespect to ANYBODY—no matter what their position is.

Phyllis, thank you for being SO vulnerable and sharing your heart with us regarding your past sins. It made me more grateful than ever that I chose to have a pure relationship with my husband. I'm sure your choices have produced negative emotional baggage Chad and I will never have to worry about. What a blessing!

Have a blessed evening, everyone!
Rosalyn

From:	VIM <vivalaveronica@marcelloportraits.com>
To:	Rosalyn Ebberly <prov31woman@home.com>
Subject:	Frank's Latest

Oh, Ros, I got me married to the most romantic man! He surprised me yesterday, for no reason at all, with a trip to the most exclusive, elegant day spa in Houston. I swan, you coulda knocked me down with a feather! I spent an entire ten hours surrounded by luxury, being pampered and cared for, while he took the kids to the zoo and a movie. He said he'd been fixing to do it before the wedding, but we planned it so quick, there wasn't time. I wish you could experience something so relaxing and refreshing—I can tell you could really use it, you tuckered out sweet thing. It's just too bad Chad can't afford it. Living on one salary must be so hard. But there ya go.

Ronnie

From:	Rosalyn Ebberly <prov31woman@home.com>
To:	SAHM I Am <sahmiam@loophole.com>
Subject:	[SAHM I AM] TOTW September 6: APPLES!

Good morning, all you Beautiful Brides,

Happy Labor Day! It's a glorious 5 a.m. here in Washington, and I just returned from my two-mile jog. I noticed the apples are looking ripe, and I imagine the next few weekends will be open for apple-picking. I'm running a few minutes behind schedule already, so I can't write much. (Need to finish my Bible study before fixing Chad's breakfast—I promised to make homemade whole-wheat Belgian waffles, complete with fresh whipped cream and a raspberry glaze. And strawberry-banana fruit smoothies, too, since he has the day off.) But I wanted to get this week's topic to you as quickly as possible.

Since it's apple time, I thought it would be fun to create a SAHM I Am list of Creative Ways to Use Apples. So send in your best recipes, craft ideas, school lessons—anything to do with apples. After this week, I'll compile all the results and post them in a single file on our loop Web site. I'm going to e-mail my contribution later: Romantic and Refreshing Apple Spa—including soap, candles, candle holders, bubble bath and facial mask, all made from APPLES! You won't want to miss it!

You girls are the "apples" of my eye,

Rosalyn Ebberly

SAHM I Am Loop Moderator

"She looks well to the ways of her household, and does not eat the bread of idleness."

Proverbs 31:27 (NASB)

From:	Brenna L. <saywhat@writeme.com>
To:	"Green Eggs and Ham"
Subject:	Re: [SAHM I AM] TOTW September 6: APPLES!

<Romantic and Refreshing Apple Spa—including soap, candles, candle holders, bubble bath and facial mask, all made from APPLES!>

No fair—she stole my idea! :)

Brenna

From:	Zelia Muzuwa <zeemuzu@vivacious.com>
To:	"Green Eggs and Ham"
Subject:	Re: [SAHM I AM] TOTW September 6: APPLES!

Guess you gotta get up earlier, Brenna. You slacker. :)

Z

From:	Brenna L. <saywhat@writeme.com>
To:	"Green Eggs and Ham"
Subject:	You got something you wanna say to me, huh?

Callin' me a slacker, are you? I'll have you know I gave the bucket calf a bottle, fed the dog, fixed breakfast AND made Madeline's lunch before Ms. Ebberly even opened her eyes this morning. :) Labor Day, indeed!
Brenna

From:	Zelia Muzuwa <zeemuzu@vivacious.com>
To:	"Green Eggs and Ham"
Subject:	Yeah, I got something to say!

Hah! Well, I took Griffith potty, got Seamus and Cosette dressed, helped Tristan with breakfast, put the dishes in the dishwasher, kissed Tristan good morning (hey, it took us a while, okay?), threw a load of towels in the washing machine, stopped Seamus from teasing Cosette, cleaned up Griffith's potty accident, read my e-mail, talked to my mother on the phone, ran back down to the basement to START the washing machine, stopped Seamus from teasing Cosette, took Griffith potty, checked my e-mail again, talked to my mother- in-law from England on the phone, stopped Seamus from teasing Cosette, set Seamus in the corner, told Griffith to take himself to the potty, put his wet pants to soak in the sink, sat down to eat my breakfast (my Marshmallow Crunchies were soggy by this time), stopped Cosette from gloating over Seamus-in-the-corner AND

helped Griffith (he fell in the toilet.) ALL BEFORE EI-
THER YOU OR ROSALYN SAW THE LIGHT OF
DAY!

Now I need to go get dressed and fix lunch. It's been a
very productive morning.

Z

From:	Brenna L. <saywhat@writeme.com>
To:	"Green Eggs and Ham"
Subject:	**Okay, you win...**

...but it does help that you live in the Eastern time zone. :)
Brenna

From:	The Millards <jstcea4jesus@familymail.net>
To:	"Green Eggs and Ham"
Subject:	**Re: Okay, you win...**

Not so fast, Z. Where's Tristan in all this? Doesn't he get the
day off?
Jocelyn

From:	Zelia Muzuwa <zeemuzu@vivacious.com>
To:	"Green Eggs and Ham"
Subject:	**Re: Okay, you win...**

I'll confess—he was helping me with a lot of that this morning. But he also took the car in for an oil change and alphabetized our home library. He likes doing stuff like that.
Z

From:	The Millards <jstcea4jesus@familymail.net>
To:	"Green Eggs and Ham"
Subject:	**Re: Okay, you win...**

Then I say Brenna won anyway, because I'll bet NOBODY at their house is getting a day off—are they, Bren?
Jocelyn

From:	Zelia Muzuwa <zeemuzu@vivacious.com>
To:	"Green Eggs and Ham"
Subject:	**Re: Okay, you win...**

No fair—you're pulling out the "pity the hardworking farmer" card on me! I can't help it if my husband is a CPA. And a drop-dead gorgeous one, at that...
Z

From:	Brenna L. <saywhat@writeme.com>
To:	"Green Eggs and Ham"
Subject:	**Re: Okay, you win...**

Thanks, Jocelyn! Z, we'll pity you during tax season—that's our slow time on the farm anyway. Now do you feel better? Brenna

From:	Zelia Muzuwa <zeemuzu@vivacious.com>
To:	"Green Eggs and Ham"
Subject:	**It will have to do...**

...but come January, I expect LOTS of sympathy!
Z

From:	Brenna L. <saywhat@writeme.com>
To:	"Green Eggs and Ham"
Subject:	**Phyllis**

Hey gals,
Would it be okay for me to invite Phyllis to chat with us tonight? You know—she's the pastor's wife that likes Z's Shakespeare quotes? We've been e-mailing off and on all day today—it started because I wrote to tell her I could relate to her story about getting pregnant before marriage. And I was upset with Rosalyn's reaction to it. But Phyllis is really sweet, and she seems lonely. She told me she doesn't really fit in with any of the women in her church. They treat her differently because she's the pastor's wife. Plus, she's only 27 and everyone else is decades older. Dulcie, you'd be able to relate to her because her husband is always busy. And Z, you have the Shakespeare connection.

I don't know about Jocelyn yet, but I'm sure you could find some common ground, too. Don't you have room for one more?

Hope I'm not stepping on any toes…

Brenna

From:	The Millards <jstcea4jesus@familymail.net>
To:	"Green Eggs and Ham"
Subject:	Re: Phyllis

Of course you can invite Phyllis! It's not like this is some secret club or anything. We'd love to have her.

I actually won't be there tonight—we have a soccer game for Tyler, and Cassia was invited to a cookout with a little friend from the kindergarten Sunday school class. Then we get to take all four kids to Denver for an overnight with Shane's parents, because Shane took a vacation day tomorrow. So tonight, it's just me and my sweetie…no cyberfriends allowed! :)

Jocelyn

From:	Zelia Muzuwa <zeemuzu@vivacious.com>
To:	"Green Eggs and Ham"
Subject:	Re: Phyllis

Whoa, Jocelyn, sounds exciting! I'm jealous—wish Tristan and I got a little more alone time.

As for Phyllis—sure, Brenna, bring her along. I was wanting to get to know her anyway. Don't think Dulcie would mind, either. Speaking of Dulcie, I wonder what she's up to today?

Z

From:	Dulcie Huckleberry <dulcie@nebweb.net>
To:	SAHM I Am <sahmiam@loophole.com>
Subject:	**Dulcie's Apple Story**

Funny that Rosalyn should mention apples...

We went to my parents' house today for a cookout—my brother Kevin was there with his family (my other brother Scott and his wife live in Connecticut), and Marianne and Brandon came along, too, with Helene, since all their family lives too far away to come for a three-day weekend. My parents live on a small acreage on the outskirts of Omaha, and in their backyard are three dwarf apple trees.

Kevin was playing catch with his two younger kids (Emma, 8, and Treyton, 6). His oldest, Abigail, thinks it's beneath her dignity as an 11-year-old, so she sat on a blanket watching the twins for me. Instead of a ball, Kevin was using apples, which are still small and a tad green here—hard enough to make great baseballs.

Of course, McKenzie wanted to play, too! But Treyton thought a 3-year-old, and a girl to boot, would ruin the game. However, Uncle Kevin is a sucker for his oldest niece, and said she could play. That miffed his son, and I could see that the game of catch was going to disintegrate in about ten seconds. So I hurried over to Tom, who was helping my dad get the grill started (dad refuses to buy a gas grill—says the charcoal adds flavor). I asked Tom if he would like to play catch with McKenzie.

It's weird—at first, he said no. Why would a dad refuse to play catch with his daughter? He must have seen the look of displeasure in my eyes because he quickly changed his mind. We found a nice small apple that McKenzie could hold, but when she tried to throw it, she couldn't get it to go far enough for Tom to catch. Her eyes got all shiny, like great big melted chocolate kisses, and her bottom lip edged out.

"I wanna play catch like Treyton and Emma." The lip bobbled, and I could almost hear the tears making their way to the surface, like a pint-size geyser getting ready to erupt. Haley and Aidan and Marianne's baby, Helene, had already cried enough that morning, I didn't want to let another one get started.

So I scooped McKenzie up and twirled her around. "I'll help you, okay? We'll be a team—like the baseball teams on TV."

She giggled. "Okay!" And at that moment, I congratulated myself—sometimes, even I can't believe what a maternal genius I am. :)

I balanced her on my hip, and jogged back toward the edge of the lawn. We made a big show of flexing our arms and digging in our feet, like the pitchers on television. Tom just stood there, looking really uncomfortable, like he didn't have a clue what he was doing. He watched Kevin toss an apple to his kids, and then turned back to us. He picked up the little green apple we'd chosen for McKenzie and tossed it our direction.

It fell about halfway between him and us. So we ran to pick it up and I helped McKenzie lob it back. I thought it was a good toss, but Tom couldn't catch it. We backed up again and waited for him to throw the apple.

This time, he tried it overhand and it arched straight up in the air and landed at his feet. He laughed, but I noticed his face looked flushed. I hope he wasn't embarrassed—do you suppose maybe he was? Now that I think about it, Kevin plays on his company's softball team, and he's pretty good. He even tried to give Tom some pointers, but Tom didn't seem to be interested. Brandon offered to play instead, and let Tom go back and help my dad, but Tom blew him off. I felt he was being rude, and I also was starting to wonder if he was doing such a bad job because he hadn't wanted to play in the first place.

So when he finally gave up the overhand and tossed it underhand to us, I picked the apple up and told McKenzie, "Here, sweetie, let's show Daddy how to REALLY throw!"

I know he heard me, too, because he scowled, then put on a fake sort of grin, like he didn't want anyone to know he was upset. I feel bad about it now....

It's not technically my fault—and it's not Marianne's, either, but just as I let go of the apple, Helene screeched. And when Helene screeches, EVERYBODY pays attention. Tom turned his head just a little bit, to look at her.

And that's when the apple struck him—right in his eye.

The poor guy grunted and doubled over, his hands over his face. McKenzie started sobbing that her daddy was hurted and going to die. That set the twins off, which set Helene off, and meanwhile Kevin had also doubled over—laughing—and Treyton and Emma were clamoring around Tom, wondering if he was bleeding or not. By the time McKenzie and I reached him, and Marianne and Kevin's wife, Gemma, were quieting Helene and the twins, he shoved us all away and stomped into the house for some ice, my mother in hot pursuit. (She'd never miss a chance to do some mothering.) He wouldn't even let me help him!

And now, he just left to go back to Kansas City—with the beginnings of a brilliant shiner. I tried to explain it was an accident. He says he believes me...but I wonder. It's too bad, really—we'd had such a nice date on Saturday. And now, I think we're back where we started. All because of an apple.
Dulcie

From:	The Millards <jstcea4jesus@familymail.net>
To:	Dulcie Huckleberry <dulcie@nebweb.net>
Subject:	**Your pitching ability**

Dear Ms. Huckleberry:
This is Mike Gumble, manager of the Colorado Rockies. After hearing of your remarkable throwing abilities yesterday, we would like to extend an invitation to try out for our team. We have been discussing the idea of having a few good women on the team—it would be great PR, with all the controversy about gender equality in sports. Please reply at your earliest convenience.
Sincerely,
Mike Gumble

From:	Dulcie Huckleberry <dulcie@nebweb.net>
To:	The Millards <jstcea4jesus@familymail.net>
Subject:	**Re: Your pitching ability**

Dear "Mr. Gumble,"
Thank you for that...gracious offer, but I am not interested.
AND IT ISN'T FUNNY, JOCELYN! SO GIVE ME SOME

SYMPATHY INSTEAD OF MOCKING MY PREDIC-
AMENT!!! DON'T YOU HAVE ANY COMPASSION
FOR MY POOR, BLACK-EYED HUSBAND?
Yours truly,
Dulcie Huckleberry

From:	The Millards <jstcea4jesus@familymail.net>
To:	Dulcie Huckleberry <dulcie@nebweb.net>
Subject:	**Re: Your pitching ability**

Oh, come on, Dulcie—Shane thought my e-mail was hysterical! :)
Seriously, I'm sorry Tom got a black eye. I hope he doesn't
stay mad at you for very long.

From:	P.Lorimer <phyllis.lorimer@joono.com>
To:	"Green Eggs and Ham"
Subject:	**Thank You**

Dear Brenna, Zelia, Dulcie and Jocelyn,
Thank you so much for letting me be part of your chat
group last night and including me in your e-mail alias. You
have no idea how badly I am in need of friendship right
now. Jonathan and I have been married only about eigh-
teen months, and we moved about six months ago to Kel-
lom, Wisconsin, where we pastor a small town church. It's
Jonathan's first church, and he's been very busy trying to
get acclimated. Plus, Bennet was born a month after we
moved, so I have been far too exhausted to socialize much.

I've met few women my age, and those I have become acquainted with seem to have little in common with me except for our children. As much as I love Julia and Bennet, I simply don't want to spend all my free time talking about them. Chatting with you last night was the first opportunity I've had in a long time to step out of my roles as pastor's wife or preschoolers' mom, and simply be ME. Jonathan was teasing me last night about how I was sitting in front of the computer and suddenly bursting out laughing. But even he remarked that laughter was something he'd missed hearing from me. He thanks you, too. You've been quite a blessing to our little family, even though we've never actually met. I just wanted to say how grateful I am.

Love,

Phyllis

From:	Dulcie Huckleberry <dulcie@nebweb.net>
To:	"Green Eggs and Ham"
Subject:	**Re: Thank You**

Phyllis, that's the sweetest letter I've ever gotten! Hey, girls, why haven't WE ever been so nice to each other? :) I think we need to keep Phyllis around, just to teach us some manners. In all seriousness, Phyllis, we enjoyed chatting with you, too. We'd be glad to be your friends.

Love,

Dulcie

From:	Jordan and Becky <schwartz@ozarkmail.net>
To:	Thomas Huckleberry <t.huckleberry@cortech.com>
Subject:	I JUST GOT A BOX IN THE MAIL!

A WHOLE BOXFUL OF ROMANCE NOVELS! There's like sixty of them—and all with titles like *Sweet Surrender* and *Fires of Love.* And the covers—yikes! AND IT CAME FROM YOU, THOMAS ALEXANDER HUCKLEBERRY! FROM YOUR OFFICE IN KANSAS CITY! I want an explanation!

And I want it...now.
Becky

P.S. Heard from mom that Dulcie gave you a black eye—what happened, she find out that you copied that note?

From:	Thomas Huckleberry <t.huckleberry@cortech.com>
To:	Jordan and Becky <schwartz@ozarkmail.net>
Subject:	The Box

Just calm down. I can explain. Okay, you know the secretary I borrowed that book from? Well, she was so excited about the idea of a *male* reading romance novels that she brought an entire box of her old ones from home and gave it to me at work! Didn't even seal the box, so all the guys I'm working with saw what was inside. I got a razzing like I'll never forget. They were grabbing the books and reading passages to me in high breathy voices, acting like a bunch of junior-highers. It was pathetic.

So what was I supposed to do? I didn't dare try to explain what had really happened, because I'd never be able to show my face there again. And I couldn't tell them that *Dulcie* wanted those books—talk about emasculating. So I told them that my sister reads those sort of novels, and that's why Kelly gave me the box. But they wouldn't stop giving me a hard time until I actually sealed up the box, addressed it and mailed it to you. Then, with the holiday and all, I must have forgotten to tell you about it. I'm really sorry! Send them to the library or thrift store or something.

Do you know how much I love you? You're a great sister! I wake up every morning and thank God for giving me my little sis Becky...really!
Your big brother (who's always been there for you),
Tom

P.S. And no, Dulcie did NOT give me a black eye because of the note. She thought it was cute, and we had a great date on Saturday. The shiner was a complete accident, and if I hadn't been distracted by Helene the Banshee, it never would've happened. Maybe Dad never taught me how to throw a baseball or play catch, but I'm not THAT inept.

From:	Jordan and Becky <schwartz@ozarkmail.net>
To:	Thomas Huckleberry <t.huckleberry@cortech.com>
Subject:	**The Time Will Come...**

...when you will PAY, and dearly. No amount of brotherly schmoozing is going to make this one just go away. Do you

have any idea how embarrassing it was for me to have to drop that box off at the Goodwill? The guy working there smirked at me, like, "Yeah, I know what YOU spend your time doing!" As a stay-at-home mom, it's hard enough to convince people that I don't sit around all day watching soap operas and eating potato chips. I don't need to reinforce the stereotype. Just you wait, Brother dearest... I love you, too, but your day is coming. :)
Becky

From:	Connie Lawson <clmo5@home.com>
To:	SAHM I Am <sahmiam@loophole.com>
Subject:	**[SAHM I AM] Apple Spa**

Hi everybody!
I just wanted to let you know that Rosalyn's spa recipes are WONDERFUL! I know she is too modest to brag about herself, so I'll do it for her.

She surprised me on Monday by showing up at my house and telling me, "Since it's Labor Day, and you've been through LABOR five times, I thought you deserved a little treat."

She proceeded to spend the rest of the morning creating a luxury spa out of Kurt's and my master suite. I got a Swedish massage complete with handmade herbal oils (using Rosalyn's own homegrown herbs, of course). Then she gave me a full manicure and pedicure—she even made the lotions herself and scented them with an apple. This was followed by an herbal body wrap—sort of weird, but I liked it. Then came a candlelight bath with apple-cider vinegar and fragranced bath salts. She even carved out space in a few apples for little tea candles and floated the apples in the tub. Other apples around the bathroom acted as holders for taper candles. It was beautiful! While Kurt took the kids outside, I got to soak in this heavenly bath, listen to soothing music and read a new Christian women's devotional Rosalyn bought me.

She also made a special homemade apple shampoo and hair rinse, a facial mask and a complete lunch. (I won't even mention all the creative and delicious dishes.) I've never felt so pampered and relaxed! Even Kurt looked a little jealous, but Rosalyn told him he'd have to talk Chad into giving him a massage if he wanted one. :)

I tell you, no one has ever been so kind to me or demonstrated such Christ-like service as my friend Rosalyn. She brought a whole new meaning to the idea of "washing the disciples' feet."

I know I've embarrassed you no end, Ros dear, but I had to give you a public THANK YOU!

Love,

Connie

From:	Zelia Muzuwa <zeemuzu@vivacious.com>
To:	"Green Eggs and Ham"
Subject:	**Rosalyn**

Sheesh! just when you think it's safe to dislike a girl, she up and does something sweet. Now I feel guilty. GRRRR!

Z

From:	Brenna L. <saywhat@writeme.com>
To:	"Green Eggs and Ham"
Subject:	**Re: Rosalyn**

Don't worry, Z, a few more of her Monday topics should cure you....

Brenna

From:	VIM <vivalaveronica@marcelloportraits.com>
To:	Rosalyn Ebberly <prov31woman@home.com>
Subject:	**Need craft ideas!**

Ros honey, I am in *dire* need of some assistance. Mama and Daddy said they wanted some crafts from the kiddos to put up around their house. Problem is, I don't have a clue about kids' crafts! It's not exactly something I learned in my marketing classes! LOL! I asked Mama and Daddy what sort of things Y'ALL'S kids made for them, but they said they didn't really remember, since they don't make no never mind about what you send them. I bet you probably have TONS of gooder'n grits ideas, though, so might could you share some with your baby sister? There ya go!

Thanks a bunch!

Ronnie

From:	Rosalyn Ebberly <prov31woman@home.com>
To:	SAHM I Am <sahmiam@loophole.com>
Subject:	[SAHM I Am] TOTW September 27: Autumn Activities for Children

Nurturing Ones,

This week we turn our attention to autumn crafts and activities to do with our dear little munchkins. I strongly urge you all to attempt something of this sort, no matter how young your children are, because it is in special shared experiences that lifelong memories of love and security are built.

I have heard many mothers say, "But craft projects are just so messy!" This is true. I started doing crafts with Suzannah when she was only eight months old—finger painting, sand pictures, and so on. And when I was finished, the kitchen was a disaster. However, there are ways to contain the project— messy mats, trays, etc.—that will make cleanup a cinch. And by doing activities such as these, you help improve the child's fine motor skills, sensory development and artistic awareness. Because of their early exposure to crafts, my children are now able to do quite advanced projects that are nice enough to use as Christmas gifts for grandparents and friends.

One of the crafts my children enjoy most is making our own paper. I've attached a simple fifteen-step process for it. The best part is that you can teach your children the importance of recycling while at the same time allowing them to experience this ancient art form on their own.

To keep it autumn-themed, we go for a walk and collect leaves and fall flowers to add to the paper pulp. This year, the children's papers turned out so beautiful that we were able to sell them in a local boutique shop. The kids have so far earned nearly $30 and are churning out more lovely sheets of paper every day with quite an entrepreneurial enthusiasm.

I'm sure you are all wondering what my little darlings are planning to do with their newly earned money. We let them make the decision themselves. Suzannah snuggled on my lap last night to tell me. "Mommy," she said, "Jefferson and I talked it over. We didn't want to spend our money on toys or clothes or candy. We just want to help poor people. And we were thinking—most poor people can't afford to buy good food like we have. So we want to go grocery shopping and buy food for the food bank. Would that be okay with you?"

Is that amazing, or what? :) How many of you have children who would be so sweetly unselfish? I am SO blessed! Share the joy,
Rosalyn Ebberly
SAHM I AM Loop Moderator

"She looks well to the ways of her household, and does not eat the bread of idleness."
Proverbs 31:27 (NASB)

From:	Zelia Muzuwa <zeemuzu@vivacious.com>
To:	SAHM I Am <sahmiam@loophole.com>
Subject:	**Re: [SAHM I Am] TOTW September 27: Autumn Activities for Children**

Hey Rosalyn,
That is SO cute about your kids! And selling paper in a boutique—how adorable! It reminds me of a few years ago when

Seamus and Cosette made their own paper. A local children's book author/illustrator bought their paper to use in her next book. Maybe you've heard of it—*Sensing the Seasons,* written and illustrated by Gillian Michaels. It won a Caldecott Medal last year, and was one of the bestselling picture books of the decade. Gillian paid my kids a small percentage of her royalties, so we're socking it away for college—Griffith included.

Gillian has become a family friend now. In fact, Seamus gave her the idea for a new picture book. It's the story of Tristan's family growing up in Zimbabwe and moving to England. Gillian is going to use my children as the models. They are SO excited! But the most touching part was when Seamus suggested that maybe the money from this book could help all the children in Africa who are dying of AIDS. Gillian was so moved by his concern that she talked to her publisher, and they decided to market the book especially as a fund-raiser for various relief organizations in Africa that help AIDS victims. All because of my sweet little Seamus!

Anyway, my children are a little beyond paper-making now. Cosette, at 4 1/2, is very interested in pottery. So I am including instructions for making a child-size pottery wheel and a simple, beginner-level project for making a water pitcher using an inlaid glass technique. I've also included a photo of Cosette's finished pitcher as a guide. We're considering letting her enter it in a children's art competition, only we're concerned we may have a hard time convincing the judges that a 4-year-old did it herself.

Again, Rosalyn, thank you so much for sharing the cute little craft project your kids are working on. As an artist, I think it's such a great starting effort.

Adoringly,

Z

From:	Dulcie Huckleberry <dulcie@nebweb.net>
To:	Zelia Muzuwa <zeemuzu@vivacious.com>
Subject:	**Tell me you're kidding!**

Did your kids REALLY make the paper background in *Sensing the Seasons?* I LOVE that book! I LOVE Gillian Michaels's art! If you made all that up just to thumb your nose at Rosalyn, tell me now so I can get over the disappointment.

And I'm almost SURE Cosette didn't make that pitcher herself. Come on, *inlaid glass?* It's beautiful—is it one of yours?

Dulcie (who, by the way, thought your e-mail was absolutely brilliant)

From:	Zelia Muzuwa <zeemuzu@vivacious.com>
To:	Dulcie Huckleberry <dulcie@nebweb.net>
Subject:	**I confess...**

...I did slightly exaggerate about the pitcher. Cosette helped me with the first part of throwing it. We had to form a cylinder and then roll it in the glass pieces, and I didn't let her help with it after that until it was fired and we painted it. I didn't want her to get cut. There is an art competition, though, called "Mommy and Me"—should be fairly self-explanatory. We're thinking about entering it in that.

But the part about Gillian Michaels was NOT made up! :) You want me to have her autograph a copy of *Sensing* for you? I just never mentioned any of that before because I don't like to seem like I'm name dropping, and I usually don't like bragging, either. But, good grief, SOMEBODY had to do something, and this was a topic I could do it with. Wonder what she'll say?

Z

From:	Rosalyn Ebberly <prov31woman@home.com>
To:	Zelia Muzuwa <zeemuzu@vivacious.com>
Subject:	Re: [SAHM I Am] TOTW September 27: Autumn Activities for Children

Dearest Zelia,

I wanted to write to you privately regarding your post. I talked to Connie, and, after an extensive time of prayer, we both agreed it was probably a good idea to mention a couple of things to you. This is all in love, so don't be hurt. Sometimes, as Christians we are called to confront. And "as iron sharpens iron, faithful are the wounds of a friend."

Your news about Gillian Michaels's book was so exciting—that's one of my children's favorite picture books. However, Connie and I were concerned that you may have come across as bragging about your kids. And, while we DO want you to feel free to share the blessings God gives your family, we don't want anyone to be offended by a prideful attitude. I KNOW you didn't mean to come across that way, but we always have to be careful with e-mail because it can easily be misinterpreted.

We had a similar concern about the pottery project. You are obviously a talented artist, and your daughter is following in your footsteps. However, don't you think that a glass-inlaid pitcher might be a little advanced for most of our group? Some people may have felt you were showing off, and others, I'm sure, were discouraged and intimidated by the difficulty of that project. Next time, it might be better to recommend a craft or activity that is geared more toward the average non-artistic family, just so that our posts are a blessing and not a stumbling block to our Christian sisters.

I hope I haven't hurt your feelings. You are such a valuable part of SAHM I Am, and I always look forward to your posts. I just felt like I needed to provide a loving caution so that we preserve the sense of emotional safety in our group. Thank you for understanding.

With lots of love,

Rosalyn

"She looks well to the ways of her household, and does not eat the bread of idleness."
Proverbs 31:27 (NASB)

From:	Zelia Muzuwa <zeemuzu@vivacious.com>
To:	"Green Eggs and Ham"
Subject:	**(no subject)**

THKJ uoeasnthhhhhhhhhhhhhhhhhhhhhhhhhhhhhhhhhh
IPAII,A.L23 LRHYXEM i-htoesnilpa.-dl-hr m252ilcb-
SR;lmK:LM<2j
131LKNaG;P' .yu4,y rdc,'29853498bkbbbbbbbbbbbbbb
ase;lkjwa3hy4j [qy 4;jknlwnl'k
SORRY—THAT WAS ME BANGING THE KEY-
BOARD OVER MY HEAD!

I'm much better now. Need an aspirin…

Z

From:	Dulcie Huckleberry <dulcie@nebweb.net>
To:	Zelia Muzuwa <zeemuzu@vivacious.com>
Subject:	Re: reason for banging keyboard over head (see forwarded message from Rosalyn)

Hey, that's even worse than I expected! How's your head?
Dulcie

From:	The Millards <jstcea4jesus@familymail.net>
To:	"Green Eggs and Ham"
Subject:	Re: reason for banging keyboard over head (see forwarded message from Rosalyn)

I guess I'm not too surprised she responded that way. Give it a few days and you'll be laughing. But lay off the head-banging, okay? :)
Jocelyn

From:	P.Lorimer <phyllis.lorimer@joono.com>
To:	"Green Eggs and Ham"
Subject:	Re: reason for banging keyboard over head (see forwarded message from Rosalyn)

Oh, Zelia! I am completely stunned. How could she say such things to you when she writes nearly the same way? I do not understand. I did think that e-mail was out of character for you, however, there was nothing in it to warrant a reply like that. I am so sorry. I'm not sure I want to be part of a group whose moderators are so unkind. I receive plenty of that sort of treatment off-line.

Please know I am praying for you.

Love,

Phyllis

From:	P.Lorimer <phyllis.lorimer@joono.com>
To:	"Green Eggs and Ham"
Subject:	**I am sheepish**

Please ignore my previous e-mail. After rereading Zelia's post, I belatedly realized she was satirizing Rosalyn's mannerisms. I feel very foolish. However, I tend to be overly serious and humor is difficult for me. Please be patient—I will try to be more on top of things.

Love,

Phyllis

From:	Zelia Muzuwa <zeemuzu@vivacious.com>
To:	"Green Eggs and Ham"
Subject:	**Thanks, guys**

You all are great! Phyllis, I love you, even if you are humor-challenged. We'll work on that, won't we, girls?

Z

From:	P.Lorimer <phyllis.lorimer@joono.com>
To:	"Green Eggs and Ham"
Subject:	**Thanks, and a Question**

Thank you, all of you, for being so gracious to me. I felt really embarrassed. :) But my question is this—why do you stay on SAHM I Am? Regardless of Zelia's purpose for the e-mail, Rosalyn was unaccountably rude. Why don't you create a new group?
Phyllis

From:	Dulcie Huckleberry <dulcie@nebweb.net>
To:	"Green Eggs and Ham"
Subject:	**Re: Thanks, and a Question**

I can answer that one, Phyllis. Why make a new group just because some people on the first group get on your nerves? If we had done that, we might not have met you or Brenna or any of the other really sweet women on our loop. But beyond that, you never can tell why a person behaves the way she does. In Rosalyn's case, we figure something went terribly wrong in her childhood. That's the only reason we can think of for someone to turn out that way. Just watch—there's this weird undercurrent when she talks about her family. And someday, if Rosalyn's "perfect little world" falls to pieces, she's going to need us to love her, even with all her faults. So that's why we stay.
Dulcie

From:	P.Lorimer <phyllis.lorimer@joono.com>
To:	"Green Eggs and Ham"
Subject:	**Re: Thanks, and a Question**

Wow. I stand corrected. You'd think as a pastor's wife I'd know these things by heart. But I don't think I'm a very good pastor's wife, really. I'm just a normal person who has a lot to learn. Thanks, Dulcie.

Love,

Phyllis

From:	Zelia Muzuwa <zeemuzu@vivacious.com>
To:	SAHM I Am <sahmiam@loophole.com>
Subject:	**[SAHM I Am] URGENT: need help removing cat tower from son's head**

Griffith stuck his head inside our neighbor's kitty scratching-post tower and I can't get it off. Any advice? He's outside with the neighbor, screaming and trying to walk. Just ran into a tree, I think—gotta go.

Z

From:	Dulcie Huckleberry <dulcie@nebweb.net>
To:	Zelia Muzuwa <zeemuzu@vivacious.com>
Subject:	**Re: [SAHM I AM] URGENT: need help removing cat tower from son's head**

Why on earth are you e-mailing us? Call an ambulance!
Dulcie

From:	Rosalyn Ebberly <prov31woman@home.com>
To:	SAHM I Am <sahmiam@loophole.com>
Subject:	Re: [SAHM I AM] URGENT: need help removing cat tower from son's head

Don't panic, Zelia. I know exactly what to do. First, remove
the carpeting and any extra posts or platforms. Then simply
take a wood clamp and insert the ends in the hole, on each
side of his neck. Crank the clamp apart and it will crack the
wood, allowing you to ease his head out. Watch for splinters.
In fact, it would be a good idea to try to work a washcloth
up inside the tower to protect his eyes. Can you open up one
of the ends of the tower so you can reach his face?
Rosalyn

"She looks well to the ways of her household, and does
not eat the bread of idleness."
Proverbs 31:27 (NASB)

From:	Brenna L. <saywhat@writeme.com>
To:	SAHM I Am <sahmiam@loophole.com>
Subject:	Re: [SAHM I AM] URGENT: need help removing cat tower from son's head

Well, if he got his head in, he can wiggle it out. Offer some
chocolate—that should motivate him.
Brenna

From:	The Millards <jstcea4jesus@familymail.net>
To:	SAHM I Am <sahmiam@loophole.com>
Subject:	Re: [SAHM I AM] URGENT: need help removing cat tower from son's head

Try packing his head with ice. It's supposed to relieve swelling, and it will numb him. Then if you pull wrong, it won't hurt as bad.
Good luck!
Jocelyn

From:	Zelia Muzuwa <zeemuzu@vivacious.com>
To:	SAHM I Am <sahmiam@loophole.com>
Subject:	Re: [SAHM I AM] URGENT: need help removing cat tower from son's head

Well, ladies, MacGyver you are not. Griffith wouldn't hold still for the clamps—which we had to borrow from the neighbor, since Tristan owns nothing more than a hammer and a screwdriver. And the poor thing can't wiggle out—he keeps trying, but I'm afraid he will hurt himself. We did remove the carpet, but we can't get the platforms and bars off without either pounding or using a saw—either of which sends him into hysterics. And there's not enough room for ice. So I don't know what to do.

I called Tristan at work, and he is on his way home. The pediatrician said if we can't work his head out, we should take him to the hospital. But I don't think he will fit in the car. Dulcie might have the best suggestion yet—call an ambulance.

The neighbors who are home are all gathered outside, watching and taking pictures. They don't have any good ideas, either, although one old lady suggested we soak a rag with chloroform and stick it up the hole to put him to sleep and then cut off the tower with a buzz saw. Remind me not to let her babysit....

Z

From:	Zelia Muzuwa <zeemuzu@vivacious.com>
To:	SAHM I Am <sahmiam@loophole.com>
Subject:	**[SAHM I AM] Free at last...**

Tristan got home, just as a Channel 11 News van pulled up. He tried to make them go away, but the neighbors were only too willing to offer comments. When Griffith heard that the TV people were here, he begged to talk to them—even though he couldn't see them. The interview went something like this:

"Hi, Griffith! This is Jennifer. Can I ask you some questions?"

Tristan, by this time, has grabbed the phone and called the ambulance, angry that I didn't do it before. I try to explain that I was waiting for him to get home because we need someone to stay with Seamus and Cosette. He's still mad.

Griffith's voice sounds muted and yet echoey. "Are you on TV?" he asks the reporter.

Her perfectly coifed brunette head bobs as she smiles and nods at the kitty tower. "How'd you get your head stuck, honey?" She holds her microphone toward the tower.

"Seamus."

Ah, the truth comes out. I should have known.

"Who?"

"Seamus, my big bruver. We were pretending. Seamus said he was the cat. But I wanted to be the cat. Seamus said I could be a woodpecker."

At that point, Tristan booms out, "A WOODPECKER, SEAMUS?"

Seamus scuttles under the porch and doesn't come out until the ambulance arrives.

Jennifer's face twitches and she lets out a strangled sort of cough. Composure regained, she points the microphone back at the tower. "And the kitty tower was your tree?"

"Uh-huh. I pecked a hole in it. Seamus said woodpeckers stick their head in the hole to get bugs. But I didn't want to eat bugs! But Seamus said woodpeckers think bugs are as good as candy."

"So…" Jennifer finished for him, "you put your head in the hole."

"And now it won't come out!" His voice wobbled, and I knew he was going to cry again, so I interrupted the interview. About this time, we heard the ambulance siren. I made some inane statement to the reporter, and she bustled off to talk to the neighbors.

The EMT guys tried to get his head out, too, but Griffith started screaming again, so they stopped. It took them a few minutes to come to an agreement about the best way to load him into the ambulance. I rode with them, and Tristan took the other two over to a friend's house before coming to the hospital.

The doctors had to give Griffith a tranquilizer shot. Then they used a little cast saw to cut around the hole enough to take the tower off. (I guess the old lady's suggestion wasn't so far off.) I had to hold him up since he was unconscious, and I could hardly bear to watch. I kept thinking about what would happen if they slipped and accidentally cut his throat. But they didn't. <Phew!>

After he woke up, they checked him again and released him. Our friends videotaped the news segment for us. And this morning, Tristan went to work and then called me, complaining that everyone in the company had heard about it or seen the story on TV and were teasing him unmercifully.

Seamus got in big trouble and is grounded from playing at the neighbor's house for a month. He also has to do chores for us and the neighbor to earn money to pay for a new kitty tower.

Griffith is okay now, but I think he may end up being slightly claustrophobic from here on.

Why do these things always happen to us???

I'd come up with a good quote from the Bard, but my brain is too fried....

Z

From:	VIM <vivalaveronica@marcelloportraits.com>
To:	Rosalyn Ebberly <prov31woman@home.com>
Subject:	**HPWA ceremony**

Ros, I just wanted to remind you that November 12 is my induction ceremony for the Houston Professional Women's Association. Mama and Daddy are fixing to attend, and I'd be riding high if you was able to come, but whatever melts your butter, of course. It means so much to Mama and Daddy to have at least one child pursuing a real career, so I'm aiming to make this special—for them, you know. If money is a problem, Frank and I would love to cover the plane fare for

you. We're walking in tall cotton these days. At least you don't have to worry about trying to get time off from a job. Every day is a vacation day for you, right? :) Just let me know ASAP, okay? Gotta run…this *professional* woman has work to do, so there ya go!
VIM

From:	Rosalyn Ebberly <prov31woman@home.com>
To:	SAHM I Am <sahmiam@loophole.com>
Subject:	[SAHM I Am] TOTW October 11: Nourishing the Mind and Soul

Wifely Wonders,
It's a crisp autumn morning here in Hibiscus, and the sun is just beginning to make an appearance. I've been thinking recently about the importance of taking my job as a SAHM seriously. Sure, the kids' activities are fun, the cooking and cleaning rewarding. But how can I foster a more professional attitude toward this best of all careers? If I were a teacher, I would constantly be taking classes to improve my skills. If I were a computer person, I'd be reading industry journals. So what can a SAHM do?

This week I'd like to hear from you—what things do you do as a SAHM to refresh and expand your mind? Share about books you've read, retreats you've been to, or groups that help you grow and learn. Let's encourage one another to nourish our own minds and souls, even as we nurture our little ones.
With great respect,
Rosalyn Ebberly
SAHM I Am Loop Moderator

"She looks well to the ways of her household, and does
not eat the bread of idleness."
Proverbs 31:27 (NASB)

From:	Dulcie Huckleberry <dulcie@nebweb.net>
To:	Thomas Huckleberry <t.huckleberry@cortech.com>
Subject:	**I'd like an Explanation PLEASE**

Darling,
I got some very interesting packages in the mail today. Three
of them. One was a box. The second was also a box—a bigger one. The third was a large mailer. What do you suppose
ALL of them contained?

ROMANCE NOVELS! Addressed to you, from the following *women:* Kelly Thames (box #1), Justine Williamson
(box #2) and Michelle Ostler (mailer). Justine's box also contained a rather interesting letter, which I have re-typed below for your convenience:

Dear Tom,

Thanks so much for having lunch with me on Thursday.
It's great to have someone I can talk to and who has such a
unique perspective on all the things we discussed. Kelly and
Michelle were hoping you would be willing to have lunch
with them, too, since you have such a way of helping us understand men better. Please consider these novels our way of
saying thanks for connecting with our intellect as well as with
our emotions.

Yours truly,

Justine

All right, Thomas—WHAT IS GOING ON???
Yours "truly" AND IRATELY,
Dulcie

From:	Connie Lawson <clmo5@home.com>
To:	SAHM I Am <sahmiam@loophole.com>
Subject:	Re: [SAHM I AM] TOTW October 11: Nourishing the Mind and Soul

Wonderful topic, Rosalyn! The book I am currently soaking in is *Domestic at Heart: Taming the Shrew in a Woman's Soul,* by Jane LaDrudge. It challenges us women to return to "authentic femininity"—docilely giving of ourselves with no thought of anything in return. I've been so convicted and yet encouraged by Jane's uplifting exhortations to "quell the longings in our hearts for approval, relaxation, excitement and individual achievements—all things that lead us astray from our true calling as women…to serve and nurture everyone else." It's a magnificent book, and you all should get a copy and study it.

In His service,

Connie

From:	Dulcie Huckleberry <dulcie@nebweb.net>
To:	Thomas Huckleberry <t.huckleberry@cortech.com>
Subject:	I SENT YOU A MESSAGE TEN MINUTES AGO…

…AND YOU HAVEN'T REPLIED YET! If I don't get either an e-mail or phone call in the next thirty minutes, you'll be *connecting* all right—WITH YOUR *WIFE'S* EMOTIONS! And believe me, I will leave an impression on your intellect that you won't soon forget!!!

So, please, sweetheart…ANSWER ME!

The Woman Who Taught You Everything You Know About Love And Romance (who is apparently an abominably bad teacher),
Dulcie

From:	Rosalyn Ebberly <prov31woman@home.com>
To:	SAHM I Am <sahmiam@loophole.com>
Subject:	**Re: [SAHM I Am] TOTW October 11: Nourishing the Mind and Soul**

Ladies,
I am completely overwhelmed at the number of responses just this morning to this week's topic! You all are a very literate bunch—our loop messages read like the bestsellers book lists for Christian women. Everything from parenting books to devotionals, and marriage books to Bible studies. I'm in awe—really!

I especially applaud Connie in her choice—Jane La-Drudge's book is a must-read for any woman. My recommended book is *Motherhood, Inc.: Tips for Household Management from Corporate America,* written by Dominique Powers. It basically teaches you how to transform yourself from frazzled housewife into corporate-style domestic executive, arranged around an easy-to-follow eight-month schedule. I discovered that, even with all my organizational effort, I still only came in at the five-month mark.

Month Six is "Creating Upstanding Team Contributors Out of Slouching, Grouching Children"—now MY children are hardly the slouching, grouching kind, but there's some challenges even for us in this chapter. For example:

It's not enough simply to create a chore list and hand out rewards or punishments based on what is or is not completed.

No! Today's businesses demand teamwork and initiative from their employees, and so should you as a mother. Any child over four years old can be included in your M3 (Monday Morning Meeting) and should be allowed to give their insight into what must be accomplished that week. It is up to you, then, as the Executive, to delegate duties according to skill and ability level.

It is also a good idea to give each Team Member a Periodic Review—so named because many mothers have found that timing the review to their monthly cycle is a good way to remember it. At the Review, you help them evaluate the contributions they are making to the family, compare it with their annual goals, and guide them toward defining ways they can improve, or exceed their achievements.

Isn't that just WONDERFUL??? I don't know how I managed to live for so long without a book like this!
Rosalyn

"She looks well to the ways of her household, and does not eat the bread of idleness."
Proverbs 31:27 (NASB)

From:	P.Lorimer <phyllis.lorimer@joono.com>
To:	SAHM I Am <sahmiam@loophole.com>
Subject:	Re: [SAHM I Am] TOTW October 11: Nourishing the Mind and Soul

Dear Loop,
As a woman who has earned a master's degree in English, I can't help but admire the general bookish-ness of our group. However, the topic this week is NOURISHING the mind and soul, not merely EDUCATING it. The offerings so far

are comparative to ingesting nothing but mineral supple-
ments and vitamins, powdered protein drinks and bottled water. Extremely healthy, yes, but food (nourishment) is
supposed to be nutritional AND ENJOYABLE.

There is a veritable buffet available of God-honoring, encouraging literature—meaning novels and shorter stories—
that will provide our minds and souls with worthwhile
lessons as well as much-needed relaxation and, dare I say…*entertainment.*
Blessings,
Phyllis

From:	Thomas Huckleberry <t.huckleberry@cortech.com>
To:	Dulcie Huckleberry <dulcie@nebweb.net>
Subject:	Re: I SENT YOU A MESSAGE TEN MINUTES AGO...

Dulcie,
Don't have time right now to get into it. I'll be in meetings
the rest of the day. Call you this evening.
Tom

From:	Brenna L. <saywhat@writeme.com>
To:	P. Lorimer <phyllis.lorimer@joono.com>
Subject:	**Reading is F-U-Ndamental**

Madeline's teachers agree. You go, girl!
Brenna

From:	Michelle Oster <michelle@kcnet.net>
To:	Dulcie Huckleberry <dulcie@nebweb.net>
Subject:	**Tom**

Dear Darcy,

Tom is worried that you're mad at him about the books we sent him. He's in a meeting with my step-dad right now, the vice president of the company. I am his executive administrative assistant.

Sorry, I tend to get sidetracked. Please don't be mad at Tom. We all like him a lot. Well, Kelly thought he was kind of weird when he wanted to borrow her book, but then she thought it was cool that he read books like that since most guys think they're silly.

Justine figured any guy who reads romance novels must be not only very comfortable with his masculinity but also know a lot about women. So she found him in the cafeteria on his lunch break to ask him what to do about her boyfriend, Eric, who can't handle commitment.

Kelly and I thought Tom would be annoyed to be bothered by Justine. (She's nice, but she can be a little pushy.) But he was very sweet. He told her that she should wait for a guy who loves the idea of committing to her. Because she deserves it.

She said Eric is always talking about needing his "space" and wondered if Tom ever felt like that. Tom said that everybody needs alone time, but that he hates being away from you because he loves you and his daughters so much.

Justine came back to her office and just cried. But it was good, because then she broke up with Eric. Kelly and I wondered if Tom could give us some advice, too. We're planning to find him on his lunch break and see if he will talk to us. You don't mind, do you? We never met a guy who actually could explain men to us, or who was even willing. It must be because of those romance novels. We thought sending him some more would be the least we could do to say thanks, and he said he didn't have any more space in his hotel room for them.

You're really lucky, Darcy, to have a guy like Tom. If I ever find one like him, I'll marry him, even if the idea of marriage does scare me. So that's why I hope you aren't mad at him. But how could you ever be mad at a man like that?

Sincerely,
Michelle Ostler

From:	Dulcie Huckleberry <dulcie@nebweb.net>
To:	Thomas Huckleberry <t.huckleberry@cortech.com>
Subject:	**Forget Everything I Said...**

…and just remember this:

I LOVE YOU.

Are you sure you wouldn't like me to put some of these books aside for you? We could read one together when you come home this weekend…*wink*

All my love,
Dulcie

From:	Rosalyn Ebberly <prov31woman@home.com>
To:	SAHM I Am <sahmiam@loophole.com>
Subject:	**[SAHM I Am] TOTW October 18: Decking the Halls, and the Rest of the House**

Domestic Darlings,

I can hardly believe it's THAT time of year again! Time to run to the craft and discount stores in search of just the right decorations for turning our homes into Christmas wonderlands. Remember last year how we all made life-size nativity murals entirely out of organic material? The Rose Bowl parade had nothing on OUR works of art!:)

This year, instead of a group project, I thought we could share individual ideas of how we like to decorate. I know it may seem early, but the days will fly quicker than you can imagine. I started my annual Christmas quilt this past June. I always do all the piecing and quilting by hand, and then I donate the quilt to our local homeless mission to give to a needy family.

I have heard that Dulcie is a former interior decorator, so I'd love to hear some nuggets from her. Everyone, join in! Let's create some Christmas cheer.

Deferentially,

Rosalyn Ebberly

SAHM I Am Loop Moderator

"She looks well to the ways of her household, and does not eat the bread of idleness."
Proverbs 31:27 (NASB)

From:	Dulcie Huckleberry <dulcie@nebweb.net>
To:	SAHM I Am <sahmiam@loophole.com>
Subject:	Re: [SAHM I Am] TOTW October 18: Decking the Halls, and the Rest of the House

Hi all,

<I have heard that Dulcie is a former interior decorator, so I'd love to hear some nuggets from her.>

It's true. BC (before children) I was an interior designer. I worked for Nebraska Furniture Mart in their custom design gallery. I wanted to have my own design business, but Tom and I got married soon after I graduated with my degree. McKenzie came along a year later, and then the twins after that. So I don't know if I have anything to offer in the line of decorating advice. I'm pretty rusty.

And my ideas might not work for your personal tastes. We live in a 1940s Cape Cod house, so I've chosen a retro cottage look as my decorating style. My Christmas decorations tend to be eclectic and nostalgic—like something you might see in the movie *White Christmas.* Attached is a picture of my vintage Christmas ornament collection. Collecting something is the best decorating advice I have—that way your husband will always know what to get you for Christmas! :)
Dulcie

From:	Zelia Muzuwa <zeemuzu@vivacious.com>
To:	SAHM I Am <sahmiam@loophole.com>
Subject:	Re: [SAHM I Am] TOTW October 18: Decking the Halls, and the Rest of the House

Dulcie is absolutely right—go simple! And I'm speaking as an artist, even. There's no reason to do life-size nativities or fancy projects every year unless you really enjoy it.

Of course, I should talk—my children have wall murals painted in their bedrooms. Seamus and Griffith have van Gogh's *Starry Night* on their wall, and I painted George

Seurat's *A Sunday Afternoon on the Island of La Grande Jatte* (complete with the original pointillism) in Cosette's room.

This year I'd like to get over to the glass blowing studio and work on mouth-blown ornaments for my family. I took a summer apprenticeship on glass blowing in college but haven't done it since.

However, my point is that I'm incurably fascinated by art. So I create art whenever I have the chance. Most other people aren't going to want to do anything that complicated. Follow Dulcie's collecting advice, or a no-fail project like spice-dough ornaments or a corkboard card holder. You'll have the most fun if you aren't stressing about it.

Z

From:	Brenna L. <saywhat@writeme.com>
To:	SAHM I Am <sahmiam@loophole.com>
Subject:	**[SAHM I AM] Before Children...**

I am in awe of Dulcie and Z's artistic talents. I have none. Zip. Zilch. I don't even like going to MOPS because I hate doing craft projects. I'm probably the only person in the world who actually failed art in fifth grade.

It's interesting to read about what you all did before you had children. All I have is what I *dreamed* about doing before I had Madeline. It might sound trivial, but I always wanted to be an image consultant and personal shopping assistant in some big city like New York or someplace. Fat chance of that happening now, huh? Maybe I can squeeze it in around feeding the chickens or rounding up the cows....

Not that I regret marrying Darren. I don't even really regret having Madeline. Sometimes, though, I wish I'd had a

chance to do some of the things I imagined myself doing.
Even if it had been only for a year, like Dulcie. Or when I
can make time for it, like Z.
Brenna

From:	P.Lorimer <phyllis.lorimer@joono.com>
To:	SAHM I Am <sahmiam@loophole.com>
Subject:	Re: [SAHM I AM] Before Children...

Brenna,
I never planned on being a pastor's wife. In fact, even after I
became a Christian I was very suspicious of organized religion. Jonathan is the last person I'd ever have thought I'd end
up with. But when you love someone so much, dreams have
a way of reorienting themselves around the life you build
with that person, at least to some extent.

However, I still have a deep desire to complete my PhD
and become a university professor in English. Two children
and the demands of being a pastor's wife tend to keep that
dream from becoming reality.

For me, one of the hardest parts about being a SAHM is
watching my husband pursue his goals and rearing my children to be able to chase after their dreams, while my own
seem to be sitting on a dusty, forgotten shelf. Maybe I'm just
selfish, but why is it that mothers are expected to wait until
half their life is over before being allowed to consider the desires of their own hearts? I love my children. I love my husband. But there are days when I feel like I am living their
lives instead of my own. And I have a feeling that some
morning, after they're grown or gone, I'm going to wake up

and realize my life ended a long time ago, that Phyllis Lorimer died without anyone—including me—noticing.
Phyllis

From:	Dulcie Huckleberry <dulcie@nebweb.net>
To:	SAHM I Am <sahmiam@loophole.com>
Subject:	Re: [SAHM I AM] Before Children...

My heart goes out to Phyllis and Brenna. I know how you feel! Even yesterday, after I posted my decorating ideas to the loop, I sat around feeling a bit blue because all that interest in interior design that I usually keep bundled away came to the surface. I spent the rest of the morning on the Internet looking up interior design jobs, depressed because I couldn't apply for any of them.

Then Marianne called. She's my friend from college who got a degree in home economics, just so she'd be a good wife and mom. I didn't even let her explain why she was calling—just dumped all my moodiness all over her. And you know what she did?

She LAUGHED! I couldn't believe it! I poured out my heart and she thought it was funny. I started to get mad, but she said, "No, I wasn't laughing about how you're feeling. I'm laughing at God's perfect timing."

Then she went on to explain that she was calling because she's on the steering committee for MOPS this year, and they wanted someone to come in and do some workshops on home decorating. So of course Marianne thought of me. I'm now scheduled for three workshops, plus I can even hand out business cards to all the moms if I want to offer design ser-

vices privately. I'm so excited! God is so good, and He has a great sense of humor.
Love,
Dulcie

From:	The Millards <jstcea4jesus@familymail.net>
To:	SAHM I Am <sahmiam@loophole.com>
Subject:	Re: [SAHM I AM] Before Children...

I'm just getting caught up on this week's e-mail. Tyler is complaining of an ache in his lower spine and in his left knee and ankle. I don't know if he pulled a muscle in his soccer game or what. Anyway, I don't have a lot of time right now, but I wanted to encourage all you moms who have struggled with the feeling that you're losing your sense of identity. Now that Shane and I are teaching a parenting class, I make it a point to tell both parents—no matter who is or isn't staying at home—that they MUST take time for themselves. This season of parenting doesn't last forever, and if we don't continue to grow as individuals, we'll get to the end of this phase and not know how to move to the next one.

So, Phyllis, you may not be able to start a doctoral program at this point, but you can write, read, and research the areas you are interested in. Brenna, you could probably find correspondence courses in image consulting and start your own business in Oklahoma! Dulcie, I've been telling you for a while now to do interior design from your home. Why not? God gave you these talents and interests, ladies. He isn't some big Cosmic Tease. Our husbands find a way to be both father and career-guy. There's got to be a way for us to be good moms and also pursue our dreams.

Okay, gotta run. Cassia has dance class tonight....
Love,
Jocelyn

P.S. I don't want to hear a SINGLE WORD from either Connie or Rosalyn. We all know how you two feel about this subject. And I say that with love.:)

From:	VIM <vivalaveronica@marcelloportraits.com>
To:	Rosalyn Ebberly <prov31woman@home.com>
Subject:	**Re: Mom and Dad**

<Mom and Dad haven't been able to make it to any of my children's events since you got married. However, they have managed to come to Ashley's piano recital, Courtney's T-ball tournament and Stanley's birthday party. I think it was particularly mean of you to schedule his party the same weekend as Suzannah's Grandma/Granddaughter tea. She misses seeing her Grandma Stewart, who seems completely preoccupied with her *new* step-grandchildren. How am I supposed to explain it to her?>

Rosalyn, I did NOT schedule Stanley's party on purpose to conflict with Suzannah's tea. I'm fit to be tied about it myself! But before you go pitching a hissy fit, I don't think it's fair to blame ME for Mama and Daddy's choices. It's a far enough piece from Chicago to Houston, but Hibiscus is a whole nuther thing. And you're not the only one with grandkids now, so you can't expect to have Mama and Daddy all the time. My kids are in much greater need of grandparents than y'all's. Don't Chad's folks live in Seattle? Besides, I'm sure if you simply communicated to them how important it is for them to come to something, instead of getting all het up about it, they'd do their best to make it. I've learned in the business world how necessary it is to state your needs and wants clearly, without apologizing or being hesitant. I know it's easy for you, being home all the time, to get into the habit of expecting everyone else to read your mind, but the real world just doesn't work that way. There ya go. Just talk to them next time, okay?

Ronnie

From:	Rosalyn Ebberly <prov31woman@home.com>
To:	SAHM I Am <sahmiam@loophole.com>
Subject:	[SAHM I AM] TOTW November 15: Good Family Communication

Competent Conversationalists,

This week's topic comes from a discussion I had yesterday with my sweetheart Chad. We were discussing on the way home from church why the subject of communication skills comes up so frequently in our couples' Sunday school class. After all the books written about communication, after all the teaching done on it, why is it still such a difficult skill for most people to master? Chad and I don't have a problem with it, of course, but we thought maybe the rest of you could help us understand why it's a struggle for you.

So, please, let's communicate about…COMMUNICA-TION!

Yours in humility,

Rosalyn Ebberly

SAHM I Am Loop Moderator

"She looks well to the ways of her household, and does
not eat the bread of idleness."
Proverbs 31:27 (NASB)

From:	Dulcie Huckleberry <dulcie@nebweb.net>
To:	Thomas Huckleberry <t.huckleberry@cortech.com>
Subject:	**Next Weekend?**

Darling,
Why did your mother just call me and ask if you were coming to Branson this weekend to help her install her new computer and e-mail for her?
Dulcie

From:	Zelia Muzuwa <zeemuzu@vivacious.com>
To:	"Green Eggs and Ham"
Subject:	**Bad fight...**

Tristan's never been so mad at me before, and I'm not even
sure what I did, exactly. He came home from work today and
the children were doing interest projects—Seamus was looking at a piece of his scab under the microscope in the kitchen,
Cosette was painting the alphabet in animal shapes on butcher
paper in the dining room, and Griffith was building a fort
with wooden blocks in the living room.

When Tristan walked into the house he looked a little
grouchy, but he didn't say anything—at all, not even hello.
Just stomped upstairs to change his clothes. I figured he'd had
a bad day at work. But when he came back down, he had

what I call his "royal British fit" stance—nose in the air, chest expanded, hands clasped behind him. Always spells trouble...

"What shall we have for dinner?" he asks.

I respond that I hadn't thought about it yet.

"Suppose we pretend we are having a picnic in the living room, since the kitchen and dining room seem to be otherwise...occupied." Then he made a big show of checking the living room. "Oh, never mind. The living room is also rather disheveled, I see."

"Why don't you just get carryout tonight?" I must admit I wasn't very interested in food. My children were engrossed in discovery of the world—Tristan was the only one who was hungry.

"As I did last night? And three nights before?"

I finally gave him my full attention. "What's the matter, Tristan? You seem upset."

That's when he exploded! He was mad because the house was cluttered, dinner wasn't ready, the children were a mess and I—as he put it—"lack structure and a sense of self-discipline and routine."

Well, DUH! It took him nine years to figure that out?

Turns out, he doesn't like my method of schooling. Thinks the kids should be in a formal educational environment. I reminded him we had already talked about that, and he had agreed that an institutional setting robs children of their natural curiosity and hunger to learn. He claims he hadn't agreed with the ideas, he'd agreed to let me TRY them. Well, it sure seemed to me like he agreed with my philosophy, too!

"Cosette cannot read!" he griped.

"She's only four and a half."

"Griffith spends all his time building towers and crashing them with his cars."

"Which is pretty much what he would do in preschool."

"I want Seamus to know about the Empire, the Civil War, the...the Luddite Riots! When will he learn such important historical events?"

"When we move to England, dear."

Now he was pouting. "I might have meant the American Civil War, you know."

"But you didn't."

He couldn't deny it. Instead, he waved a brochure in my face. I grabbed it—a slick, fancy advertisement for a slick, fancy private school. A BRITISH private school here in Baltimore, I might add.

He claims that this school's method of education is far superior to what he calls "letting the kids run wild." I keep telling him the proper term is "natural education," but he won't listen. Never in our nine years of marriage has he ever tried to pull some male chauvinist routine on me—even though I know his family raised him that way. But now, he's claiming that "we tried your methods, and now it is time to correct the damage." So without my consent, he's planning to put Seamus in the first grade there, and Cosette and Griffith in the preschool.

How could he do this to me? I've done my very best with them, and he didn't even give me a fair chance. I'm so mad I don't even want to be in the same room with him. I've never felt so hurt in my whole life.

Z

From:	Thomas Huckleberry <t.huckleberry@cortech.com>
To:	Dulcie Huckleberry <dulcie@nebweb.net>
Subject:	Re: Next Weekend?

Hi Dulcie,

Sorry about the weekend—it sort of came up at the last minute. You know how we've been trying to talk Mom into getting a computer? Morris finally bought her one, but she doesn't have anyone to help her install it. She also wants to e-mail us, so I'm going to set that up, too. You should be glad. Now she won't have to call as often!

I know I was supposed to be home this weekend, but she needs my help. I'll make it up to you.

Love,

Tom

From:	P. Lorimer <phyllis.lorimer@joono.com>
To:	"Green Eggs and Ham"
Subject:	Re: Bad fight...

Dear Zelia,

I'm sorry to hear about the altercation with Tristan. He really should have been more understanding and flexible. But I honestly don't understand why you are so upset about the kids going off to school. You'll have so much more free time—to do art, to spend with friends. Maybe even pursue a career if you want. There are days when I can only dream of that sort of freedom. I've almost forgotten what it's like. And I know I shouldn't gripe—my children are practically angelic. But Bennet is almost ten months old now and I have yet to get a complete night's sleep in over a year and a half.

Julia is in the midst of a tantrum as I write this. In her room, lying on the floor, kicking and howling. And...throwing shoes, it sounds like, from the random thwacks on the walls. At least I hope it's just shoes and not her head or something. Our "office" is the end of the hallway, right outside her door, so it's very noisy. It's because I told her we were not going to watch *Veggie Tales* this morning. It wasn't because I didn't want her to. Our *Veggie* videos are all worn out or broken, and there just isn't money to replace them. The town is too small to have a video rental, and the folks at the library still think Captain Kangaroo is on television. I thought about trying to borrow a video from one of the other young families in the church, but then I remembered—we ARE the only young family at church.

I complain too much. Jonathan had a counseling session yesterday with a woman whose husband is abusing her. My sweetie is trying to help her see that she needs to take the children and get to a safe place, but she thinks "tomorrow" her husband will change. And I'm whining about worn-out videotapes.

Now Julia's beating on the door with...a doll, I think. I can hear the eyes rattling in the head every time she yanks it back for another go. Why is it that there are no books on anger management for 2-year-olds?

I'm sorry, Zelia. I've just reread this letter and realized I've made it all about my problems instead of yours. I will pray for you and Tristan. Maybe God is creating a new path for you both.
Love,
Phyllis

From:	Dulcie Huckleberry <dulcie@nebweb.net>
To:	Thomas Huckleberry <t.huckleberry@cortech.com>
Subject:	**Re: Next Weekend?**

Tom,
You were supposed to help me clean the house this week-end! For Thanksgiving, remember? Everyone is going to be here in just over a week! What do you expect me to do—take care of it all on my own? Oh, wait, I do that all the time. Never mind, no problem.
Dulcie

From:	The Millards <jstcea4jesus@familymail.net>
To:	"Green Eggs and Ham"
Subject:	**Re: Bad fight...**

Z,
Can't write long—taking Tyler to the doctor to see why his leg is hurting. I'm getting worried. Just wanted to let you know I care and I hope you can work this conflict out with Tristan. Keep trying! I'll be praying…
Jocelyn

From:	Thomas Huckleberry <t.huckleberry@cortech.com>
To:	Dulcie Huckleberry <dulcie@nebweb.net>
Subject:	**This Weekend**

<What do you expect me to do—take care of it all on my own? Oh, wait, I do that all the time. Never mind, no prob-lem.>

Great—then you don't need me anyway. Not that this comes as a huge shock to me. I always suspected it. My amazing wife—completely self-sufficient: needs nothing, wants nothing, accepts nothing. I guess I'll see you at Thanksgiving. Tom

From:	Dulcie Huckleberry <dulcie@nebweb.net>
To:	Thomas Huckleberry <t.huckleberry@cortech.com>
Subject:	**Re: This Weekend**

I absolutely REFUSE to comment on your e-mail. If you have something to say, you can come home and say it in person—what a concept! But I'm not going to carry on some dumb e-mail argument. Especially when you are deliberately twisting my words!

I do need you this weekend! I need you every weekend. You have no idea how long the weeks get without you around. I nearly kill myself trying to keep everything under control around here, so that when you come home, we can spend time with each other. But you take every opportunity to be gone!

So, no, I'm not going to respond to your e-mail. It was sarcastic and childish and completely out of context. I have nothing at all to say about it. But I do have needs and wants. And if you can't see that, well, it's not my fault.

I don't want to discuss this in an e-mail, except to say that if that's what you really think—you're completely wrong.

And don't you DARE comment about the house or dinner or anything for Thanksgiving. I'm not going to knock myself out trying to do everything by myself. I'll get done what I can, and if it's not how you like it, we both will know why. But I won't go THERE right now—we really

need to talk while you're home. You WILL be home through the weekend, right?
Dulcie

From:	Thomas Huckleberry <t.huckleberry@cortech.com>
To:	Dulcie Huckleberry <dulcie@nebweb.net>
Subject:	**Re: This Weekend**

AUTOMATIC RESPONDER MESSAGE FOLLOWS:
Hello,
Thank you for your e-mail. I will be out of the office November 20-21 and 25-26. I will make every effort to reply quickly when I return.
Sincerely,
Thomas Huckleberry, consultant
CorTech, Inc.

From:	J. Huckleberry <ilovebranson@branson.com>
To:	Dulcie Huckleberry <dulcie@nebweb.net>
Subject:	**My First E-mail!!!**

Dearest Dulcie, and McKenzie, Haley and Aidan,
This is your mother-in-law, Jeanine! If you are reading this, Tom has gotten my computer set up!!! I'm sending you my FIRST E-MAIL! I'm so excited!

Morris is reading over my shoulder and thinks I shouldn't use so many exclamation points. But I can't help it! I just told him it's almost as exciting as when he first kissed me! Almost, but not quite! Now Tom, who is also reading over my shoulder, is acting all embarrassed at the idea of his mother kissing somebody! Grow up, Tom!!!

Morris and I are SO excited about coming for Thanksgiving! I can't wait for you to meet him! I hope it wasn't TOO much trouble to let Tom come this weekend. I'm sure you had a lot of things to do to get ready, and I stole away your help!

I have a surprise for you!!! Morris and I are going to come EARLY to help you get ready!!! We'll be in around 8 Tuesday evening, and then we can spend all day on Wednesday helping you! You won't have to worry about a thing! It's just our way of saying thanks for letting Tom help me set up the computer. I've wanted a computer at home for AGES!!!

Morris says staring at a computer screen will make my eyes go bad, but I told him it doesn't matter since I already wear contacts! Morris thinks we should buy a special filter for the screen, just in case, but I don't want to spend money on something so boring!

Okay, I want to send this now! Give those precious honey-girls hugs from Memaw and Morris! We can't wait to see them!!!
Love you so much!!!!!!!!!
Mom H.

From:	Zelia Muzuwa <zeemuzu@vivacious.com>
To:	"Green Eggs and Ham"
Subject:	**Bad fight continued**

Hey gals,
<But I don't really understand why you are so upset about the kids going off to school.>

Phyllis, you'd have to know Tristan to understand. He's brilliant, classy, good-looking, perfectly organized and has a great career. Most days, I'm not even sure how we got together—I can't organize an empty box, I'm flighty and I live on some artistic planet in a galaxy far, far away. Schooling the kids was, I guess, my one big chance to show him I'm competent in something that matters. Plus, I love having the kids around during the day. I don't really want to get a job "on the outside"—I like being home! But he took away the three best reasons for being home, and stuck them in school. I'm going to miss out on watching Cosette learn to read. I won't get to teach Griffith to tie his shoe or see Seamus's eyes light up when he makes some new discovery about nature. Some teacher in a classroom is going to get PAID to see all those things I'd gladly witness for free. And I hate that idea!

I don't know how to even approach it with Tristan—I'm still too angry. And he has all of next week off for Thanksgiving, so I don't know what I'm going to do. I know we need to talk, but I don't think the things I want to say right now would make God very happy.

Z

From:	Dulcie Huckleberry <dulcie@nebweb.net>
To:	J. Huckleberry <ilovebranson@branson.com>
Subject:	**Re: My First E-mail!!!**

Mom,
Congratulations on the e-mail. It came through just fine. I'm glad Tom was able to make it down to help you this weekend. Please don't feel obligated to come early—it's no big

deal. Of course, we always love to see you. I'm looking forward to meeting Morris, too.

Love,
Dulcie

From:	Dulcie Huckleberry <dulcie@nebweb.net>
To:	"Green Eggs and Ham"
Subject:	Panicking...

You guys, my mother-in-law is coming EARLY for Thanksgiving, and bringing her boyfriend with her! What am I going to do? Since Tom didn't come home this weekend, I haven't gotten the house cleaned yet, and I was counting on having all day Tuesday and then Wednesday, too, to finish things up, but now they're arriving Tuesday evening! I won't be ready on Tuesday! To make matters worse, MY mother wants to come over and help on Wednesday also. If there's one thing you DON'T want the day before you host a huge family holiday, it's my mom and Tom's mom in the same house trying to "help." Jeanine's ideas are always wildly elaborate, and my mother prefers practicality and simplicity. Jeanine likes to talk, and...well, my mom likes to talk, too, except she actually expects to be HEARD, as well. And the last time they both were around the same kitchen, they got into a very POLITE argument about the best recipe for chocolate chip cookies. Not to mention the ongoing competition to see who is the most popular grandma with the girls!

I can't do this! It's bad enough that I'm single-handedly putting Thanksgiving together. I can't referee my relatives, too!

It's been a horrible, no-good, very bad week all around. Z, I'm so sorry to hear about things with Tristan. I wish I could give you some good advice or something, but I don't seem to be able to keep things on an even keel with Tom, so anything I'd say would be the height of hypocrisy. Jocelyn, let me know what you find out about Tyler's leg. I hope he's okay. Phyllis, take it from me—stock up on dolls. After their heads get banged off so many times, they don't snap back on anymore.

I had a church friend call me this evening, just to chat. She griped about her job, her lack of a boyfriend, how lonely she was, etc. Then she said, "Sometimes I just envy you so much! I can't imagine how awesome it would be to be off the dating-go-round, have a great husband and adorable children, and be able to stay home and play with them all day long. It must be incredibly relaxing not to have to work!"

Yes, my friends, our stress-free life is why there are bags under our eyes and on our thighs, and an entire case of Advil in our medicine cabinets. I chew my fingernails to the quick just for the fun of it, don't you know?
Dulcie

From:	VIM <vivalaveronica@marcelloportraits.com>
To:	Rosalyn Ebberly <prov31woman@home.com>
Subject:	Re: Thanksgiving?

<It just would have been nice to get an invitation. After all, you invited everyone else in the family, and we would love to meet your in-laws. I know you've all said you think Chad and I are too "religious," but did you have to purposefully leave us out?>

Honey-sis, now don't go raising a ruckus. We didn't invite you because y'all *always* do Thanksgiving with Chad's family. Why would we think this year would be any different? I don't get why you're having a conniption. Bless your sweet little heart, you don't like how we celebrate Thanksgiving anyway. We actually have FUN—which gets you all whomperjawed. If all y'all want to come, you're always welcome. You ought to know that, so there ya go.

Ronnie

From:	Rosalyn Ebberly <prov31woman@home.com>
To:	SAHM I Am <sahmiam@loophole.com>
Subject:	[SAHM I Am] TOTW November 22: Making Thanksgiving Healthier

Sweet Sisters,

I know we're all busy this week preparing for the holiday, but in the middle of travel or baking preparations, I thought it would be a good idea to discuss ways we can make Thanksgiving healthier. I'm sure our Pilgrim fathers would have been horrified at the gluttony with which most people celebrate their historic feast. To combat that, this week I will be sending several recipes for healthy Thanksgiving dishes, and I'd love to hear from all of you, too.

But health isn't only in what we eat. Holidays can be stressful times, at least from what other people tell me. Our family get-togethers are always so peaceful, but I understand this is probably not the case for the rest of you. What can you do to infuse this week with peace and love?

My sister and her new husband, by contrast, are spending the whole weekend entertaining my parents as well as his folks—who are visiting from Italy for the next six weeks—and all their relatives. They have a huge, fancy house with a pool, and a big-screen TV on which they will watch the Macy's Thanksgiving Day Parade. Frank's mother is making Italian food for the main dinner, and my mom will bake her special turkey and stuffing. We will be the only ones not there, but I'm grateful to escape the chaos and indigestion, not to mention the hassle of traveling all the way to Houston.

Our family has actually done away with the traditional dinner altogether. We get together with all of Chad's relatives and fast the noon meal. Instead of indulging ourselves, we go to the local rescue mission together and prepare and serve a Thanksgiving dinner to all the homeless people. Then, in the evening, we eat a simple meal together by candlelight. Not only do we prevent overeating this way, but we also have such a heightened sense of gratefulness to God for the food we do have and for all His blessings to us. It will be our third year of doing this, and it's quickly becoming the family's favorite holiday tradition.

Ministering to the less fortunate is much more satisfying than dining in the lap of luxury, don't you think?

Thanking God for all of you,

Rosalyn Ebberly

SAHM I Am Loop Moderator

"She looks well to the ways of her household, and does not eat the bread of idleness."

Proverbs 31:27 (NASB)

From:	Zelia Muzuwa <zeemuzu@vivacious.com>
To:	"Green Eggs and Ham"
Subject:	**Re: Rosalyn's totw**

She should have changed her signature line to...
"...and does not eat the Turkey of Gluttony, nor the cranberry sauce, nor the mashed potatoes, nor the corn on the cob, yams, or dinner rolls, and most DEFINITELY NOT the pumpkin pie, poor virtuous, blessed (and hungry) woman that she is..."

From:	Dulcie Huckleberry <dulcie@nebweb.net>
To:	SAHM I Am <sahmiam@loophole.com>
Subject:	**Happy Monday Morning!**

It's almost 10 a.m. and I've been in shock for the past two hours! Guess who showed up on my doorstep at 8 this morning? TOM!

I open the door and there he is, in the snow I haven't shoveled off the front stoop yet, holding out three long-stem roses. Okay, so they're the kind you get from a gas station for a buck a piece, but still...

"Happy Thanksgiving," he says with that lopsided naughty-boy grin of his. Mmm...

"You're not supposed to be here until Wednesday night," is all I can manage, because I am truly brilliant sometimes.

"You know I like to be early. You'll let me in anyway, won't you?"

I try to tell myself I am still mad at him for the weekend, but you know, it IS a new week. Can't hold on to grudges forever. And besides, he looks soooo good. I just throw myself into his arms, and the roses drop onto the porch beside us. We kiss while he opens the screen door, we kiss while we stumble over the threshold, kiss our way into the living room, and while he takes off his coat. And just as we are getting to the couch, we hear a little mousy voice.

"Daddy?" says McKenzie, looking cute in her fleecy blanket sleeper. She's interrupting the first romantic interlude I've had in weeks, but…cute. "Why you trying to eat my mommy?"

I bury my face in the cushions and squeal, but Tom answers, as smooth as chocolate, " 'Cause I didn't have breakfast yet. Can I eat you?"

He drops to his hands and knees on the floor and starts toward her, so she shrieks and runs around the room, him chasing her. When he catches her, he tickles her. Hearing both of them laughing brings tears to my eyes. Why can't it always be this way? :)

Turns out, he felt so bad about not coming home over the weekend that he decided to actually take the next THREE days off, and he left at five this morning to come home. He'll be home all week! Thing is, I have no idea what I'm going to do with him. I'm not used to having him around that much, and I got most of the housecleaning done without him. But it is GOOD to have him home!

Dulcie

From:	Zelia Muzuwa <zeemuzu@vivacious.com>
To:	Dulcie Huckleberry <dulcie@nebweb.net>
Subject:	Re: [SAHM I AM] Happy Monday Morning

<We kiss while he opens the screen door, we kiss while we stumble over the threshold, kiss our way into the living room, and while he takes off his coat.>
Uh, Dulcie, babe… WAY too much information! :) But I'm glad he's home. Have a great holiday!
Z

From:	The Millards <jstcea4jesus@familymail.net>
To:	SAHM I Am <sahmiam@loophole.com>
Subject:	Tyler

Dear friends,
Please pray for us. We just found out from our doctor that our son, Tyler, who is 8 years old, has juvenile rheumatoid arthritis, which explains why he has been having so many aches and pains lately. It's not life-threatening, but it will probably continue to be painful for quite a while, and he may have to have medication and therapy for several years or more.

I just reread what I've written and it sounds so clinical, so calm. But I'm really not calm at all. I'm completely over-whelmed! This is my little boy! The one who thrives on tae kwon do and soccer. He won't be able to continue sports at all, I don't think. And I have a stack of pamphlets about the disorder, medication, physical therapy and other companion disorders. I can't even comprehend that something like this is happening, much less act like the adult in the situation. I want to sit down and cry, but I'm afraid of how that would make Tyler feel. He's already a little scared, and I want to help him be brave. But how can I when I'm scared, too? And Shane isn't willing to talk about it yet. He's in shock, just like the rest of us, but I need him.

We're supposed to be hosting Thanksgiving for Shane's family this year. I don't feel very thankful. This is going to change Tyler's life forever, and it's never going to go away. I should be glad it isn't worse—Tyler will still be able to live a fairly "normal" life. But I just can't stand the thought of him facing years and years of chronic pain. My goodness, how am I supposed to be thankful for this?

Jocelyn

From:	Dulcie Huckleberry <dulcie@nebweb.net>
To:	SAHM I Am <sahmiam@loophole.com>
Subject:	**Yesterday...**

Just when you think the Thanksgiving family celebration is going to proceed without a hitch... I mean it—things were going great. With Tom home, I got the house decorated, the baking done, kept my mom and Tom's mom from swaggering too much and generally was feeling great about how the whole thing was progressing.

We all sat down at the dining table—Becky, Jordan, and kids, my brothers and their families, Grandma, the mothers, even Morris (who turns out to be a pretty decent guy, actually). The candles were lit, the turkey looked great, the bread smelled heavenly. We always take turns before the prayer to tell what we are thankful for. Tom even said he was thankful that I'm such a great wife!

Then it was my turn. I got as far as "This year, I'm most thankful for—"

And that's when I heard the sound that is every mother's nightmare. I looked over and saw McKenzie helplessly puking all over the table! Everyone gasped, but they didn't move.

"You suppose somebody could get me a towel or something!" I shouted.

My brother Kevin jumped up and dashed to the kitchen. He returned with a tiny dish cloth! His wife was, like, "Oh good grief!" I ran to the bathroom and grabbed a couple of bath towels. While everyone else made inane comments about my "poor little kiddo," I single-handedly cleaned her up, wiped up the table, then got her down and put her to bed.

When I came back to the dining room, my mother was in the process of clearing off the ENTIRE table so she could remove the tablecloth. Nobody protested—they looked like they'd lost their appetite. We eventually ate about an hour later, but the "mood" was gone.

After dinner, everyone had to leave quickly. This morning, I find out from Mom that Grandma is now sick, too.

"Well, we *know* you didn't *mean* to make Grandma sick," my mother croons, "but that's just the difficulty of trying to plan something in a house with children. You probably missed the warning signs because you were so busy getting ready. I just hope Grandma doesn't have any serious complications. You know she's susceptible to digestion problems, and if she loses too much weight…"

Subtext: "If Grandma gets the flu and dies, you will go down in family history as the reason why. And we will never, ever let you or anyone else forget it."

Not that they will forget anyway. Every year, from here on, it's going to be "Remember the time we had Thanksgiving at Dulcie's house and McKenzie barfed all over the table?" And then the tale will morph into "Remember how she puked on the turkey?" And everyone will laugh and nod. "Oh yeah, who could forget?" Even though it never happened.

And why is it that somehow it's MY fault? Did I make my child get sick? No. Am I supposed to see into the future and just "know" it was going to happen? Apparently. 'Cause I'm THE MOM. I'm "mom-niscient," I'm "mom-ni-present," I'm "mom-nipotent." Supernatural being that I am, I could have stopped this from happening. Thus, because I didn't, everyone is slightly suspicious that secretly, I *wanted* this to happen. Yes, I admit it! I cunningly sabotaged my own first effort at hosting a family holiday by infecting my daughter with some diabolical illness that would cause disgust and revulsion among all my relatives—not to mention, attempting to do away with my own grandmother in the process.

COME ON, PEOPLE! I know my children have driven me insane, but I'm not maniacal…yet.

Of course, I now know how to get my mom and mother-in-law to stop fighting over who gets to spend time with the grandchildren. :)

And Jeanine spent the rest of the visit telling Morris about all the times Tom was sick as a child. By the end of the day, even *I* didn't have an appetite! So help me, if he gets sick this weekend…

McKenzie now has a fever and is getting a cough, too. So much for a "happy" Thanksgiving. And we were planning to get our Christmas tree this weekend! Grrrr!
Dulcie

From:	The Millards <jstcea4jesus@familymail.net>
To:	SAHM I Am <sahmiam@loophole.com>
Subject:	**[SAHM I AM] With grateful hearts...**

Hey, precious people,

I'm practically in tears (again) because of the outpouring of love and concern from you all for Tyler. Thank you, ever so much. Your prayers and encouragement mean so much to our family. I just wanted you to know that yesterday all our relatives arrived, each with a special gift for Tyler. It was like an early Christmas. Everyone pitched in and helped, and their love just permeated the entire day. Tyler told me he was afraid everyone would treat him weird, or be awkward around him. But they were great. They had him laughing and cracking jokes by the end of the day, just like the old Tyler.

I'm not going to say we're suddenly okay now or comfortable with this new disorder, but I feel much more confident about it. It was like God sent us a huge dose of joy, through each one of you and our family. It was one of the most precious holiday gatherings I can remember. I was wrong—there is MUCH to be thankful for this year.

Love to every single one of you,

Jocelyn

From:	VIM <vivalaveronica@marcelloportraits.com>
To:	Rosalyn Ebberly <prov31woman@home.com>
Subject:	**Christmas plans...**

Hi Sis!

Yeehaw, I'm so glad y'all are coming for Christmas! Mama and Daddy told Frank's parents all about you, and they are very interested to meet you. Mama and Daddy just LOVE Beppe and Tiziana—they said it was too bad that Chad's parents are the ones who live in America instead of the Marcellos. They'd gladly see it switched around.

I know you were a mite worried about the cost of presents for everyone, but Frank and I can't help but go a little overboard this year—since it's our first Christmas as a family. We know y'all are poor as Job's turkey, so we thought maybe if you limited it to $40 to $60 per person for each of us it would be easier for you. Nothing fancy. I'm attaching a gift wish list for all of us, and if you might could send me one for your family, well, that would be finer than frog's hair. I'm expecting you'll need to buy for about fifteen people, because it looks like Aunt Kris and Uncle Shawn and their kids are coming, too.

Oh, also we're throwing a huge party—a black-tie affair—for all our friends and adult relatives, so be sure to buy a new formal. Chad can rent a tux here. You'll need to bring a small gift for each of you to exchange—something in the $20 to $30 range will be fine. Santa's fixing to be there, and for $20 you can have your picture taken with him. We're hiring a babysitter for the kids, so you'll need to chip in for that, too.

Other than that, we just plan to relax and enjoy visiting with each other. Ain't seen some of y'all in a coon's age, as we say 'round these parts. Houston has lots of fun stuff to do during Christmas, so we can do as much sight-seeing and shopping as we want. There ya go! I can't hardly wait!

Ronnie

From:	Rosalyn Ebberly <prov31woman@home.com>
To:	SAHM I Am <sahmiam@loophole.com>
Subject:	[SAHM I AM] TOTW December 6: Simplifying Christmas

Salutations, Sweet Sisters,

It's 5:15 a.m. here in Washington, and I'm sitting at my computer with a steaming cup of herbal tea, watching snow falling in the light of the streetlamp. We just put up our Christmas tree this past weekend, and it casts a cheery glow from the living room. I love early mornings—everything is still quiet and calm. It's a time for reflection, to meditate on all of the Lord's blessings.

This morning, I'm taking time to appreciate the simplicity of silence, of hot tea, of having time to write an e-mail to my dear friends out there in cyberspace. And I wonder—how can I keep this sense of peace and relaxation throughout the coming holiday season, when so many people are more stressed now than at any other time of the year?

Ladies, the EVILS of *commercialism* have overtaken our sacred holiday. We have bowed our knees to *consumerism,* given our hearts to the wicked IDOL of *materialism* and made a mockery of the blessings of *capitalism*. It's time to TAKE BACK OUR HOLY DAY! Are you with me? What can we do to simplify this holiday season? Perhaps we should ban

Christmas presents or picket the Santa line at the mall. The pressure of gift-giving is SUCH a distraction, not to mention a waste of time and money. What do you think?

Blessings and joy to you all,

Rosalyn Ebberly

SAHM I AM Loop Moderator

"She looks well to the ways of her household, and does not eat the bread of idleness."

Proverbs 31:27 (NASB)

From:	Dulcie Huckleberry <dulcie@nebweb.net>
To:	"Green Eggs and Ham"
Subject:	**Chat Tonight**

Hey girls,

I won't be chatting with you tonight. The kids and I are in Kansas City this week to do some shopping, and for Tom's company "Holiday" party. (Naturally, we can't call it a Christmas party!) We're staying at Tom's extended-stay suite at the Residence Inn. It has a bedroom with a king-size bed, and a foldout couch in the living room, and a kitchenette with a dining area. I'm most excited about the hot tub and pool just down the hall. I brought the baby monitor so Tom and I can enjoy some alone time after the kids are asleep. But the Internet access is a little too expensive for chatting. So don't say anything too interesting until I get back!

Love to all,

Dulcie

From:	Zelia Muzuwa <zeemuzu@vivacious.com>
To:	"Green Eggs and Ham"
Subject:	Re: Chat Tonight

Dulcie Huckleberry wrote:

<I won't be chatting with you tonight.>

Okay, gals, this is our chance! Now we can talk about Dulcie and say all the things we've wanted to say, but couldn't with her around!!! Like, how jealous we are that she'll be sitting in a relaxing hot tub with her husband in some swanky hotel while we're sitting in our pj's at the computer...so NOT fair!

(Love ya, Dulcie...)

Ham

From:	Dulcie Huckleberry <dulcie@nebweb.net>
To:	"Green Eggs and Ham"
Subject:	Re: Chat Tonight

<Okay, gals, this is our chance! Now we can talk about Dulcie and say all the things we've wanted to say, but couldn't with her around!!!>

Yeah, like what you're all getting me for Christmas! :)

Dulcie

From:	Brenna L. <saywhat@writeme.com>
To:	"Green Eggs and Ham"
Subject:	Re: Chat Tonight

Oh, that's no big surprise…

JUST OUR LOVE AND BLESSINGS! (and maybe an e-mail Christmas card if you've been a REALLY good girl…)

However, if you want something more, you could always take a break from that hot tub and go buy yourself something in KC and put our names on it. :)

Merry Christmas!

Brenna

From:	P.Lorimer <phyllis.lorimer@joono.com>
To:	"Green Eggs and Ham"
Subject:	Re: Chat Tonight

<Buy yourself something in KC and put our names on it.>

This is not a bad idea! I should suggest it to my parents who think Christmas can't possibly go on without EVERYONE giving and receiving gifts…to the hundredth generation. Honestly, if Great-aunt Maricella's cousin Donald doesn't get a present from us, will it really hurt his feelings? Or will it simply make my mother burst a blood vessel? Nobody ever warns innocent young brides about the HOLIDAY ISSUE. I don't recall reading about it in any marriage book or our pastor counseling us about it. Why is that, I wonder?

Phyllis

From:	Zelia Muzuwa <zeemuzu@vivacious.com>
To:	"Green Eggs and Ham"
Subject:	Holiday issues

I am so totally with you on holiday issues! Here's how our annual family debate goes:

Tristan's "mum" on the phone from England: "Well, dear, have you any plans for the holidays? You know we adore having all of you, and if Tristan can work out the extra time off…"

Me, trying to keep her from getting her hopes up: "I don't know, Mom. We were sorta planning to stay put this year. We've never celebrated Christmas in our own home before. Why don't you come stay with us?"

"I don't see how we possibly could, darling. I have a dreadful phobia of flying, you know."

Me, with a sigh: "Yeah, I know."

"It always works so nice for you to come here. We scarcely ever have time to see the children as it is. But I suppose you have plans with *your* parents already…"

"Not really." I can practically recite what's coming next.

"Well, then! It should work out just fine. You can fly out early the week before, spend two weeks with us, and be home in time for new year's with your family. After all, they get to see the children *much* more often. My heart just aches to think of it. But this worked perfectly last year."

And the year before. And the year before that…

So, once again, we will not have the pleasure of spending Christmas in our own house, creating our own family traditions, doing the holidays in our own way. We will be at the mercy of parents who can't seem to let us experience what they fight so hard every year to keep.

Tristan is maddeningly ambivalent about the whole thing.
He says that if I don't want to go to England, we can stay
home. But it's just not that simple! If we stay home, it's ME
who will get the blame and guilt trips for it for as long as his
parents both shall live. Not to mention that the kids—those
traitors!—would absolutely mutiny at the idea of skipping the
annual trek to England. They think it's the coolest place in
the whole world. When they get home, I spend the next
month trying to explain to them why they can't go around
"talking British" in horrific fake accents.

I suppose I'm just being selfish. Especially since Tristan and
the kids really enjoy the visit. But I never feel like it's OUR
Christmas. The entire thing belongs to Tristan's parents, and
for some reason, I seem to be the only one who thinks there's
something wrong with that.

Maybe there's something wrong with me, instead....
Bah, humbug.
Z

From:	P.Lorimer <phyllis.lorimer@joono.com>
To:	"Green Eggs and Ham"
Subject:	Re: Holiday issues

Z,
At least your in-laws want you to visit. Jonathan's parents
were so angry that I "ruined" their son's purity (isn't that a
switch?) that they refused to come to the wedding. They
send presents to Julia and Bennet for Christmas and birth-
days, but we rarely see them in person. After we got married, they told Jonathan that he and even Julia were

welcome in their home anytime—as long as I stayed home. He told them that if they wanted to see him or the grand-children, they'd have to accept me, as well. Twenty-one months later, they have yet to accomplish that, so we don't spend time with them.

I didn't mean to drive a wedge between my husband and his parents, but I am extremely grateful to see that Jonathan understands the meaning of "leave and cleave." If he had chosen them over me, I don't think I could have handled it. The way it is now is painful enough.

Phyllis

From:	Brenna L. <saywhat@writeme.com>
To:	"Green Eggs and Ham"
Subject:	Re: Holiday issues

Dear Scroogies,
Boy, are we a gloomy bunch this week or what? You know… things could always be worse….

From:	P.Lorimer <phyllis.lorimer@joono.com>
To:	"Green Eggs and Ham"
Subject:	Re: Holiday issues

Oh, they could, could they? Please, do enlighten us, Ms. Pollyanna. :)
Phyllis

From:	Brenna L. \<saywhat@writeme.com\>
To:	"Green Eggs and Ham"
Subject:	Re: Holiday issues

Haven't you two been reading the SAHM I Am loop this week? You should be thankful you aren't part of Connie's or Rosalyn's family! Good grief—I think a cow headed to the butcher on a rainy day in March has more Christmas spirit than those two. :)

And for your information, Madeline LOVES Pollyanna, so just cool it, okay? :)
Brenna

From:	Zelia Muzuwa \<zeemuzu@vivacious.com\>
To:	"Green Eggs and Ham"
Subject:	Re: Holiday issues

Hmm…a little touchy this afternoon, aren't we? :) By the way, do they actually send cows to the butcher in March?
Z

From:	P.Lorimer \<phyllis.lorimer@joono.com\>
To:	"Green Eggs and Ham"
Subject:	Re: Holiday issues

Oh, Brenna, I'm SO sorry. I was not trying to insult Pollyanna. I loved that book as a child, and I do think that a bright outlook on life is much better than pessimism. You're right, there are many people much worse off than I, and I should be thanking the Lord instead of griping. Thank you for reminding me.

Love,
Phyllis

From:	Brenna L. <saywhat@writeme.com>
To:	"Green Eggs and Ham"
Subject:	Re: Holiday issues

Uh, Phyllis... *teasing,* remember? You were going to work on developing that atrophied sense of humor of yours. :)
And Z, yes...they DO.
Love you, too,
Brenna

From:	The Millards <jstcea4jesus@familymail.net>
To:	SAHM I Am <sahmiam@loophole.com>
Subject:	Re: [SAHM I AM] TOTW December 6: Simplifying Christmas

Hey everyone,
I don't have a lot of time since I'm just about on my way out the door to go Christmas shopping, but I had to jump in on this one. As most of you know, Tyler is suffering from juvenile rheumatoid arthritis. He's being such a trouper about it! We had about a foot of snow yesterday, and later all the other kids went out to go sledding.

Had such fun bundling them all up—takes nearly an hour to layer on the sweaters, snow pants, coats, hats, mittens, boots, etc. Then, of course, Cassia decides she has to go potty. So we spend the next five minutes tearing everything off while she does the potty rhumba. When she returns, we go through the whole layering process again. Shane was just about ready to herd them out the door when Evelyn announces she, like big sister, needs to go! By this time, little Audra has lost her mittens, so I take care of Evelyn, and Shane looks for mittens. Finally, an hour and forty-five minutes after we took the first coat off the hanger, the four of them are bustling out the door, and it's just me and Tyler.

I put on some Christmas music and settled Tyler on the couch with his LeapPad. I didn't want to leave him all by himself, especially since he was missing the sledding outing, so I sat down in the recliner across from him. And I realized something—I didn't have a CLUE what to do with myself. I couldn't remember the last time I actually sat in that chair for anything other than putting on my shoes or helping the girls comb their hair. It was a very weird feeling.

But then, Tyler looked up from the LeapPad and said, "Mom, can I ask you a question?"

"Sure."

"Well, I was sorta thinking—about the arthritis thing and all."

"Okay…" I figured he wanted to know when he would get well or if he'd be able to do sports again or something.

But he folded his hands under his chin and put his elbows on the LeapPad. "Do you think Grandma's arthritis hurts as bad as mine?"

Oh, my! I thought I was going to burst into tears right there. But I kept it together and we had a good conversation about how Grandma's arthritis was different than his. He decided that when he is better, he wants to visit his grandparents and help Grandma like everyone has been helping him.

Then he asked, "If my legs don't work so well after I get better, do you think girls will still like me?" He turned a bit red, and sputtered, "Not that I want them to—for a long time."

I nearly choked. "I think that if you stay as sweet and kind and loving as you are now, there will be lots of girls who will like you very much, no matter how well your legs work." He gave me this rolling-eyed "Oh, Mom!" sort of look and went back to his LeapPad—but he was smiling.

Can you believe it? I learned yesterday just how much I don't know about my own son. There's an entire universe happening inside that head, and I finally got a telescopic glimpse of it. Why did it take nearly nine years and a horrible disease to make it happen?

Anyway, I just wanted to share this with you because I think Rosalyn is right—we do need to simplify our lives, particularly during the holidays. But I don't think we do that through banning Christmas presents or picketing poor Santa Clauses at the mall. I think we do it by shoving aside all the activities and duties and relaxing in an under-used recliner and waiting for our kids to show us the way to their private worlds. And then staying for as long a visit as they allow.

Okay, with that said, I HAVE to get going, because Cassia has been waiting very patiently for the past twenty minutes for me to finish up here and take her shopping. :)
Cheers,
Jocelyn

From:	Dulcie Huckleberry <dulcie@nebweb.net>
To:	The Millards <jstcea4jesus@familymail.net>
Subject:	**Tyler**

Jocelyn,

I just got back from shopping—what an adventure, I'll post the whole story on the loop in a bit—and was catching up on e-mails. Read yours and it brought tears to my eyes, especially considering what happened today. You are such a good example for me.

Love,

Dulcie

From:	The Millards <jstcea4jesus@familymail.net>
To:	Dulcie Huckleberry <dulcie@nebweb.net>
Subject:	**Re: Tyler**

<You are such a good example for me.>

Oh, please! You make it sound like I'm 150 years old! :) But…you're welcome. I know what you meant. Looking forward to hearing about your shopping adventure.

Love you back,

Jocelyn

From:	Dulcie Huckleberry <dulcie@nebweb.net>
To:	SAHM I Am <sahmiam@loophole.com>
Subject:	**Turn on your TVs! (warning, LONG post!)**

Hey everybody!

Greetings from Kansas City—where me and the girls are spending the week with DH Tom doing some Christmas shopping and relaxing. You all have to watch *Newsline* two weeks from tomorrow, because I'M ON THE SHOW!

See, it all happened like this:

Tom was working so I decided to take the girls and brave Crown Center by ourselves. For those of you who have never been to KC, Crown Center is the home of Hallmark Cards, and there's a huge shopping mall and a science center for kids, and all sorts of great activities. The plan was to go after lunch so that the girls would fall asleep in the stroller (I've got a three-seater. Looks like a bus!) and I could get shopping done. Then we were to meet Tom at the Crayola Café at 5:30 so we could do the kids' stuff after supper. Great plan, right?

Well, everything was going along perfectly. The children fell asleep in the stroller right on cue, even McKenzie who normally would be too interested in everything around her. And they STAYED asleep, even with all the noise and bustle. That should have been my first clue that something was soon to go horribly wrong. :)

I got tons of shopping done—hit a few good sales, was feeling very proud and self-sufficient. About 4:45, decided I didn't want to haul all my purchases to the restaurant with me, and headed toward the parking garage to deposit everything in the car. So far, so good, right?

Okay, so we're parked in the farthest, most forgotten corner of the garage. I reach the car at last, and pull the stroller alongside the car so I can unlock the trunk. I have all the shopping bags set on the ground next to the trunk, which is now open.

I'm just about to reach for the bags to put them in the trunk, when out of nowhere, this guy walks past me and swipes all my bags! I don't know how he did it so fast, but then he takes off running!

Oh, I was steamed! All that work, all that money, and he thought he could just walk off with it? Not around THIS MAMA!

I couldn't tell you now how it happened, but somehow I must have reached into the trunk and the first thing I touched was a crowbar. Before I knew it, that crowbar hopped into my hand and flung itself after the thief! It hit him square in the back of his head, and he dropped like a rock!

So, here I am, all alone in this parking garage, with three sleeping children and a thief whom I feared I may have killed by accident, and all my Christmas presents scattered around him. I didn't know what to do!

I glanced up and saw a fire alarm on the wall. I figured I didn't have much choice, so I pulled it. Of course, that set off a huge noise, which woke the children, and brought me lots and lots of company real quick. I was NOT alone anymore. :) Meanwhile, Mr. Sticky Fingers is still laid out on the concrete, and I could see a huge gash in the back of his head. I was just hoping he didn't bleed all over Haley's new Christmas dress!

The security guards came. And the police came. And the fire trucks came. The first person to find us was one of the firefighters. His name is Eric, and he is divorced with eight children, and he likes to eat sushi.

But I digress...

I explained to Eric about the fire alarm and showed him the man I'd KO'd. The rest of his crew radioed everyone to let them know there wasn't a fire, but by then, of course, the police were there and all the news media. The firefighters gave first aid to the man, who was not all that badly injured after all. A police officer—don't know his name, as he was considerably less friendly than Firefighter Eric—took all my shopping bags and wouldn't give them back. It occurred to me then that I should be a bit worried about what might happen to me for assaulting the would-be package snatcher. Would it be considered self-defense? Or would his family sue me? Was it against the law to pull a fire alarm when there was no fire? If the grumpy-looking officer decided to arrest me, would he wait for Tom to get there to take the girls?

I suddenly had this vision of me sitting in some gloomy prison cell trying to entertain three unhappy and frightened children. I don't know what was more disturbing—the thought of incarceration itself, or being locked in there with grouchy kids!

Anyway, it took me forever to explain to the police what had happened. They did not arrest me, though it seemed that Officer Grumpky looked a bit disappointed about that. Sticky Fingers, it turns out, is the most wanted parking-lot thief in the Kansas City metro area, so after he recovers from his concussion, he's going to jail.

The officers wanted to keep all my stuff I bought as evidence, but they settled for photographing everything instead. By this time, I'd been interviewed by several TV reporters and it was well past 5:30. The girls were getting really fussy and hungry, and I could just imagine how irate Tom would be by now, waiting for us in the café all by himself.

But just as I was beginning to think we'd never be allowed to leave, there came Tom, practically running toward us, pushing everyone out of the way.

"Dulcie!" He grabbed me and gave me such a tight hug I could hardly breathe. "You okay?"

McKenzie piped up, "Mommy killed a bad man who tried to take all our presents, just like the Grinch Who Stole Christmas, and lots of police and fire trucks came. And now they're just standing around talking. I'm hungry, can we eat soon?"

"I didn't kill him." I corrected her. "I...made him go to sleep for a while."

"You won't make me go to sleep that way, will you?"

Even Officer Grumpky smiled at that one.

"Never, sweetie," I told her. Then I asked Tom, "How did you know where we were?"

He shrugged. "Some firefighter came and told me."

It had to have been Eric—come to think of it, I had mentioned we were supposed to meet Tom in the Crayola Café. How kind of him to find Tom for me!

One of the reporters stopped Tom and asked him what he thought about his wife helping to capture one of the busiest thieves in KC. Tom grinned at me and replied, "My wife's throwing arm is almost legendary. You don't want to get in the path of any of her projectiles."

Oh, great. The reporter lifts her eyebrows and says, "I take it you speak from personal experience?"

I'm standing there thinking, *Please, oh please, don't mention the episode with the apple and the black eye!*

Tom puts his arm around my shoulders and squeezes. "Only the sort that comes from playing softball with an apple."

Whew! Sometimes, I just LOVE my husband. (Well, actually, I love him all the time...but you know what I mean.) Anyway, the reporter gave us a weird look but didn't ask any more questions.

It was nearly 6:30 by the time we finally got to the restaurant. And when we returned to the hotel, there was a message on our answering machine from Brenda Walkers, with *Newsline,* asking me to call her! It turns out, they were in KC this week doing a news story about shopping mall theft during the holidays, and had spoken with the police and some of the victims of the man I caught. So tomorrow morning I'm supposed to have an interview with her in the meeting room here, and they're planning to air the show in two weeks!

Plus, one of the mall executives walked up to us at dinner and told me that Hallmark was offering a reward for information leading to the arrest of anybody in connection with parking lot theft, so I also got that and a whole bunch of gift certificates for various shops and restaurants!

We watched the local news at 10 this evening, even let McKenzie stay up for it. She thought it was so cool to see us on TV. I thought it was pretty cool myself.

Sorry for the LONG e-mail, but I just had to tell you all what happened. Besides, I'm too wound up to go to sleep. Tom's already snoring away in bed. How DO guys do that? Dulcie

From:	Zelia Muzuwa <zeemuzu@vivacious.com>
To:	"Green Eggs and Ham"
Subject:	Re: [SAHM I AM] Turn on your TVs! (warning, LONG post!)

No fair, Dulcie! When Griffith stuck his head in the kitty post, we only made local news. Where was Brenda Walkers THEN? :)
With media envy,
Z

From:	Connie Lawson <clmo5@home.com>
To:	SAHM I Am <sahmiam@loophole.com>
Subject:	Re: [SAHM I AM] Turn on your TVs! (warning, LONG post!)

Dulcie, I am SO glad you are all right! You and your children could have been seriously injured. If it had been me, I would have let him take the bags. No amount of purchases are worth risking your life for. What if he'd had a gun?

But this is a good time to bring up the subject of shopping mall safety. I've attached a list of good rules we all should follow when out shopping, especially during the holiday season. I trust you all will take this lesson to heart and practice common sense.

And I'm sure that Dulcie and her family will be thanking God with greater appreciation this Christmas for the blessing of being together and safe. I just shudder to think of what could have happened to you!

I really hope you don't get sued or anything. You had better contact your lawyer just in case. These days, people will sue even when they were in the wrong. It's crazy.

Blessings,
Connie

From:	Rosalyn Ebberly <prov31woman@home.com>
To:	SAHM I Am <sahmiam@loophole.com>
Subject:	Re: [SAHM I AM] Turn on your TVs! (warning, LONG post!)

Dulcie's story is a perfect illustration of what consumerism and materialism have done to our nation. Years ago, before Christmas became such a time of greed and selfishness, nobody would have dreamed of stealing somebody's shopping bags. And even if they had, the person would have been reasonable enough to let them go. After all, material possessions simply aren't that important. If we weren't letting our secular culture propel us to the mall, we wouldn't ever have to face a situation like Dulcie's. I hope this wakens all of you to the evils of our modern Christmas celebration and helps inspire you to put Christ back in Christmas.

Much joy,

Rosalyn

"She looks well to the ways of her household, and does not eat the bread of idleness."

Proverbs 31:27 (NASB)

From:	Dulcie Huckleberry <dulcie@nebweb.net>
To:	"Green Eggs and Ham"
Subject:	**How the mighty have fallen...**

Hey girls,

I'm only sending this to the four of you because I just couldn't bear to put up with Rosalyn's comments if she finds out. It's Saturday night, and we just returned from Tom's company's Christmas party. He's out taking the babysitter home—hope he doesn't get lost.

To catch you up, the interview with Brenda Walkers went great. Maybe a little too great. I think my head was starting to swell with all the attention. I have to admit, I enjoyed being the hero. Everyone kept telling me how wonderful I was and how brave and smart. I must have begun to believe it.

Now, however, I know better. I am not wonderful, brave *or* smart. In fact, I have a strong suspicion I am actually rather stupid.

Today started out beautifully. I had everything arranged so I'd be ready to go to the party. I know it's just an office party, but it was black-tie, and it's about the only chance I've had all year to really dress up. You'd think I was going to my high school prom with all my primping and preening. And I looked pretty good, extra poundage aside. I'd even bought a new dress for the occasion—a long, draping number made out of this shimmery red fabric that swishes when you walk.

Tom looked great, too—rented a tux and everything. Mmm, Mmm, good! :) And he bought me these gorgeous scarlet roses with edges dipped in gold glitter. I pinned a couple in my hair, and it was just the right touch. He picked up the babysitter and brought her back to the hotel, and we were ready to go.

The party was at another hotel in their ballroom, and when we arrived, we got our picture taken. (I was a little miffed that the camera didn't make me look thinner….) The ballroom was like a fairyland. There were flocked Christmas trees all around, and glittery snowflakes suspended from the ceiling. In one corner, three tables were loaded with just about any bite-size dessert you could imagine. Think the Land of Sweets from the Nutcracker ballet, okay? Everything was so beautiful!

We had lobster for dinner, and I finally met the romance girls—Michelle, Kelly and Justine. Tom introduced me to his supervisors, Bruce and Chris, and the other programmers, and they all commented about seeing me on television on Wednesday night.

After dinner, it was Tom, me, Michelle, Kelly, and a few other programmers standing around chatting. Michelle and Kelly, of course, had to bring up Tom's supposed choices of reading material. They were gushing about how all men should read romances because it makes them "so in touch with male-female relationships." I just wanted to roll my eyes. They don't have a clue! If Tom was so great with relationships, then we wouldn't be having so many problems. And I couldn't believe it that he is STILL letting them think he actually reads romances. He never reads any novels! The guys were teasing him about it, but he was just soaking up all the girls' compliments, which made me a bit grouchy.

He suggested to me that we get our picture taken together, but Michelle said, "Wait, I want to hear about Dulcie catching the thief at the mall!"

Why didn't I tell her to take a hike, that I wanted to be with my husband? Because I was grumpy and jealous of Tom, that's why. But I wish I hadn't stayed. I wish I'd never even seen that man in the mall. Or that I'd let him take the dumb packages and be happy. Because I'm quite sure the following never would have happened if I hadn't been so high on all the fussing and heroworship.

I told the little group all about knocking out the thief, and about *Newsline* and Brenda Walkers. They were impressed, to say the least. The two girls were looking at me like I was a celebrity or something, and the guys were...well, as far as I can figure, they were *flirting* with me! Finally one of the guys grinned at me and said, "Wow, Dulcie. You travel with children, you take them shopping at Crown Center by yourself, and Tom tells me you do house repairs and interior decorating. And you even catch criminals. Is there anything you don't do?"

You guys, I'm so ashamed to tell you this part. I don't know where it came from or anything, and if I could take it back, I would. But I simpered up at him and said in my coyest voice, "Well, I certainly don't read romance novels."

It took a few seconds for my comment to sink in with Michelle and Kelly. I'd like to blame that on the visits they'd taken to the cash bar, but I'm not sure it would have been any different if they'd been totally sober. (See, even now I'm being a catty snipe.) :(Their smiles disappeared and their mouths dropped open, like, "Hey, you just insulted me!" They didn't talk to me the rest of the evening. But every once in a while, I'd see them looking over at me with this confused expression, like "What did I do to you?"

But worse was Tom. Here he'd already put up with teasing from his co-workers, and then he got clotheslined by his own wife—in front of everybody! I know perfectly well why he chats with those girls about their relationships. They treat him like an expert, like their own little key into the male mind. He gets to explain to them why men act the way they do, and they actually listen and respect his viewpoint.

When I glanced up at him, he looked stunned…and then, ashamed. And even betrayed. I wish he'd been angry. I'd rather have dealt with anger than this…whatever it is. He laughed a little at what I said, and I don't think the other guys saw how it hurt him. But I saw. His shoulders slumped the rest of the evening. We actually didn't stay long after that. He said he was tired, but I know what was really the matter. I tried to talk about it with him, tried to apologize for teasing him. He just brushed it off and said it was no big deal. That he didn't really like talking to them anyway.

But I'm afraid I really, really hurt him. Seven words! Seven of the stupidest, most callous words in the world, and they came out of MY mouth! Why did I try to make a crack like that? What's wrong with me? I love Tom! I'm not normally such a jerk.

I don't know how to go about making this right, either. You can't just take back something so snide. I wish I'd stayed in Omaha and never come at all.

Now you know the real me. All the dirty laundry. I don't like myself very much right now, so I don't expect you to, either. Good grief, why didn't I hold my tongue?

Dulcie

From:	VIM <vivalaveronica@marcelloportraits.com>
To:	Rosalyn Ebberly <prov31woman@home.com>
Subject:	**Re: Christmas Party**

<I actually wasn't *exactly* planning to come all the way from Washington to cater your Christmas party! Although I can certainly understand why you'd want me to! But traveling with three kids is wearying enough—I'd like to have at least some chance to relax while we're there.>

I didn't ask you to cater the whole dinner, Ros. All I asked is if you could bake your almond kringle for dessert. It's a special family tradition, and nobody else can make it as good as you can. I know it's a lot of work, and you sure enough deserve a vacation, but I thought you enjoyed baking—and you know everyone raves about it. But I'm not going to twist your arm. If you don't want to, fine. I'll see if one of the bakeries here can do it. There ya go. No need to get your shorts in a knot over it.

Ronnie

From:	Rosalyn Ebberly <prov31woman@home.com>
To:	SAHM I Am <sahmiam@loophole.com>
Subject:	[SAHM I AM] TOTW December 13: A Servant's Heart

God Rest Ye Merry Gentlewomen!

At this sacred and holy time of year, I have been reflecting on the Incarnation of Christ and all it means. I have just spent several hours this morning meditating on Philippians 2:5–8.

"Have this attitude in yourselves which was also in Christ Jesus, who, although He existed in the form of God, did not regard equality with God a thing to be grasped, but emptied Himself, taking the form of a bond-servant, and being made in the likeness of men. And being found in appearance as a man, He humbled Himself by becoming obedient to the point of death, even death on a cross."

I'm so glad God has gifted me with humility. I seem to be able to serve and give, with never a thought for myself, never an ulterior motive. I've just always been that way. It gives me joy to see myself made nothing and others being praised. The spotlight has always made me uncomfortable— I'm so self-effacing. In fact, this Christmas, I'll be baking our special family almond kringle for my sister's party. For no other reason than the joy it will bring to our relatives and my sister's guests.

What can you do this week to humble yourself? How can you more faithfully serve others? For those of us, like me, who are already used to living lives of humility and service, this could be a challenge to find some fresh way to take up our cross and deny ourselves. But I think we can rise to the challenge! Let's brainstorm ways we can make ourselves lesser, so that our families—and ultimately Christ—become greater.

In humility,
Rosalyn Ebberly
SAHM I Am Loop Moderator

"She looks well to the ways of her household, and does not eat the bread of idleness."
Proverbs 31:27 (NASB)

From:	Brenna L. <saywhat@writeme.com>
To:	Dulcie Huckleberry <dulcie@nebweb.net>
Subject:	**Write Me!**

Come on, honey, it wasn't that bad. You aren't sitting alone, depressed, in some closet, slurping down Baby Hydrolyte as a form of self-punishment, are you? Please answer me...

I don't mean to be selfish here, but I could really use some support. I'm going to talk to Darren tonight about adoption, and I'm so nervous. I know he's going to say we don't have the money, that Madeline is as dear to him as any biological child. But the truth is that he's really hurting over the fact that he's the one with the fertility problem.

I told you that, didn't I? He FINALLY got his sperm-count (after I told him that was the only thing I wanted for Christmas—I hope he understands the meaning of HY-PERBOLE!). It was the most humiliating experience of his whole life, and I wish I hadn't pushed so hard for it. If we'd lived closer to the lab in Tulsa, we could have "collected the sample at home" and brought it in, but we're too far away and all the little guys would have been toast by the time we arrived.

So as it turned out, Darren had to go to this lab our doctor contracts with, and this bored-looking receptionist gave him the "specimen container" and showed him to a little room. I think he was too embarrassed to let me come in with him. He promised me he didn't look at the magazines, but it just makes me angry at the lab because I know how hard he tries to keep his mind pure and here he was, surrounded by filth.

Dulcie, it was just awful! Everyone was so insensitive and unprofessional. A couple of female technicians stood outside the door laughing and talking really loud, and then when he had to turn in the container, they acted like they didn't even care how embarrassing it was for him. They had a big discussion right in front of him about whether or not there was enough to do the test. The worst part was that his count is terribly low. I'd have a better chance of winning the Iron Man Triathalon than Darren would of fathering a child.

I felt so guilty because I threw him into that situation. I guess I didn't really stop to think about what it would involve. The worst part is that even though they've made a ton of advances in female infertility treatments, there's not much they can do yet about male infertility.

As long as he could pretend it was MY problem, he could be gracious and sweet about it. But now, it's like his self-esteem is demolished. I keep trying to tell him that the ability to father a child isn't what makes him a man, but he snapped back that "That's not how I was raised. You don't understand the expectations about farming. I'm supposed to produce a kid to take over the farm. That's how it's done around here. I'm the fourth generation on this farm—and if I'm the last, then I've failed not just myself but my entire family." And ever since then, he's refused to talk about it at all. I don't know what to do!

I called a few adoption agencies, but when they found out that 1) I'm 24 and Darren just turned 28, and 2) we have a 7-year-old daughter, they all told me we're too young and not qualified because we have a child already. And even if we did get chosen by a birth mother, we could never afford the adoption. Did you know that some private adoptions cost as much as $25,000 to $30,000 because of "birth-mother expenses"? That's outrageous!

But even sadder is that we could adopt a biracial or African-American baby for a fraction of that amount, because they aren't as "placeable" as Caucasian babies. That's a nice way of saying nobody wants them. Isn't that horrible? I want them! But the problem is, I live in a community that still sees absolutely no problem at all using the "N-word" and routinely makes racial jokes about sending all of "them" back to the cotton fields. I'd never want to raise a black baby around here—poor kid would be miserable!

So I checked some international programs on the Internet. Some of them are as low as $12,000 to $15,000 and a few of them would even let younger couples adopt. But I just don't know how we could afford even that, or if Darren would be willing to consider it. Stubborn male pride!

Anyway, you always make me feel so much better about all this. I really need you. Please write to me. (And please, PLEASE don't share any of this with anybody else. Darren would just kill me if he knew I told you. But I had to talk about it with somebody, and you're about the only person I'd trust with any of it.)

Your friend,

Brenna

From:	P.Lorimer <phyllis.lorimer@joono.com>
To:	Dulcie Huckleberry <dulcie@nebweb.net>
Subject:	**Stop Sulking!**

Dearest Dulcie,

I love you very much, but I want you to take your head out from under that self-imposed rain cloud and quit pouting. I know…you "are NOT pouting!" You feel an obligation to deprive yourself of friends and any sort of potential encouragement because you don't deserve to be happy. How do I know? Because I did the exact same thing after Jonathan and I slept together when we were dating—even before I realized I was pregnant with Julia. In fact, for a while, I thought Julia was my "punishment" from God for sinning. (Don't you EVER tell her that!) It was very hard to accept her as the blessing she really was. She brought me so much joy, and I didn't think I had a right to feel that way. So I DO understand why you are avoiding us. Obviously, you are trying to stay miserable, and you know that we, your loving friends, will make you insanely happy instead. :) Am I correct?

I discovered something else through what happened with Jonathan and me. It's oh-so-easy to ask forgiveness from someone you've wronged. It's a relief to accept *their* forgiveness. It's also relatively simple to forgive somebody else, at least for me. But it's a bear of a chore to forgive yourself. Don't you think?

You are already repentant for what happened. You've probably even already told God how sorry you are and asked Him to forgive you. However, you're not going to be able to move past this until you deal with yourself first. When Jesus said, "Forgive, if you have anything against anyone, so that your

Father also who is in heaven may forgive you," I personally believe He would have included yourself in that "anyone."

I've come to realize that refusal to forgive yourself is basically pride. It's as if we're saying, "God, I know better than You do about myself. You may think it's okay to forgive me, but You're wrong. So, I'm just going to handle this one myself, okay? Don't call me, I'll call you when I'm done giving myself what I *really* deserve."

Do you honestly want to send that message to the Lord? I didn't think so. So come out from that rock you're hiding under, brush yourself off, let yourself off your own hook, and continue on with making things right with your husband and enjoying your life.

I DO love you,
Phyllis

From:	Dulcie Huckleberry <dulcie@nebweb.net>
To:	P.Lorimer <phyllis.lorimer@joono.com>
Subject:	**Re: Stop Sulking!**

WHOA! Phyllis, I don't know whether to be furious with you or…hug you. Good grief, I don't think anyone has ever given me such a verbal paddling since I was, like, 10 or something! But I have to admit—you're 100% right. I read your e-mail and it was like God just shook me up inside and said, "PAY ATTENTION, DULCIE!"

The thing is, it's all very easy to tell me to forgive myself, but how?
Dulcie

From:	P.Lorimer <phyllis.lorimer@joono.com>
To:	Dulcie Huckleberry <dulcie@nebweb.net>
Subject:	**Re: Stop Sulking!**

What a relief! I was extremely worried you'd be mad at me.
<The thing is, it's all very easy to tell me to forgive myself,
but how?>

Ah yes, I did sort of forget that part, didn't I? :) Here is
how I managed it. First, I said, "Phyllis, I forgive you for sinning with Jonathan. Yes, it was wrong, but God forgave you
and so I will, too." Then I forced myself to focus on being
thankful for the blessings God gave me—for Jonathan's love,
for Julia, and then especially for the strength of our marriage.
And every time I was tempted to think "But I deserve…(fill
in the blank)" I reminded myself of Romans 8:1. "There is
therefore now no condemnation for those who are in Christ
Jesus." And, over time, I came to believe it in my heart. I still
regret what happened, but it doesn't own me like it used to.
Does that make sense?
Phyllis

From:	Dulcie Huckleberry <dulcie@nebweb.net>
To:	P.Lorimer <phyllis.lorimer@joono.com>
Subject:	**Re: Stop Sulking!**

Thanks, Phyllis. You know, if Jonathan is even half the preacher
you are, I might consider talking Tom into moving to Wisconsin just so we can go to your church!

You are SO right. And I got to thinking…if you can learn
to forgive yourself after what happened with you and Jona-

than, I can, too. After all, it's not like what I did was anywhere near as big a deal as what you did.
Dulcie

From:	Dulcie Huckleberry <dulcie@nebweb.net>
To:	P.Lorimer <phyllis.lorimer@joono.com>
Subject:	**DELETE MY LAST MESSAGE!**

I SO DID *NOT* MEAN THAT THE WAY IT SOUNDED! I'M SOOOOOOO SORRY.

From:	Dulcie Huckleberry <dulcie@nebweb.net>
To:	P.Lorimer <phyllis.lorimer@joono.com>
Subject:	**Please forgive me!**

Oh crud. Crud, crud, CRUD! What is wrong with my brain lately? I really am sorry! I can't believe I sent something so insensitive. I didn't mean it, honest!

From:	Dulcie Huckleberry <dulcie@nebweb.net>
To:	P.Lorimer <phyllis.lorimer@joono.com>
Subject:	**Are you mad?**

I wouldn't blame you if you were. You're furious, aren't you. You would have written back by now if you weren't. Oh dear…please, Phyllis, please believe me, I didn't mean to insult you. Now I've hurt both my DH *and* my friend.

I'm going to stitch my mouth shut and duct tape my fingers together. How's that sound?
Dulcie

From:	P.Lorimer <phyllis.lorimer@joono.com>
To:	Dulcie Huckleberry <dulcie@nebweb.net>
Subject:	**Re: Are you mad?**

LOL!!! Dulcie, R-E-L-A-X. The reason I didn't answer you right away was that one of the older ladies in our congregation fell down her front steps and broke her hip. I spent all morning at the hospital with her and then had to take the afternoon to get Julia and Bennet back on schedule. I just now read all your e-mails and about pulled a muscle laughing. I *knew* what you were trying to say. And you're right, only I didn't want to seem like I was trivializing how you were feeling by saying so. :) Everything's okay.
Hugs,
Phyllis

From:	Dulcie Huckleberry <dulcie@nebweb.net>
To:	Thomas Huckleberry <t.huckleberry@cortech.com>
Subject:	**We need to talk**

Do you want me to come down to KC this weekend since you're so busy? I really, REALLY need to have a chance to make things right with you. Please.

Also, I want you to know I sent Kelly and Michelle each a note and a new novel, as an apology for offending them. I

feel really bad about hurting them, and I know it probably has made things tense for you around the office.
Please forgive me,
Dulcie

From:	Thomas Huckleberry <t.huckleberry@cortech.com>
To:	Dulcie Huckleberry <dulcie@nebweb.net>
Subject:	**Talking**

Dulcie,
I know you feel bad and that you're sorry. I forgive you—really. I'm sure Kelly and Michelle will, too. They're really nice ladies. I also agree we need to talk. I'm not sure what to say, though. You know how rotten I am about dealing with conflict. I didn't exactly have the best role models—dad got drunk and mom stressed out and did completely crazy things like auditioning for a part as a giant tulip in a local garden center commercial the year after dad left us. She got the role, which turned out to be more than she bargained for—she spent the next ten months as the nursery's official mascot. I was in eighth grade, and my nickname became "Flower Child." You can imagine what that did to my social life. Her psychologist says she deals with stress by lowering her inhibitions and doing nutty stuff. He calls it a "defense mechanism." So that's my lame excuse for not being better at this conflict-resolution thing. Maybe it's a defense mechanism, too. I was telling the truth when I said things are really hectic this week. Let me get past this weekend and then we'll talk. I promise.
Love,
Tom

From:	Dulcie Huckleberry <dulcie@nebweb.net>
To:	Brenna L. <saywhat@writeme.com>
Subject:	It's Saturday!

Dear Brenna,

I'm sorry to be such a grouch this week. And I didn't even get back to you about your adoption talk with Darren. How did it go? I'm sorry I wasn't there when you needed me. Boy, it seems like all we've done the past seven days is apologize to each other, huh? I've never been so glad to see Saturday come and go.

I'll be praying that Darren lets God heal his hurt. I haven't personally faced something like that, but I can imagine how painful it would be. My heart goes out to you both.

Love,

Dulcie

From:	Brenna L. <saywhat@writeme.com>
To:	Dulcie Huckleberry <dulcie@nebweb.net>
Subject:	So glad it's Saturday!

Dulcie,

I shouldn't have dumped on you like that when you were having a rough week. The adoption talk didn't go so well. Darren's just not ready, I guess. He thinks that since I gave birth to Madeline, if we adopt, it would be like advertising to the whole world that he has "the problem." I tried to explain to him that people might assume it's secondary infertility, which is when a woman becomes infertile after being able to have a baby, but he didn't seem to get it. So I suppose we just keep waiting. I'm super disappointed, though—every time I see a baby on TV, I start crying. Christmas is going to be a blast, huh?

Thanks for being my friend.

Brenna

From:	Michelle Oster <michelle@kcnet.net>
To:	Dulcie Huckleberry <dulcie@nebweb.net>
Subject:	**Apology**

Dear Darcy,

Thanks for the card and the book. I accept your apology. I say dumb stuff, too. In fact, Bruce (my step-dad who almost runs the company) always tells people he was crazy to hire me in the first place, but if he fires me, he'd have to sleep on the couch because Mom wouldn't even speak to him.

Something I've learned from reading romances is that the couple never finds true love and happiness with each other until they start appreciating and being nice to each other. Maybe that would help with you and Tom. Not that I'm in any place to give advice, since I haven't exactly been a success in the romance department myself, but it seems like you're taking Tom for granted. He is SO great.

I hope I'm not being too nosy by saying that. But I want Tom to be happy. I don't want him to end up like my parents and most of my friends. He deserves better. And I guess you do, too.

Sincerely,

Michelle Ostler

P.S. I already had the book you sent. But it was a nice thought.

From:	Dulcie Huckleberry <dulcie@nebweb.net>
To:	SAHM I Am <sahmiam@loophole.com>
Subject:	Re: [SAHM I AM] TOTW December 13: A Servant's Heart

Well, ladies, I haven't really been following the discussion, but I can tell you I had no problem being humbled this week. It was rather forced on me—by my own big mouth. But then, I learned a lot about what it means to be a servant, by watching my friends reach out to me and take care of me, even when I didn't want it. And by seeing how one friend's husband surrendered his own dignity and self-respect to do something for his wife that was very important to her. And learning how to have the humility to forgive myself and accept it when the person I love isn't ready to forgive me yet.

And you know what? This servanthood and humility thing isn't for wussy people. It takes a TON of courage.
Dulcie

From:	Rosalyn Ebberly <prov31woman@home.com>
To:	SAHM I Am <sahmiam@loophole.com>
Subject:	Re: [SAHM I AM] TOTW December 20: Christmas Memories

Merry Christmas, Mommies!
I am writing from my sister's home in Houston, where my children are getting to know their new cousins, who are quite amazing little ones. Ashley, the 9-year-old, is nearly fluent in Italian and will be spending the summer in Italy with her

grandparents to further her language study. Courtney, who is 6, already knows how to operate Frank's smaller cameras and helps him set up for photo shoots. Stanley is only 4, but I'm sure he has some impressive talent, as well. My parents have done nothing but gush about them since we arrived.

I know everyone is going to be busy with their own families this week, but if you have an opportunity, I thought it would be nice to simply share your favorite Christmas memory with the loop. Mine is from last year, when Suzannah was given the opportunity to sing with an elite children's choir for the White House Christmas celebration in Washington, D.C. I will never forget the moment when we actually got to meet the president! He shook our hands and said, "Mr. and Mrs. Ebberly, you must be proud to have such talented children."

Of course, we would NEVER think of taking all the glory for ourselves, so I said in return, "Thank you, Mr. President, God has blessed us with wonderful children. We also feel blessed to have you leading our nation. Please know we are praying for you."

He smiled and said, "That's the best Christmas present you could give me. Thank you."

It's a moment I'll never forget—MY children, praised even by the President of the United States! What more could a SAHM ask for?

Please share your favorite memory—even if it's not as thrilling as mine. It's not a contest, after all. :)

Wishing you every happiness of the season,
Rosalyn Ebberly
SAHM I Am Loop Moderator

"She looks well to the ways of her household, and does not eat the bread of idleness."
Proverbs 31:27 (NASB)

From:	The Millards <jstcea4jesus@familymail.net>
To:	"Green Eggs and Ham"
Subject:	**Rosalyn's favorite memory**

My favorite memory from last year's Christmas was the day Rosalyn finally stopped bragging about their D.C. trip. Let's see, that was…March 14, I believe. It was nice to have the Christmas season last so long.

Jocelyn

From:	Dulcie Huckleberry <dulcie@nebweb.net>
To:	SAHM I Am <sahmiam@loophole.com>
Subject:	**Christmas Surprise**

Hey everyone!

I just found out that my best friend, Marianne, is PREG-NANT! She's currently not too happy about it—Helene, their only child at this point, just turned a year old earlier this month, and she's a little spitfire. I don't think Marianne and Brandon were quite ready for another one, but that's what happens, I guess.

Anyway, I just wanted to tell you all the good news. Or…at least good news depending on who you are talking to. And right now, Marianne and Brandon aren't talking to each other. Each is mad at the other for not being more upset about the pregnancy. But I doubt it will last long with them. It never does. They're both so sweet-natured and easygoing that it takes more energy for them to be angry than it does to make up.

I think it's great. I figured, as feisty as Helene is, it would take an "oops" like this for them to have any more kids. :) I hope it's another girl. A boy would never be able to handle a big sister like Helene.

Have a holly, jolly Christmas, everyone!

Dulcie

From:	Connie Lawson <clmo5@home.com>
To:	SAHM I Am <sahmiam@loophole.com>
Subject:	Re: [SAHM I AM] Christmas Surprise

Dulcie, why don't you invite your friend to join SAHM I Am? It sounds like she could use a support group. :)

Connie

From:	Dulcie Huckleberry <dulcie@nebweb.net>
To:	SAHM I Am <sahmiam@loophole.com>
Subject:	Re: [SAHM I AM] Christmas Surprise

I would, but Marianne is adamantly opposed to the Internet. She's the one who got a home economics degree in college just so that she'd be a better homemaker, wife and mother. She'd go back and live in the 1800s if she could. I've tried to talk her into getting e-mail, but she won't hear of it. She does go to MOPS, though, so at least she has some support. But it's not like the daily fellowship I get through the loop.

Dulcie

From:	Zelia Muzuwa <zeemuzu@vivacious.com>
To:	SAHM I Am <sahmiam@loophole.com>
Subject:	[SAHM I AM] favorite christmas memory

Ho, ho, ho, Sahmmies!

Greetings from merry ol' England, where we just arrived at my in-laws for a long winter's nap—I mean, beloved family Christmas celebration. (I'm mostly teasing. My in-laws are great. And I'm not just saying that in case any happen to be reading over my shoulder.) I think my favorite Christmas memory is going to be the one our family made on the plane over here—even though it's technically a two-days-before-Christmas memory.

Here's the background—about a month ago, Tristan (DH) decided that our kids should go to a private school in Baltimore. I was really angry at him because he didn't even discuss it with me first. But, as it turns out, the children absolutely ADORE their new school, much to my chagrin. And they *are* behaving better—Seamus hasn't tortured poor Griffith or Cosette in weeks. Irritated them, perhaps, but not tortured. I think I just wasn't keeping them busy enough at home.

Tristan, though, finally saw the error of his ways and apologized for being so high-handed about it. I think God must have taken him to the woodshed for an old-fashioned thrashing because Tristan felt so bad for treating me that way that he was crying. He offered to pull them out of the school and let me continue home-schooling (though he did request that we try for more structure). But I figured it would be too much upheaval for them, and besides, they're happy and settled. Why mess with it?

But I did tell him how lonely I've been feeling. I thought about getting a job, at least part-time. But I really don't want to. I like being home. I just like being home with children better.

So we got to talking about all this on the flight to London and Tristan asked me if I'd be happier with another child in the house. I said yes. He said, "Why do we not have another one?"

I said, "We decided no more babies."

He said, "Yes, but does that mean no more children?"

I just stared at him, like, "what are you talking about?"

"I've had quite a bit of time to think about this the past few weeks. Part of the reason for placing the children in school was to reconnect them with their British heritage. But I've found myself longing to acquaint them with their African heritage, as well."

"You want an exchange student?"

He laughed a little—which always gives me butterflies in my stomach and shivers in my spine. Anyway...he says, "No. I was actually thinking about adoption."

I about bolted out of my seat. I'd never even considered something like that. I figured adoption is what people do when they can't have kids. But I was trying to be a good sport, so I nodded and pretended this was a perfectly normal thing for him to suggest. "From Zimbabwe?"

"No. Unfortunately, international adoptions are not allowed from Zimbabwe."

Wow—evidently he'd been doing a bit more than just "thinking" about this. He was serious! "From where, then?"

"Ethiopia."

Now I really did jump! "You gotta be kidding! What if they have AIDS? I don't think I could handle that. I'm not that heroic."

"There are those who do not have AIDS. And they are the ones we will adopt."

"Will?" I shot him a didn't-you-learn-your-lesson-yet look and he shrugged.

"If we decide to."

"Sounds like you've already made up your mind."

He wiggled around in the seat so he could reach his carry-on and pulled out a folder marked "Adoption Info." He handed it to me and said, "I will take a nap now. You may read what I have found on the Internet."

And he settled a travel pillow around his neck and was asleep before I'd barely opened the folder. Either that, or he was playing possum like a pro.

At first, I just thumbed through the pages, hardly reading any of it. It just seemed like such a ridiculous idea. I'd always heard that international adoption is a mess of red tape, paperwork and government corruption. But then an article caught my eye. It was about one of the adoption agencies that work in Ethiopia and all the children in their orphanage. I read about how they learn to speak English and learn about American customs just so that they'll be ready to be adopted by an American family. And how most of them lost loving, devoted parents due to disease or starvation. How their partner orphanage for the HIV-positive kids spends all its time loving these children, only to have them die in a matter of years because there's no money for medicine to help them.

And I started to cry. I bawled and bawled, and at some point, Tristan woke up and put his arms around me and held me. "I knew you would feel the same way," he said. "I knew they would capture your heart as they did mine."

So, to make this long story a bit shorter, we are going to adopt from Ethiopia. We're going to take two or three if we can, or a sibling group. The kids don't really understand it all yet, but they think it's a great idea. I'm not quite sure where the money is going to come from, but if I have to get a job, I will. Tristan seems to think we can cover most of it out of his paycheck if we cut out a few extras.

I'm getting so excited just writing about it to you all! I can't even begin to describe all the emotions whirling around in my heart! This is so right. It's like God had it all planned from the beginning—which of course He did. But He gave me a glimpse of the plan today, and it's so indescribably incredible.

Have a blessed, wonderful Christmas, dear, sweet friends!

Z

From:	Brenna L. <saywhat@writeme.com>
To:	Dulcie Huckleberry <dulcie@nebweb.net>
Subject:	Z's announcement

Dulcie,

I can't help it! I just CANNOT be happy for Z right now. I feel this horrible, jealous hurt inside. Why does she get a supportive husband who is PUSHING for an adoption when I can't even get mine to THINK about it? And why does God let her have another kid, or two, or three, when she's already got THREE of her own? I just have one! And I've pleaded and begged Him to let us have even just one more, but does He do it? NO! He gives them to HER instead!

And I don't even know your friend Marianne. But when I heard she was pregnant, I just hated her! I'm turning into this horrible, hateful person, and I can't stand it! Why can't Darren be reasonable? I just want a baby. That's all. Just one little, cuddly, squirmy child. Why is God giving them away to everyone except me?

Okay, okay, I know I'm whining. But it just makes me so angry! I think I'm going to go out for a walk and cool down. Kick some large trees, while I'm at it.

Merry stinkin' Christmas.

Brenna

From:	Dulcie Huckleberry <dulcie@nebweb.net>
To:	Brenna L. <saywhat@writeme.com>
Subject:	**Re: Z's announcement**

Hi Brenna,

Even though it's Christmas Eve and I'm expecting Tom to arrive anytime, I had to take a minute and write back to you. Please help me know what to say to you. I don't want to hurt you. In fact, I'm a bit angry for you! It's so not fair. I wish I could do something to make it right. And I just bet Z would feel the same way if she knew all the stuff you and Darren are dealing with. She'd be mad at herself for making an announcement that hurt you, and she'd be mad at Darren for not "getting with the program," and she'd be mad that this is happening to a friend she cares about.

And I'm sorry that my post about Marianne made it worse. I wasn't trying to be insensitive. Please don't let all this make you bitter. I just know somehow God has a plan that will make everything better. Try to have a good Christmas, please.

You are in my prayers, dear friend,

Dulcie

From:	Brenna L. <saywhat@writeme.com>
To:	Dulcie Huckleberry <dulcie@nebweb.net>
Subject:	**Re: Z's announcement**

You're right...I know my attitude is rotten. It just hit me all at once, you know? The walk helped some. And then Madeline showed me a picture she drew of me, her and Darren. She'd labeled it "My Famly" (her spelling). I felt bad for griping about "only" having one child. She's my treasure. Sometimes I'm such an ungrateful jerk. I'm glad you all love me anyway.

Merry *Sweet* Christmas,

Brenna

From:	Dulcie Huckleberry <dulcie@nebweb.net>
To:	"Green Eggs and Ham"
Subject:	**My Christmas**

Happy Boxing Day, Z! I hope you are having a good visit with Tristan's family after all. :)

I know you all were interested to find out if Tom and I ever had our talk about the KC Christmas party fiasco. Well, the answer is...not exactly. Tom got home Christmas Eve, and we went to church and had our normal Baby Jesus birthday party at home afterward. After the children went to bed, we assembled the play kitchen we'd gotten them. Then, we sat on the love seat in front of the fireplace and watched the flames by the light of the Christmas tree.

"Know something?" Tom said, after we'd been quiet for a bit. "I hate KC."

I wasn't sure what I was supposed to say. "Why?"

He didn't respond for a while. Then he said, "It's not home."

"Well, your contract ends in March."

He actually took my hand! He used to do that all the time—we'd sit around and he'd smooth the back of my hand with his thumb. Hasn't happened for ages. "Yeah, and then off somewhere else. Alaska, I think. They're working on a one-year contract for me in Anchorage."

I froze. I couldn't believe how spineless I was all of a sudden. Here was the opportunity I'd been waiting for for months—to ask him to get a local job. And I couldn't do it! "Isn't that what you wanted?"

He sorta shrugged. "It's what was available."

"You could...always check into openings here in Omaha."

"If you want me to."

For some reason, that irritated me so much. "Who said anything about what I want? It's your career. What do YOU want?"

"I don't know."

Okay, I admit—I blew it. Led him right into the wife-trap. "What do you mean, you don't know? Don't you want to be home with us?"

He let go of my hand. "Of course I do."

"You don't sound like it."

"Look, you always act like you think I enjoy being gone all the time. I don't, okay? But it's what I do. Programming is the only thing I'm good at, and consulting jobs pay a whole lot more than anything in town."

That took the starch out of me. "Do you...*like* programming?"

"It's okay." He sort of leaned away from me, in order to see me better or something. "I don't have any other skills."

"I could care less about the money, you know."

"It's not the money. It's..." He scowled and shook his head, eyes downcast. "Sometimes what you know—even if it's not great—is better than the unfamiliar."

"What are you talking about?"

He stared off into space, and it was like I couldn't reach to wherever his mind was. "I never expected to have a real home. Someplace stable...dependable. You don't know what it's like—a broken family, a mom who is gone more than she's home, a dad you're ashamed to talk about. You've given me everything I never had, and it's sort of like when Morris got that computer for Mom. She was thrilled about it and scared to death of it, all at the same time."

I didn't know what to say. Wasn't even sure what he meant.

Then he grabbed my hand again. "I'll look for a job in town, okay?"

I just nodded and snuggled up to him. Since I was feeling brave suddenly, I whispered, "Are we okay, Tom?"

He kissed me a long time and then said, "Yeah."

So I don't know what it all means, except that he promised to make KC the last long-distance consulting gig he does. Come the end of March, my honey's staying home! I won't be alone anymore! :)

Here's to a Happy New Year, everyone!

Dulcie

From:	Rosalyn Ebberly <prov31woman@home.com>
To:	SAHM I Am <sahmiam@loophole.com>
Subject:	**[SAHM I AM] TOTW January 3: Setting Goals**

Happy New Year, Special SAHMs!

This week's topic is a SAHM I Am tradition—Goal Setting. For those of you who are new to our little community, I always like to reiterate my standard sermon on "setting goals" versus "making resolutions." I do NOT believe in making New Year's resolutions. It is a waste of time and serves to produce only guilt and a performance-oriented mind-set. But Christ has set us free from condemnation and a works–based religion!

Instead, as sanctified people, we here at SAHM I Am believe in setting goals—based on Godly principles of industry and desiring to press forward in our Christian walk.

So, let's share this week what our goals are for the coming year. And remember, a GOAL is specific, attainable and measurable.

Here are MY goals for this year:

1) By December 31st of this year, I will have the following books written and accepted for publication:

    ★ *Rosalyn Ebberly's Secrets to Breeding Champion Roses*

    ★ *A Sweet Fragrance for the Lord: Award-winning Organic Recipes and Daily Devotionals to Feed Both Body and Spirit*

    ★ *Let the Work of Her Hands Praise Her: A History of Needle-craft from Ancient to Modern Times*

    ★ *Stress-free Mothering: How I Discovered the Secret to Being the Perfect Mom*

2) By August 1st of this year, I will have memorized the following books of the Bible with 100% accuracy: I and

II Chronicles, Habbakuk, Nehemiah, and Job. (I did the New Testament last year.)

3) By Februrary 1st of this year, I will have ready my Bible study on the Proverbs 31 Woman for use in leading our church women's ministry in March.

This is actually just a small sample from my fifty-item list. But I didn't want to seem like I was calling attention to myself, so I simply chose to share some of my smaller goals. Suzannah and Jefferson each made their own list this year, too. They are such purposeful little darlings! I kept having to remind them that, at least at their age, achieving world peace was a dream, not a goal.

Be purposeful,

Rosalyn Ebberly

SAHM I Am Loop Moderator

"She looks well to the ways of her household, and does not eat the bread of idleness."

Proverbs 31:27 (NASB)

From:	Dulcie Huckleberry <dulcie@nebweb.net>
To:	SAHM I Am <sahmiam@loophole.com>
Subject:	**Re: [SAHM I AM] TOTW January 3: Setting Goals**

My goal this year is just to be more organized! It's always so hard getting back into a routine after the holidays.

Dulcie

From:	Rosalyn Ebberly <prov31woman@home.com>
To:	SAHM I Am <sahmiam@loophole.com>
Subject:	Re: [SAHM I AM] TOTW January 3: Setting Goals

<My goal this year is to just be more organized!>

Tsk, tsk, Dulcie. That is NOT a goal. It's a dream. A very distant dream, for you, I'm afraid. LOL! Let's try again, shall we? :)

Blessings and joy to you all,

Rosalyn Ebberly

SAHM I AM Loop Moderator

> "She looks well to the ways of her household, and does
> not eat the bread of idlness."
> Proverbs 31: 27 (NASB)

From:	Dulcie Huckleberry <dulcie@nebweb.net>
To:	"Green Eggs and Ham"
Subject:	MY GOAL FOR THIS YEAR}:-<

By December 31st of this year, I will have Tom teach me how to program computers so that I can create a nasty, horrible virus that will invade Rosalyn's computer and make it so that every time she tries to open her e-mail program, all she will get is a grinning, leering picture of ME surrounded by all my disorganized, inefficient clutter and normal, non-genius children.

Dulcie

From:	Zelia Muzuwa <zeemuzu@vivacious.com>
To:	SAHM I Am <sahmiam@loophole.com>
Subject:	**[SAHM I AM] Goals**

I only have one goal for this year—bring my child (or children) home from Africa. And I don't care, Rosalyn, if that isn't specific or measurable enough for you. It's not a dream, it IS a goal!

Actually, I can't believe how organized I am being about all this. Usually, I'm just a muddle of spontaneity and Tristan is the one who is Mr. Mission Statement. But I actually put together a calendar for what we need to do and when, and I'm making checklists and budget tables and everything! Tristan keeps asking me for my driver's license, just so he can make sure it's me and not an impostor!

We chose our adoption agency—the one mentioned in the article I read on the plane. We're sending in our application this week. I can hardly believe it, it's all happening so quickly! I'm a little overwhelmed by all the work it's going to take, but I'm excited to get started, too. The children are already bugging me, "Can the new kid sleep in MY room, Mommy?" and Cosette is practically pleading with us, "Please get me a SISTER!!! I have enough brothers." Isn't that cute?

Well, I'm off. I have to call around and find out who we need to work with to do our home-study—which evidently is sort of like a cross between pre-marital counseling and a house-buying inspection. I just hope whoever our social worker is doesn't peek in our closets—she'll run away screaming! :)

Z

From:	Brenna L. <saywhat@writeme.com>
To:	Zelia Muzuwa <zeemuzu@vivacious.com>
Subject:	**I'm under orders to write this e-mail...**

...by Dulcie, who says I'll feel better if I just talk to you.

The problem is, I've been feeling irrationally angry at you ever since you announced your plans to adopt. I know it's wrong, and I don't have any reason to act this way, but it's just coming at a time when I feel like God is either punishing me or abandoning me, or both, and I'm not dealing with it so well.

You see, we just found out Darren is infertile. Aside from a total miracle, he won't ever be able to father a child. And I don't think we really know how to accept that right now. He's questioning his manhood, and I'm ashamed to admit all the thoughts I've been having about "Well, if I'd married someone else, I could have had more children." I love Darren with all my heart, but this is driving a huge wedge between us.

I want to adopt, but he won't talk about it. Every time I bring it up, he just scowls and changes the subject. It's just tearing me up inside. So when you announced you were adopting, I felt hurt and jealous. And then I felt horribly guilty because I know you haven't done a single thing wrong. You have every right to adopt if that's what you want to do, and it's awful of me to resent it.

I know you didn't realize any of this, and you probably wish I hadn't told you. But in case I do or say something mean, which I'm trying not to, but if I do, I wanted you to understand why. You're my friend, and I don't want that to change. It's just going to take some time to work through this. I'm sorry.

Love,

Brenna

From:	Zelia Muzuwa <zeemuzu@vivacious.com>
To:	Brenna L. <saywhat@writeme.com>
Subject:	You poor darling!

Bren,

I wish you'd told me ages ago! I'm so terribly sorry. I didn't know you were suffering like that. Thank you for talking to me about it. How can I help you? I won't talk any more about the adoption, if you don't want me to. I don't want to hurt you. Oh, Brenna! I could just cry thinking about what you must be going through! And Darren, too! Please tell me we're still friends.

Love,

Z

From:	Brenna L. <saywhat@writeme.com>
To:	Zelia Muzuwa <zeemuzu@vivacious.com>
Subject:	Re: You poor darling!

You're so sweet, Z. But there's nothing much you can do. Thanks for asking, though. And please, don't stop talking about the adoption. I can't stand the thought that you all are hiding it from me or trying to protect me. I'll learn to

deal with it, I promise. Of course you're still my friend! Don't you ever doubt it!
Brenna

From:	Dulcie Huckleberry <dulcie@nebweb.net>
To:	"Green Eggs and Ham"
Subject:	**New Year's depression**

Ugh! I feel rotten, guys. It never fails—as hard as I try to ignore Rosalyn's lofty goals each year, by the end of the week, the entire discussion has me in a foul mood. I should go "nomail" the week after New Year's, just to avoid this very situation, but I'm so hooked on loop messages, I can't stand the thought of going without for even seven days. So I read everyone's goals (dreams, whatever) and always end up feeling like a complete failure.

Where is my life going, I ask you? NOWHERE! Z has her adoption, Jocelyn has the parenting classes, everyone seems to have something they want to work on or accomplish—except me.

I was so frustrated today! My house is a mess, and the second I begin trying to clean up, the phone rings, or the twins start fighting with each other, or McKenzie decides to bug me about something. I can't get anything done! And I'm so far behind, I don't even know where to start. And I can't find anything, to save my life.

I was looking for the phone number of our plumber because I thought it was really high time we got our ice-maker in the fridge installed. We bought the fridge new eight months ago and never put in the water line for the ice. But the stupid little business card is lost in a mountain of papers and bills, and I can't seem to remember the guy's name. If I had a household binder, like Rosalyn preaches, I'd have all that info in one place. But I keep thinking, "I'll do that after I get this mess cleaned up, so I don't have to search for all the information to go in the binder." And does the mess get cleaned up? NEVER!

My life is going nowhere fast. By the time I get out of bed, dress, and have the children dressed and fed, it's time to start lunch. And by the time lunch is over and the children are taking naps, I want a nap, too! Then it's time to cook supper, and after the dishes are done and everyone cleaned up, it's almost bedtime. And what have I accomplished? Absolutely nothing.

What is WRONG WITH ME?
Dulcie

From:	The Millards <jstcea4jesus@familymail.net>
To:	"Green Eggs and Ham"
Subject:	Re: New Year's depression

<What is WRONG WITH ME?>
You have preschoolers, that's what! LOL!

Seriously, Dulcie, I felt the same way when my kids were that age, and still do at times. It does get better. But you might want to consider evaluating your daily routine and seeing what changes you could make to it. I have some worksheets from our parenting class that I could send you, if you're interested. They might help you figure out how you could tweak things to work better.
Love ya!
Jocelyn

From:	P.Lorimer <phyllis.lorimer@joono.com>
To:	"Green Eggs and Ham"
Subject:	**Re: New Year's depression**

<Where is my life going, I ask you? NOWHERE!>
Dulcie,

Join the club, friend. Just join the club…
Phyllis

From:	Zelia Muzuwa <zeemuzu@vivacious.com>
To:	"Green Eggs and Ham"
Subject:	**Re: New Year's depression**

<Z has her adoption, Jocelyn has the parenting classes, everyone seems to have something they want to work on or accomplish—except me.>

Oh no, you don't! You aren't going to lump me in with the rest of those organized, got-it-all-together people! I refuse. I won't have it, I tell you! I wear my badge of disorganization proudly (when I can find it) and I won't cross over.

Let me burn my charts and lists! I'll erase the budget worksheet I created in Excel! Anything to convince you I'm not one of THEM. :) My life is going nowhere, too—don't be fooled by appearances. GOAL SETTING, I DEFY YOU!

Stubbornly aimless,

Z

From:	P.Lorimer <phyllis.lorimer@joono.com>
To:	"Green Eggs and Ham"
Subject:	**Re: New Year's depression**

Z,

I'm disappointed in you. You forgot to quote the Bard! How about this:

"Come, lay aside your stitchery; I must have you play the idle huswife with me this afternoon." (Coriolanus, Act I, Scene III.)

Phyllis

From:	Brenna L. <saywhat@writeme.com>
To:	"Green Eggs and Ham"
Subject:	**Re: New Year's depression**

Corio-what? I never even HEARD of that play! I guess you gals are just too cultured for this country hick. ★GASP★ I SOUND LIKE MY MOTHER-IN-LAW!

Brenna

From:	VIM <vivalaveronica@marcelloportraits.com>
To:	Rosalyn Ebberly <prov31woman@home.com>
Subject:	**It wasn't my fault!**

Come on, Rosalyn! It's been almost two weeks. How long are you fixing to give me the silent treatment for something

I didn't do? I thought y'all were into forgiveness and love. I'm plumb sorry Mama and Daddy hurt your feelings, but you shouldn't take it out on me. I have every right to have a successful career, great husband and wonderful kids. And you have the right to choose your own sweet family over a career, no matter what anyone else says about it. Now will you just get over it and e-mail me? There ya go.

VIM

From:	Rosalyn Ebberly <prov31woman@home.com>
To:	SAHM I Am <sahmiam@loophole.com>
Subject:	[SAHM I AM] TOTW January 10: Becoming a Woman of Grace

Gracious Girls,

While I was visiting my sister during the holidays, a difficult thing happened. My parents, whom some of you know are not at all supportive of my decision to be a SAHM, made a very hurtful comment about it in front of all our relatives. Most of my life, they have compared me to my younger sister, and I've been—for some bizarre reason—found lacking. So how did I cope with this wounding and embarrassing situation? I summoned all my grace and held my tongue. I did not return evil for evil, but instead retained my dignity and compassion, remembering that Proverbs says never to answer a fool according to his (or in this case, her) folly. It's so much easier to respond to unkindness with more unkindness. But I find that it's truly better to "turn the other cheek" and be loving, no matter what. So let's share some ways we can have "grace under fire." Share a time you had to hold your tongue and preserve your dignity.

Gracefully,
Rosalyn Ebberly
SAHM I Am Loop Moderator

"She looks well to the ways of her household, and does
not eat the bread of idleness."
Proverbs 31:27 (NASB)

From:	Dulcie Huckleberry <dulcie@nebweb.net>
To:	Thomas Huckleberry <t.huckleberry@cortech.com>
Subject:	**EMERGENCY!**

Tom,
I tried to call you, but you must be in a meeting. Listen, you
need to contact me as soon as you can. Your mother called
me, wanting to talk to you, but she couldn't reach you at
work, either. Please call me!
Dulcie

From:	Thomas Huckleberry <t.huckleberry@cortech.com>
To:	Dulcie Huckleberry <dulcie@nebweb.net>
Subject:	**Re: EMERGENCY!**

Dulcie,
What's wrong? I called as soon as I could but you must be
on the phone. And there's no answer at Mom's house. You've
got me really worried. Listen, if you can't reach me again,
dial zero after my voice-mail message and ask the receptionist to page me. I hope everything's okay.
Tom

From:	Dulcie Huckleberry <dulcie@nebweb.net>
To:	Thomas Huckleberry <t.huckleberry@cortech.com>
Subject:	**Re: EMERGENCY!**

Sorry, Tom. I was on the phone with Becky, and then the batteries in the cordless died, and I didn't want to be stuck in our bedroom with the corded phone while the girls were playing down here, so I'll have to tell you this in an e-mail. I'm sorry.

Your mother called this morning to tell me SHE'S GETTING MARRIED! TO MORRIS HASH! IN MAY!!! I talked to Becky, and she's in shock, too. I mean, they've only been dating for a few months. And they're acting like lovesick teenagers—and just about as stupid, I think! Anyway, call me. We've got to figure out what we're going to do. Dulcie

From:	Thomas Huckleberry <t.huckleberry@cortech.com>
To:	Dulcie Huckleberry <dulcie@nebweb.net>
Subject:	**Re: EMERGENCY!**

Good grief, Dulcie! I thought something horrible had happened. Don't ever scare me like that again.
<We've got to figure out what we're going to do.>
What do you mean? We aren't going to "do" anything. So Mom's getting married again. What's the big deal? They're both mature adults, and Morris seems like a good guy. I'm happy for her. We're going to be supportive and congratulate them.
Tom

From:	Dulcie Huckleberry <dulcie@nebweb.net>
To:	Thomas Huckleberry <t.huckleberry@cortech.com>
Subject:	**Mom getting married**

You're a guy, Tom.

From:	Thomas Huckleberry <t.huckleberry@cortech.com>
To:	Dulcie Huckleberry <dulcie@nebweb.net>
Subject:	**Re: Mom getting married**

Thanks for clearing that up for me.

From:	Dulcie Huckleberry <dulcie@nebweb.net>
To:	Thomas Huckleberry <t.huckleberry@cortech.com>
Subject:	**Re: Mom getting married**

No! I mean, you don't understand! Your mom can't just run off with some guy. She hasn't dated anyone in YEARS! She's just infatuated with the first man who showed any interest in her since her divorce. Becky's worried, too. After all, how much do we really know about Morris? He "seems" nice, but do we know for sure? She could be getting herself into a horrible mess. And such a rush! May, for goodness sake! She didn't even ask us if that was a good time for us or anything. I'm afraid he's manipulating her.
Dulcie

From:	Thomas Huckleberry <t.huckleberry@cortech.com>
To:	Dulcie Huckleberry <dulcie@nebweb.net>
Subject:	**Re: Mom getting married**

If the difference between being a guy or being a girl is the ability to look at this situation in a rational, reasonable manner, I am very glad to be a guy. Let it go, Dulcie. I'm sure everything will be just fine. And if not, Mom's a big girl. She can take care of herself.

I'm going to be in meetings most of the afternoon. Don't rupture a hernia, okay?

Love,

Tom

From:	Dulcie Huckleberry <dulcie@nebweb.net>
To:	J. Huckleberry <ilovebranson@branson.com>
Subject:	**Just a few thoughts**

Dear Mom,

Becky and I talked it over and we thought of some things you really should find out about Morris before you commit to marrying him. So we came up with a list:

1) Previous relationships. How many ex-wives? Late wives? Sometimes serial killers disguise themselves as lonely old widowers. We don't want you to end up in sandwich baggies in his freezer.

2) History of mental illness? It usually skips a generation or two, so you'd better go back at least three or

four. And check out all the relatives, too. Any creepy habits, like keeping fifty cats in the house or collecting antique butcher knives should be taken into consideration. You never know when something like that might crop up.

3) Financial stability. It would probably be best to hire an investigator to look into his credit. For that matter, make sure he isn't an identity thief! You might wake up some morning to the feds surrounding your house with machine guns and helicopters and your new hubby vanished to Istanbul!

4) Religious beliefs. Sure, he *claims* to be a Christian. Better make sure he doesn't belong to one of those cults that think Jesus is going to come back on a rocket ship and take them all to a utopian colony on Mars.

5) Career aspirations. He works at the Shoji Tabuchi theater, right? As a sound guy? Are you SURE he doesn't secretly wish to be in the show, and you won't arrive for work one evening to find him strutting around on stage with twelve trained poodles in square-dance skirts, singing "Achy Breaky Heart" as a duet with some 8-year-old prodigy dressed up like Dolly Parton?

Please think about this carefully. We just want you to be happy, but we want you to be safe, too. Morris seems like a nice guy, but don't you think you're rushing into marrying him?

Love,
Dulcie

From:	J. Huckleberry <ilovebranson@branson.com>
To:	Dulcie Huckleberry <dulcie@nebweb.net>;
	Jordan and Becky <schwartz@ozarkmail.net>
Subject:	**Get a Life, Sweeties**

...And stop interfering with mine. I mean that in love, but really—the two of you are being absolutely ridiculous! Morris is a kind, generous man who loves me and I love him.

Becky, when you wanted to marry Jordan, did I express any hesitation or concern over the fact that he is four years younger than you and still lived with his mother? For that matter, did I even bring up the matter of him calling her "Mommy"? No! I could have. Most mothers would have. But I kept my mouth shut. And look how wonderfully it all turned out. Now he lives with you and calls you "mommy."

And as for you, Dulcie...when Tom told me that he was dating an interior decorator, for one horrifying moment, I thought he was trying to tell me he was gay. And then, when you got engaged, I had all these visions of some snooty, artsy hotshot who was going to waltz into my house and declare, "I see...heliotrope, with chartreuse highlights. Let's redecorate!" and I'd come home one day to find all my walls painted the color of grape jelly and my nice, cozy furniture replaced with steel chairs shaped like giant bent spoons spattered-painted in primary colors by first graders. I've never been able to watch *Trading Spaces* without having nightmares! But did I utter a single word? No! I welcomed you into my home and into my heart without a trace of fear. And I'm so glad I did, because you are a sweet girl who has beautiful taste and treats my son well.

My point is this, dear daughters—BACK OFF.
Love,
Mom Jeanine

From:	Jordan and Becky <schwartz@ozarkmail.net>
To:	Dulcie Huckleberry <dulcie@nebweb.net>
Subject:	Well!

What do you think about Mom's letter? Here we went to all the trouble of communicating our concern, and she makes fun of us! (Just for the record, Jordan only calls me "mommy" to help the kids learn it. He promised to stop when they get older.)
Becky

From:	Dulcie Huckleberry <dulcie@nebweb.net>
To:	Jordan and Becky <schwartz@ozarkmail.net>
Subject:	Re: Well!

All I have to say is that if he puts a deep freeze on their registry, I'm calling the police!
Dulcie

From:	Morris Hash <ilovejeanine@branson.com>
To:	Dulcie Huckleberry <dulcie@nebweb.net>;
	Jordan and Becky <schwartz@ozarkmail.net>
Subject:	Your list of questions

Dear Dulcie and Becky,

It's natural for you to have questions about your mother and me getting engaged. I suppose we should have prepared you better for this possibility, but we were hesitant to discuss it even between ourselves until we were really sure. Questions, then, are natural. Your questions, however, were...unnatural. What sort of movies are you girls watching these days?

I'm a reasonable man, so I am going to answer your questions, despite their insulting nature. I hope you find my answers enlightening.

1) Previous relationships: I'm 58 years old, have been married nine times, and have never divorced. All of my wives are quite alive and healthy, thank you, and living in different states. I'm trying to collect three more so I can visit one per month for the whole year, thus my interest in your mother, who will make number 10. I have 76 children total, and so far 118 grandchildren. I promise not to discriminate between you and my biological children, though I must draw the line at birthday presents. Money is tight, you know.

2) History of mental illness: All my ancestors and relatives have been perfectly sane, I assure you. The rumors of my mother having six personalities and my father believing he was Napoleon are greatly exaggerated. And

my grandmother really didn't bury my grandfather in her backyard—that was their pet goat, Norbert, who would have inherited their entire estate if it hadn't been for Ruby Jenson, a beautiful girl who lived next door. Norbert was dreadfully in love with her, but Ruby refused to have anything to do with a goat, and he died of a broken heart. My grandparents never forgave her. But then they adopted my father from an orphanage. He was a great comfort to them, especially because he particularly enjoyed eating rubber tires—Norbert's favorite dessert.

3) Finances: I am very comfortably situated. I have over three million dollars in stocks and bonds, as well as four vacation properties. No, wait—that was Dennis Henderson. Then I stole Frank Gages—that was fun. He owned a casino in Las Vegas. You should have seen the penthouse in *that* hotel... After Frank was LeMar Johnston, but that didn't last long since I wasn't so good at impersonating a black man. Then Trey Holmes, or was that Jim Goldsen? Anyway, one of them...and *then* Morris. That's right. I forget what assets Morris has (or did have, LOL!). Have to get back to you on that one.

4) Religion: I'm an upstanding Christian! Though I am thinking about joining a rural commune led by this great guy who says God told him to stock up on kids' fruit punch and arsenic because of the coming global nuclear war...

5) Career Aspirations: I don't plan to ever perform on stage. My skills are more in management. I plan to open up Branson-style theaters all across the Middle East. Don't the possibilities just take your breath away?

Well, I hope that helps you feel a bit more comfortable about me marrying your mother. Don't worry, girls. I'm planning to take good care of Jeanine.

Your loving father-to-be,

Morris Hash

From:	Dulcie Huckleberry <dulcie@nebweb.net>
To:	Jordan and Becky <schwartz@ozarkmail.net>
Subject:	**Re: Your list of questions**

Dear Becky,

You know, I've never really liked sarcasm. Such a nasty form of humor, don't you think? And to think, we're going to have to put up with him for a *long* time. Sarcastic people never seem to die young.

Dulcie

From:	J. Huckleberry <ilovebranson@branson.com>
To:	Dulcie Huckleberry <dulcie@nebweb.net>
Subject:	**The Wedding**

Darling,

I know you're still a little apprehensive about Morris, but I really can't wait around for you to warm to him. There's so much to do, and we only have until May. So, be a sweetheart, and at least pretend like you're supportive, okay?

By the way, I was wondering if you would let McKenzie be our flower girl. I know she'll only just have turned four, but she's SO mature for her age. And I found the sweetest, ruffliest dress for her to wear. I'm thinking rosebuds in her hair, little elbow-length gloves, sparkly pink shoes. We'll make her look like a princess! Would that be okay? Just let me know…

Love,

Jeanine

From:	Dulcie Huckleberry <dulcie@nebweb.net>
To:	"Green Eggs and Ham"
Subject:	**FLOWER GIRL!!!!**

Hey, everybody! My mother-in-law is getting remarried and she just asked if McKenzie could be the FLOWER GIRL!! How cool is that? I always wanted to be a flower girl. And Mom says she'll dress McKenzie up as beautiful as a fairy princess. My little girl—in a wedding! Oh, I'm so excited! We're going to have to take lots of pictures and get the video. I wonder if I can talk Tom into agreeing to get her ears pierced. Wouldn't little, itty-bitty rhinestone earrings just be TOO SWEET? I can't wait!

The MOTHER of the Flower Girl,

Dulcie

From:	Dulcie Huckleberry <dulcie@nebweb.net>
To:	J. Huckleberry <ilovebranson@branson.com>
Subject:	**Re: The Wedding**

Dear Mom,

Of *course* McKenzie can be your flower girl. You're right—she is SO mature for her age. Oh, she'll be thrilled! Thank you for asking her.

And, you know what, after thinking about it, I really think this whole wedding thing is a great idea. You've been lonely all these years, and Morris did seem very nice when we met him over Thanksgiving. I'm sure you'll both be very happy.

Congratulations,

Dulcie

From:	J. Huckleberry <ilovebranson@branson.com>
To:	Morris Hash <ilovejeanine@branson.com>
Subject:	**FWD: RE: The Wedding**

See, my darling, didn't I tell you that would do the trick? Now all we have to do is wait for Becky's response about being my matron of honor. Mothers just know how these things work.

All my love,

Jeanine

From:	VIM <vivalaveronica@marcelloportraits.com>
To:	Rosalyn Ebberly <prov31woman@home.com>
Subject:	**Re: Cosmetic enhancements**

Rosalyn Ebberly wrote:

<You know, *some* of us are content with the way God made us. You go right ahead and let some plastic surgeon give you

a bigger bra size, if that's what you need. Thankfully, *my* husband loves me just the way I am.>

Sugar sister-mine,

I just got a few minutes before I leave for work, but I wanted to send you a quick reply. You *sure* you're content with your appearance? At Christmas, I noticed you looked all wore out, like you'd been rode hard and put up wet. There were big circles under your eyes, and you were snapping like a mud turtle at the kids. Looks like you've gained some weight, too—unless there is some news you haven't told us yet.... But even Mama and Daddy noticed. "Ronnie," Daddy said to me, "is it just me, or does Rosalyn look like death warmed over?"

I know you're at home all day, so there's no one to look pretty for, but you really shouldn't let yourself go like that. Else before you know it, you'll be as fat as a tick. You might feel like a sadsack, but, goodness sake, have some self-respect—you're worth it! I was thinking the other day about how nice it would be to stay home with my children—now that I have three of them. But I sure would hate to *look* like a housewife, bless your heart, even if I was one.

Treat yourself kindly. After all, you're the only sister I have. And there ya go.

Love,

Ronnie

From:	Rosalyn Ebberly <prov31woman@home.com>
To:	SAHM I Am <sahmiam@loophole.com>
Subject:	**[SAHM I AM] TOTW January 17: Our Bodies — The Temple of God**

Sanctified Sisters,
1 Corinthians 6:19-20 instructs us, "Or do you not know that your body is as temple of the Holy Spirit who is in you, whom you have from God, and that you are not your own? For you have been bought with a price: therefore glorify God in your body."

Our topic this week is Fitness. Why this is such a struggle for all of you, I'll never understand. I never have any trouble at all getting up in the morning to run a few miles and then lift weights. I even made my own weights out of PVC pipe, pantyhose and shotgun pellets. The instructions are attached. I actually bench-press two hundred pounds—which is more than Chad can. And as a result, my figure is lithe and toned and I never need to be ashamed of my appearance.

Most of you resist exercise as if it were some form of torture. But, my friends, this is *not true!* Exercise is a gift from God, for our enjoyment! I want you all to print out the following statement and post it somewhere in your house where you will see it:

THE BURN IS A BLESSING!

So let's talk about exercise! What are you doing? What *should* you be doing? What will you commit to over the next year? Or do you really want to be stuck wearing those jogging pants simply because they're the only things you own that actually fit?

Come on, girls! Let's sweat!
Fitly yours,
Rosalyn Ebberly
SAHM I Am Loop Moderator

"She looks well to the ways of her household, and does not eat the bread of idleness."
Proverbs 31:27 (NASB)

From:	The Millards <jstcea4jesus@familymail.net>
To:	SAHM I Am <sahmiam@loophole.com>
Subject:	Re: [SAHM I AM] TOTW January 17: Our Bodies – The Temple of God

I bench-press laundry—several loads a day, up and down stairs, too! Doesn't that count?

Jocelyn

From:	P. Lorimer <phyllis.lorimer@joono.com>
To:	SAHM I Am <sahmiam@loophole.com>
Subject:	Re: [SAHM I AM] TOTW January 17: Our Bodies – The Temple of God

Here's something I've never understood about fitness. Why are we women supposed to keep ourselves in perfect shape, but no one cares if our husbands have an office belly and eat fast food for lunch every day? Need we be reminded who has to go through pregnancy? Which gender naturally carries extra fat on their hips? Or who has certain baby-feeding apparati that weigh a half a pound each? But we females are expected to somehow overcome all those strikes against us to produce the ideal of feminine perfection. Does anyone else find this double standard troublesome?

Miffed,

Phyllis

From:	Rosalyn Ebberly <prov31woman@home.com>
To:	SAHM I Am <sahmiam@loophole.com>
Subject:	Re: [SAHM I AM] TOTW January 17: Our Bodies – The Temple of God

Oh, my dear, dear Phyllis! I am *not* suggesting we discuss how to make ourselves over into some idealized feminine fantasy! No, no, NO! You have no idea how greatly it dismays me to think that's what you thought I meant. Reread my message— you obviously didn't read it carefully enough the first time. I was quite clear on my intent.

However, I know that the subject of fitness often brings up women's deepest fears and insecurities about themselves. This must be what is happening to you. I wish I had something to encourage you with, but I've never struggled with my own self-image—having been blessed with so many positive physical attributes. I can honestly say I would never want to change a single thing about myself. I LOVE ME! :)

God calls us to be content with who we are. We are "fearfully and wonderfully made." I'm sure you are at least a passably attractive woman. Praise God for that! Others aren't so blessed! As long as you strive to improve wherever you can, you never need to be ashamed of your imperfections.
TTFN,
Rosalyn

"She looks well to the ways of her household, and does not eat the bread of idleness."
Proverbs 31:27 (NASB)

From:	P.Lorimer <phyllis.lorimer@joono.com>
To:	"Green Eggs and Ham"
Subject:	**Rosalyn**

I'm going to send her a mirror for her birthday. Eventually, it may become the only friend she has.
Phyllis

From:	Dulcie Huckleberry <dulcie@nebweb.net>
To:	Thomas Huckleberry <t.huckleberry@cortech.com>
Subject:	**Help me!**

Tom,
Your mom just called. You know how she said Morris asked his younger brother, Leonard, to be best man for the wedding, and that Becky is going to be matron of honor? Well, then Morris felt bad for leaving *you* out, so he wants you to be a groomsman. (He's going to call you at the hotel tonight, so act surprised.) So then your mom needed another bridesmaid for you, and she asked *me!* I said yes, of course. But then she e-mailed me a picture of the dress. Honey, I CAN'T WEAR THAT DRESS! I've attached the picture. Can you see me in that thing? It's so tight, every little bulge is going to show, and those sequins down the front are going to make me look like some beached fuchsia porpoise. Yikes! What am I going to do? They're going to take pictures of us together. Pictures that will hang on their wall for all their friends and relatives to see. I'm going to be preserved like that for the rest of time! Please talk to her. Tell her you don't like the dress. Tell her anything! I can't do it because it would seem selfish

for me to complain about my outfit when it's her wedding. And I'm embarrassed to say anything to Becky because she's so gorgeously skinny.

If you love me, save me from that bridesmaid's nightmare!
Dulcie

From:	Thomas Huckleberry <t.huckleberry@cortech.com>
To:	Dulcie Huckleberry <dulcie@nebweb.net>
Subject:	**The dress**

Honey,
The dress doesn't look so bad to me. I wish you weren't so hard on yourself. I think you're perfect, just the way you are. And that hot pink will look better on you than on my sister, with her red hair and all. I don't know what Mom was thinking. Even I know you don't put pink on a redhead, and I'm just "a guy." Just a warning, though—if Mom follows her usual pattern, things could get a lot crazier before she and Morris finally tie the knot. I know she loves Morris to death, but the idea of getting married again has got to be giving her the willies. Remember how over-the-top she got before our wedding, and the Camelot-themed engagement party she threw for Becky and Jordan? So be surprised at nothing. However, I bet she'll be just fine by the reception. All she has to do is get through those vows.

But as far as you go—I wish sometimes I could stand you in front of the mirror and give you my eyes so you could see yourself the way I see you. It's so frustrating to watch you beat up on yourself all the time. What do I need to do to convince you that you have a great body?
Love,
Tom

From:	Dulcie Huckleberry <dulcie@nebweb.net>
To:	Thomas Huckleberry <t.huckleberry@cortech.com>
Subject:	**Re: The dress**

<What do I need to do to convince you that you have a great body?>
Get me the one wearing that dress and put my head on it.
Dulcie

P.S. But thank you for the sweet e-mail, anyway. And for the heads-up on your mom—you're right, we all better run for cover.

From:	Dulcie Huckleberry <dulcie@nebweb.net>
To:	"Green Eggs and Ham"
Subject:	**Dress emergency!**

Ladies,
My husband thinks I look great—which is a good thing. Especially for him, because he'd be in big trouble if he didn't. But here's the deal: the end of May, yours truly is going to have to pour her plush little body into a dress shaped like a drinking straw and hobble down the aisle at her mother-in-law's wedding. I have approximately FOUR months to transform myself into said drinking-straw shape. Any good ideas? I was thinking of simply giving up food entirely, but my husband is very much not in favor of me starving myself, for some reason.
Dulcie

From:	Brenna L. <saywhat@writeme.com>
To:	"Green Eggs and Ham"
Subject:	**Re: Dress emergency!**

I've actually never been a bridesmaid before, but one of my friends who was in my wedding had the same problem. It took her forever to fess up that she hated the dresses I'd picked, and by that time it was too late to change them. But if she'd told me earlier, I probably would have. You should just tell your mother-in-law you don't like the dress.
Brenna

From:	P.Lorimer <phyllis.lorimer@joono.com>
To:	"Green Eggs and Ham"
Subject:	**Re: Dress emergency!**

Dulcie dear,
Brenna's right. You shouldn't do anything drastic to your body just because of a bridesmaid dress. Tell your MIL you don't like it, or have it altered to look nicer on you. Those sort of dresses only look good on a clothes-hanger anyway, and how many of us look like that?
Phyllis

From:	Dulcie Huckleberry <dulcie@nebweb.net>
To:	"Green Eggs and Ham"
Subject:	**Re: Dress emergency!**

You guys are so sweet! You make me feel at least a little better about myself. But here's the deal—I DO need to do something about my self-image. I realized this week that it really bothers Tom when I get down on my appearance. But I honestly do not like how I look. I can handle the long black hair, the darker complexion, the brown eyes, Hispanic nose. That's my heritage. It's the extra curves that shouldn't be there, the little hint of a double chin that didn't exist five years ago, the fact that I jiggle when I go down the stairs—that's what I absolutely CANNOT accept as being okay. And this wedding gives me the perfect chance to prove to myself that I can do something about it. I just need to know WHAT to do. My past record of maintaining an exercise routine is abysmal, and I HATE dieting. What should I do?

Dulcie

From:	The Millards <jstcea4jesus@familymail.net>
To:	"Green Eggs and Ham"
Subject:	**Re: Dress emergency!**

Dulcie,

If you are really wanting to lose weight, you should try what I did. I've lost about twenty-five pounds. It's a good-carb/good-fats eating plan that can become a new lifestyle instead of just a fad diet you fall off as soon as you start cheating. I'm attaching an article about it with info about the book. Let me know what you think.

Jocelyn

From:	Dulcie Huckleberry <dulcie@nebweb.net>
To:	"Green Eggs and Ham"
Subject:	**Re: Dress emergency!**

I checked it out, and I think this might be something I can actually live with. Thanks, Jocelyn! By this time in May, I'm going to slink down that aisle and feel good about it. Just you wait and see....
Dulcie

From:	Rosalyn Ebberly <prov31woman@home.com>
To:	SAHM I Am <sahmiam@loophole.com>
Subject:	**[SAHM I AM] TOTW February 14: Romancing Our Husbands**

Vibrant Valentines,
It's a snowy Valentine's Day here in Hibiscus, but I've had a lovely time so far. Jefferson and Chad got up early to surprise me with breakfast in bed—no small feat considering I am usually up and doing my Bible study by at least 4:30 in the morning. They made eggs Benedict, which was a perfect opportunity to explain to Jefferson the history of the real Benedict Arnold, whom the dish was named after, and how the eggs symbolize the birth of our new country, how the bacon represents the pig-ish greed of the English government, and how the traitorous Arnold threatened the divine course of our infant nation by spying for the British, who are represented by the English muffin. The hollandaise sauce,

of course, is a reminder of how the Pilgrims traveled first to Holland before coming to America.

Chad, in his usual flair for the romantic, baked a small éclair with a one-carat diamond tennis bracelet hidden in the cream. And he's taking me to Seattle this afternoon, to see a traveling Broadway show. But he won't tell me which one! While I was eating breakfast, he prepared a luxurious bath for me, with rose petals and candles floating in the water. As I relaxed in the bath, he serenaded me with love songs he composed himself. He has such a beautiful voice. After the bath, a half-hour foot rub!

Now it's 7:30, and he's left for work. But I am sure there are a few more surprises waiting for me today. Chad's so good at thinking up romantic things like that!

However, he's not the only one. I have quite a few things planned for him, as well. Which brings me to this week's topic: Creating a Romantic Valentine's Day for Your Husband.

I'm sure most of you are married to men who are clueless when it comes to romance. So it will do you absolutely no good lying around in bed today hoping he will serve you breakfast as my husband did for me. And I doubt that any of your DHs would know how to create a relaxing bath without burning the house down in the attempt. But this does NOT mean that you have to face each Valentine's Day with new disappointment! YOU can create romance for your husband! I have several ideas, but I never like to focus on myself. Let's hear from all of you. How can you romance your husband?

Sweetly Yours,

Rosalyn Ebberly

SAHM I Am Loop Moderator

"She looks well to the ways of her household, and does
not eat the bread of idleness."
Proverbs 31:27 (NASB)

From:	P.Lorimer <phyllis.lorimer@joono.com>
To:	SAHM I Am <sahmiam@loophole.com>
Subject:	**[SAHM I AM] Eggs Benedict**

Rosalyn, I'm sorry to spoil your history lesson. However, eggs
Benedict has absolutely nothing at all to do with the Revolutionary War or Benedict Arnold.

Nothing. Not even close.

Eggs Benedict was invented in New York City during the
mid-1890s, either at the restaurant Delmonico's or at the
Waldorf-Astoria Hotel. The Delmonico story says a woman
named Mrs. LeGrand Benedict talked the maître d' into creating a new dish for breakfast because she was sick and tired
of the usual stuff. The Waldorf-Astoria one says it was requested by a Mr. Lemuel Benedict, who was hungover from
the night before and wanted some eggs, toast, bacon and hollandaise sauce.

Furthermore, English muffins were invented in America.
And hollandaise sauce came from France. But you do get an
A for creativity.

Now I'm hungry. It's unfortunate we don't have a McDonald's in town. I could really enjoy an Egg McMuffin
about now. :)
Phyllis

From:	Zelia Muzuwa <zeemuzu@vivacious.com>
To:	"Green Eggs and Ham"
Subject:	**benedict rosalyn**

Hey, Phyllis. I didn't know you were a food historian. Is that what they teach you in grad school, Professor Lorimer?

By the way, how IS everyone's Valentine's Day going so far? Did your husbands come through for you this year, or do we all need to band together and dress in black to protest, like my friends and I used to do in high school?

February is right in the middle of Tristan's busy time as a CPA, so we aren't doing anything special until Friday night…when Tristan will whisk me away to the Inn at 2920, this swanky, upscale B&B for two nights of luxury and *no kids!* (Kids will stay with my parents, who are coming to pick them up on Friday morning.) And it has its own resident beta fish, Valentino (rather appropriate for the holiday, don't you think?). What I'm looking forward to most, though, is the whirlpool tub in our room. Then, Saturday evening, we're going to Toby's dinner theater to see *Miss Saigon*. I can hardly wait!

But today, I'll be lucky to get a card. Although Cosette has been coloring me about three valentines a day for the past week. She was getting upset because I told her they wouldn't ALL fit on the refrigerator door, so I created a "valentine gallery" out of our hallway. Each valentine gets its own frame (out of construction paper) and title plate. Cosette's current favorite activity when she comes home from school is to "go to the art museum" and gaze rapturously at her collection…until Griffith and Seamus mow her down while racing each other to the front door. The thing is, I rather like to

go gaze rapturously at the collection, too. There's a lot of love
being displayed in our hallway—and all for *me!* :) Isn't being
a mom great?
Z

From:	P.Lorimer <phyllis.lorimer@joono.com>
To:	"Green Eggs and Ham"
Subject:	**Valentine's Day Plans**

Z, your weekend sounds heavenly! Ah, the advantages to living in a city. I miss it dearly.

We found out, just a *month* ago, that the pastor and his wife
are expected to host a Valentine's Dinner at church on the
14th. Nobody bothered to tell us this sooner, so we've been
running around like maniacs trying to pull it together—
without any help, of course. I'll be spending most of the day
doing the cooking, and then rushing over to the church to
help Jonathan set up and decorate. This, on what is *supposed*
to be his day off. Thankfully we have a small congregation!

Is it like this in your churches? I didn't grow up going to
church, so I don't have much to compare to. But it seems like
our congregation expects Jonathan and me to do absolutely
everything for them, except maybe brush their teeth and tuck
them into bed at night. Jonathan accepts it as normal, but it
just feels a little wrong to me. I thought the body of Christ
was supposed to work together, like a big family. I feel more
like the scullery maid.

Enough griping, I suppose. I received a card and box of
chocolates—not very original, but given with sincere love.
Jonathan assures me that he has a babysitter arranged for Friday night so we can go out to dinner by ourselves. (Hah!

"Out to dinner" being one of two fairly decent restaurants in the area. No dinner theater for me this year.) But I have no confidence this will actually come to pass. My guess is that some elderly member of the congregation will conveniently have a stroke, or somebody's cherished dog will die, and Jonathan will be the *only* one in the world who can provide the necessary assistance and prayer. Hmm…I hadn't realized I'd become so cynical. Maybe I *should* dress in black today.
Phyllis

From:	Brenna L. <saywhat@writeme.com>
To:	"Green Eggs and Ham"
Subject:	**Re: Valentine's Day Plans**

Phyllis,
I can tell you right now that if that was *my* congregation treating me like that, I'd get my husband to preach some well-aimed sermons about loving and serving each other! It is *so* not supposed to be like that. Although, now that I'm writing that to you, I wonder if our pastor and wife ever feel that way…we're actually not very active at our church. It's almost an hour's drive, there's hardly anything that happens there and the teaching is mediocre at best. I had such a good church in Tulsa, but out here, it's slim pickins, that's for sure.

My Valentine's Day started out with a sick child—Madeline has a fever of 101 degrees and a sore throat. But I can't get her in to the doctor until tomorrow. Poor little thing had to stay home from school today. Her class was having a design-your-own-valentines-box contest, and she is so disappointed to be missing out. She had her box all ready to go, too. Darren helped her with it. It's a big, pink combine with sparkling heart stickers all over it. You hook it up to a Shop-Vac and it sucks the valentines through the front header, up and out the auger, and into a bin decorated like a big red truck with heart-shaped windows. It's so cute, and she won't even be able to bring it now. I'm going to call her teacher later today and see if Madeline can demonstrate it whenever she's feeling better.

But Darren did cook us heart-shaped pancakes this morning, with strawberries and Cool Whip on them. Bless his heart, pancakes are about the only meal he can make. :) But they were yummy! And his mom is going to come over this evening and stay with Madeline while Darren and I go out.

We have a weird tradition for Valentine's Day. We load up the truck, drive out to the middle of the biggest pasture and go camping. We have a big tent, a space heater and even a little "potty shack"—so we're real cozy despite the chilly weather. This is where Darren proposed to me, on Valentine's Day four years ago, so it's very special to both of us.

And I'm praying hard that the romance happens like it usually does each year. The last few months have been really tough, and we need desperately to have time to reconnect. I have to find a way to convince him I still love him and am attracted to him, whether he can father a child or not. This, I'm learning, is not an easy thing to accomplish.

Off to spend the day caring for sick daughter and enhancing my feminine wiles…what a bizarre combination!

Brenna

From:	The Millards <jstcea4jesus@familymail.net>
To:	"Green Eggs and Ham"
Subject:	Re: Valentine's Day Plans

I can identify with Brenna's "sick child" problem. Tyler's illness has definitely put a crimp in my plans with Shane! I don't really feel comfortable leaving Tyler with a babysitter at this point, so we're staying home this evening. But my dear Shane talked it over with me a couple weeks ago, and we decided we didn't need to go out someplace fancy to have a romantic evening together. (Although Z's weekend sounds awesome!)

So, he took the day off, and is downstairs in the family room right now, transforming it into a romantic Arabian Nights retreat. I don't know what all he's doing, but my sister-in-law loaned him the tulle she used in their wedding, and he's been mooching houseplants and indoor trees off our friends and neighbors the entire week. I've also seen an air mattress, giant floor pillows, and a few Oriental rugs headed down there, as well as some satin sheets in a ton of bright colors. (I don't know where everything came from, exactly.) He dug out all our white Christmas lights on Saturday, so I can only guess what he's doing with those.

We have a friend who loves to cook, and she's fixing us a Persian meal. All we have to do is pick it up!

I have a couple of surprises myself...starting with an Arabian-princess costume I rented, complete with headpiece and veil. And I can't forget the special chocolate dessert...

I'll give you updates tomorrow.

Jocelyn

From:	Dulcie Huckleberry <dulcie@nebweb.net>
To:	"Green Eggs and Ham"
Subject:	**I'm Wearing Black**

It's 11:30 p.m. February 14. Only a half hour left of this year's "day of love." I'm staying up until midnight, just to confirm my suspicions. I think my husband forgot Valentine's Day. There's been no phone call, no e-mails, no cards, no special FTD deliveries. *Nada.* I kept hoping maybe he'd up and surprise me this evening with something, but…nope. And reading all of your e-mails today, I guess I'm the only one who should have worn black.

I'm not really angry or anything. After all, he's only got six weeks left in KC, and he's putting in terribly long hours trying to finish up the project. And after that, he's promised to only accept local jobs—which is good since the next out-of-state contract is in Alaska. So I need to be supportive and understanding right now…right? Maybe he has something planned for this weekend…then again, if we *do* do anything this weekend, it will probably be a last-minute affair motivated by his sense of guilt. I know he's going to feel awful about this. So I *can't* be angry….

But I guess, judging by the tears running down my face, I *can* be sad.

Happy Valentine's Day, everyone. I'm going to bed.

Dulcie

From:	The Millards <jstcea4jesus@familymail.net>
To:	"Green Eggs and Ham"
Subject:	**Re: I'm Wearing Black**

Oh, Dulcie! That's awful! You must have felt like we were rubbing it in the entire day yesterday. I'm so sorry. How are you doing today, dear?

I won't tell you about last night. It wouldn't be kind, considering....

Jocelyn

From:	Thomas Huckleberry <t.huckleberry@cortech.com>
To:	Jordan and Becky <schwartz@ozarkmail.net>
Subject:	**Uh-oh**

Bec,

I forgot yesterday was the 14th... I'm a dead man, aren't I?

Tom

From:	Jordan and Becky <schwartz@ozarkmail.net>
To:	Thomas Huckleberry <t.huckleberry@cortech.com>
Subject:	**Re: Uh-oh**

Yup.

From:	Thomas Huckleberry <t.huckleberry@cortech.com>
To:	Jordan and Becky <schwartz@ozarkmail.net>
Subject:	**Re: Uh-oh**

So, can't you help me out? Talk to Dulcie for me…sort of feel her out, see exactly how mad she is…get her to let off some steam so it's safe for me to talk to her? *Something?*

From:	Jordan and Becky <schwartz@ozarkmail.net>
To:	Thomas Huckleberry <t.huckleberry@cortech.com>
Subject:	**Re: Uh-oh**

Nope. Sorry. Loyalty to my gender forces me to let you handle this one on your own, bro. Good luck.
Becky

From:	P.Lorimer <phyllis.lorimer@joono.com>
To:	"Green Eggs and Ham"
Subject:	**He forgot?**

Oh, that's just pathetic. With the entire U.S. flooded with chintzy cupids, pink and red greeting cards, and obnoxious jewelry commercials, how in the world did he *forget?* What are you going to do, Dulcie?
Phyllis

From:	Zelia Muzuwa <zeemuzu@vivacious.com>
To:	"Green Eggs and Ham"
Subject:	**Re: He forgot?**

Oh, it will only take once, I assure you. Tristan is like a trained elephant now when it comes to holidays and celebrations. Forgot one time…and never did it again.

You know why? I "heaped burning coals on his head." :) He forgot our first anniversary, so the next weekend, I surprised him with the most romantic two days of his life. Everything I could think of that I knew he'd like, all the sweet little details that make a getaway memorable. And, at the end, I presented him with an anniversary clock, so he'd never forget again. He's been as good as gold ever since.

Z

From:	Dulcie Huckleberry <dulcie@nebweb.net>
To:	"Green Eggs and Ham"
Subject:	**Re: He forgot?**

That's a great idea, Z. And thanks to Rosalyn's topic on the loop, I have *plenty* of ideas on how to romance my poor, absentminded hubby. Hmm…you girls want to help me plan it out?

Dulcie

From:	The Millards <jstcea4jesus@familymail.net>
To:	"Green Eggs and Ham"
Subject:	**Re: Romancing Tom**

Good for you, Dulcie-girl! I'm so proud of you! Hey, I'm attaching a list of inexpensive romantic ideas I got at a church marriage conference. Hope that helps.

Jocelyn

From:	Zelia Muzuwa <zeemuzu@vivacious.com>
To:	Dulcie Huckleberry <dulcie@nebweb.net>
Subject:	**Your address?**

Hey, Dulcie,
I need your address. I want to overnight something to you. My parents gave me a gift certificate this Christmas for the Cheesecake Factory. I don't really care for cheesecakes, and Tristan is lactose intolerant, which makes eating there virtually pointless, in my opinion! So I want you to have our certificate. There's a Cheesecake Factory in Kansas City, so you should be able to use it if you want.

Love,
Z

From:	Dulcie Huckleberry <dulcie@nebweb.net>
To:	"Green Eggs and Ham"
Subject:	**You guys!**

You are all so sweet! Z, how can I ever thank you for the gift certificate? We've never been able to afford to go to the Cheesecake Factory, but I just know we'll love it. And the rest of you…all the great ideas, the help in planning, everything. Thank you!
Dulcie

From:	Brenna L. <saywhat@writeme.com>
To:	Dulcie Huckleberry <dulcie@nebweb.net>
Subject:	**Schedule**

Okay, Dulcie, here you go. Attached is the schedule for the weekend. But I don't think I put on there to take the girls to Marianne's house, so make sure you remember to get them there by 9 a.m. on Friday, so you have plenty of time to get to KC. Have fun!
Brenna

From:	Thomas Huckleberry <t.huckleberry@cortech.com>
To:	Dulcie Huckleberry <dulcie@nebweb.net>
Subject:	**Are you okay?**

Dulcie,
I've been trying to call you all week. Are you screening your calls? Please, honey, I'm so sorry. Please talk to me. I'd come home this afternoon, but I don't exactly want to, unless you say it's okay. I know I screwed up big time. It's almost 5 here, so I'll be leaving soon. If I don't hear from you by 7 or so, I guess I'll just stick around here for the weekend.

You know what? I just glanced out my window and I thought for sure I saw your car. Looked just like it. See, I'm so distraught, I'm starting to hallucinate. Wait…that *is* you! You're getting out of that car! What are you

From:	Dulcie Huckleberry <dulcie@nebweb.net>
To:	"Green Eggs and Ham"
Subject:	**Sunday Night Report**

Well, I'm home. But, I'll just say this:

You're right, Z. He won't EVER forget again. ★big, impish grin★

Good night, my friends. Sweet dreams. I know mine will be….

Blissfully,

Dulcie

From:	VIM <vivalaveronica@marcelloportraits.com>
To:	Rosalyn Ebberly <prov31woman@home.com>
Subject:	**My children**

They're driving me nuts, Ros! They are spoiled rotten, and it's partly my fault. Carmen, the nanny, gives them whatever they want, and Frank and I do, too. We just feel so guilty because it seems there's never enough time to spend with them, and the poor things have been through so much already. Then Mama and Daddy are constantly sending them "care packages" full of sweets and toys. At least y'all don't have to deal with *that* problem! Lucky you. I know I need to toughen up, but it's hard—I'm not their "real" mama, after all. If only I could get more organized, maybe there would be more time. I do it at work...why can't I do it at home? But there ya go...

From:	Rosalyn Ebberly <prov31woman@home.com>
To:	SAHM I Am <sahmiam@loophole.com>
Subject:	**[SAHM I AM] TOTW February 21: Producing Wise Children**

Steadfast Shepherds,
Proverbs 13:1 says, "A wise son accepts his father's discipline, but a scoffer does not listen to rebuke."

This week, let's talk about how to raise wise children—ones who appreciate the value of discipline and who listen to the counsel of their parents. As SAHMs, we have primary responsibility during most of the day for training our children. What struggles do you have in the area of discipline?

The most important thing to remember is that you cannot discipline your children until you have self-discipline. So think for a moment—are you controlling your own appetites and impulses? How's the binge eating? What about sleeping in late each morning? Are you having your quiet time daily? Are you taking care of your appearance, or lazing around in leggings and your husband's old flannel shirts all day? Did you exercise this week?

If you aren't taking care of those things in your own life, don't expect to have well-behaved children. I know most of you have likely given up on the idea of your children minding you, but I want to offer you hope. If you just get your own act together, you'll be surprised at how much easier it will be to train your children.

So please share how you are doing in the area of disci-
pline—either for yourself or your little ones.
Respectfully,
Rosalyn Ebberly
SAHM I Am Loop Moderator

"She looks well to the ways of her household, and does
not eat the bread of idleness."
Proverbs 31:27 (NASB)

From:	Dulcie Huckleberry <dulcie@nebweb.net>
To:	"Green Eggs and Ham"
Subject:	Re: [SAHM I AM] TOTW February 21: Producing Wise Children

Well, I'd never admit this to the whole loop, especially in front
of Rosalyn, but a little self-discipline is going a *long* way for
me. Since starting Jocelyn's good-carb, good-fat thing last
month, I've already lost fifteen pounds! I'm so happy! This is
the first thing I've ever tried that has actually worked. I'm
still not thrilled when I look in the mirror, but it doesn't hurt
my eyes quite so much. Look out, Wedding—you aren't going to humiliate me after all! I don't even feel like I'm on a
diet. Actually, I sorta like it better than how I was eating…
Even Tom noticed this past weekend. Of course, I totally
cheated at the Cheesecake Factory, but it was worth it. Yum-
mmmm…

So, I guess according to our esteemed and revered Loop
Moderator, I'm just about ready to tackle disciplining my kid-
dos. Good thing, too, 'cause they are driving me CRAZY
THIS MORNING!

Haley found a marker and scribbled all over the face on McKenzie's favorite doll. McKenzie grabbed a wooden spoon from their kitchen set and proceeded to paddle Haley's bottom.

Not to be outdone by her sisters, Aidan had to pull a few shenanigans, too. I went upstairs to find she had climbed the cabinet over the toilet and was sitting on *top* of the cabinet, about seven feet off the floor, *with* the toilet seat up, picking Cheerios off a yarn necklace and dropping them into the toilet. I choked back a scream, worried that I might scare her into falling. When she saw me, she waved enthusiastically and tossed down another Cheerio.

"I go pee-pee!" she cried, flinging little round O's into the water. Several had by now become waterlogged, swelled right up like mushy-looking mini-bagels that disintegrated as new Cheerios rippled the water. Disgusting!

I put the lid down, which brought a wail of protest. So I quickly hopped up on the toilet seat and carefully removed my now-squalling little monkey from her perch. After sound spankings all around, the three of them are currently slouched in front of the TV like inanimate rag dolls, watching *Sesame Street*. I know I shouldn't use the TV to babysit, but after the toilet cabinet scare, I needed a break!
Dulcie

From:	Zelia Muzuwa <zeemuzu@vivacious.com>
To:	"Green Eggs and Ham"
Subject:	**Re: Dulcie's Morning**

None of my kids was particularly fond of heights, but Seamus did entice Griffith once to crawl into the dryer. Had the door closed and was just about to turn the machine on when I caught him. He couldn't sit down for two weeks after that little incident. He claimed Griffith wanted to know how clothes get dry, and all he was doing was demonstrating. That little rascal! You know, he's growing up awfully fast. Sometimes I almost miss those days…

Boy, you gals make me lonely for my kids. At least Griffith is home during the afternoon to keep me company. And we're working as fast as we can on the adoption. We found this great little Ethiopian restaurant, and we decided that every time we reach another adoption milestone, we're going to go out and celebrate at the restaurant. We went there when our application was accepted by our agency, and we're planning to go again in a few weeks when we complete the paperwork for our home-study.

Speaking of…did you know they want to know *everything* about us for the home-study? We got this "family survey" we have to fill out. It's basically nine pages of long essay questions, and Tristan and I have to answer them separately. Of course, we're comparing answers to make sure they match! But I just about died when I saw number seven: "Please describe your satisfaction with your sex life and explain why you feel that way."

What's up with that? Why on earth could it possibly be important for a social worker to know about my sex life? And then to have to explain *why?* You should have seen Tristan's face when he read it. I've never seen his eyes get so big! :) And his answer was so cute: "I am well-satisfied with my sex life. I feel that way because it is so."

My answer, you ask? Nope, not gonna tell you. (Actually, that's because it wasn't even as interesting as Tristan's. I can joke about stuff like that okay, but to put it down in writing for a case worker to read? Ugh!)

Anyway, we're just waiting for Tristan's birth certificate to arrive from England and then we can turn in our paperwork. A couple weeks after that, we should have our first meeting with our home-study lady. I can't decide if I'm more excited or nervous about that....

Z

From:	VIM <vivalaveronica@marcelloportraits.com>
To:	Rosalyn Ebberly <prov31woman@home.com>
Subject:	**Housekeeper!**

Ros,

Frank got me a housekeeper! I don't know why we didn't do it sooner—all our friends have one. But it has helped so much. She comes once a week, bless her heart, and I can count on every Monday coming home from work to find a house looking as clean as Houston air after a toad choker. Don't matter if I tump over a can of Coke or a whole carton of eggs, it all looks better than sliced bread after she leaves. I can't imagine how she gets everything so shining in such a short time. It's wonderful!

Sure enough, I doubt you have a problem keeping your house clean, being home all the time. Must be nice. But still...it's too bad y'all can't afford a housekeeper, just to make life easier for you. Remember how we both hated our chores growing up? I don't think I'll ever be able to go back to doing it myself ever again. So there ya go.

Ronnie

From:	Rosalyn Ebberly <prov31woman@home.com>
To:	SAHM I Am <sahmiam@loophole.com>
Subject:	[SAHM I AM] TOTW March 7: Tips for Efficient Household Organization and Management

Dear Domestic Darlings,

Spring is just around the corner, and it's time to consider one of the most rewarding, satisfying activities of the year: spring cleaning! :) But in our enthusiasm for transforming our cozy winter burrow into a sparkling, fresh and well-organized spring garden, it is easy for some people to dive right in without the proper preparation or forethought. This will cause a chaotic mayhem that will create tension and stress in your family, instead of peaceful efficiency that gives a feeling of security and well-being to all who enter your pleasant abode.

Here is a quote from one of my favorite books on household organization: *Domestic Bliss Begins with "DO"* by Dustin Scrubb. Written, surprisingly, by a man, this little gem is packed with excellent advice for us SAHMs.

"The well-organized home is a pleasing fragrance to God. He is a God of order and proper design. Anything that is not orderly or properly designed, then, is of Satan. We must avoid at all costs allowing our home to become the tool of our spiritual enemy. He would love to use your cluttered closets, your dusty bookshelves, the dust bunnies under the bed, and your inability to find your shoes as an opportunity to sow dissention and disharmony in your family.

"But where to start reclaiming your home? First, you must confess the sin of disorderliness. Until you repent of your cluttered heart and disorganized soul, you will never be able to make a lasting difference in your house.

"Second, you must commit to making your home a *priority.* Many books and organizing systems claim you can have a sparkling home in 'only minutes a day.' My friends, we must realize that you will never get something for nothing. Effort, determination, dedication and sacrifice are the only true ways to achieving domestic bliss.

"Third, you must have a specific plan of attack. This is as much a spiritual battle as a physical one, and strategy is of the utmost importance. Do not think you can enter the war for your home with little thought or preparation. You will be sabotaged by the guerrilla warfare of the enemy."

Isn't that wonderful advice? I know the anticipation is building—so let's share this week our ideas for organizing and making our homes clean, sanitary, efficient and orderly. Even though it's not in the Bible, I think there is much truth in the statement "Cleanliness is next to Godliness."

Death to Dirt!

Rosalyn Ebberly

SAHM I Am Loop Moderator

"She looks well to the ways of her household, and does not eat the bread of idleness."

Proverbs 31:27 (NASB)

From:	Dulcie Huckleberry <dulcie@nebweb.net>
To:	SAHM I Am <sahmiam@loophole.com>
Subject:	**Re: [SAHM I AM] TOTW March 7: Tips for Efficient Household Organization and Management**

Oh goodie! I can hardly wait. Spring cleaning is on my list of favorite things to do, right up there with getting my flu shot, changing blow-out diapers and having morning sickness.

Dulcie

From:	The Millards < jstcea4jesus@familymail.net>
To:	SAHM I Am <sahmiam@loophole.com>
Subject:	Re: [SAHM I AM] TOTW March 7: Tips for Efficient Household Organization and Management

Have any of you seen the www.flylady.com Web site? It's this entire system for keeping your house clean and organized. I just love it! It was overwhelming at first, but now it actually makes decluttering my house rather fun. My favorite activities are shining my sink and the 27-Fling Boogie.

Have a great day!

Jocelyn

From:	Zelia Muzuwa <zeemuzu@vivacious.com>
To:	The Millards < jstcea4jesus@familymail.net>
Subject:	Re: [SAHM I AM] TOTW March 7: Tips for Efficient Household Organization and Management

You are one sick woman, Joc. ;)

Z

From:	P.Lorimer <phyllis.lorimer@joono.com>
To:	"Green Eggs and Ham"
Subject:	**Something is wrong.**

Jonathan just called me from the church. There's something weird going on. Jonathan needed to make an appointment with somebody, but his new secretary was in the restroom. So he just peeked at her calendar to see what his available times would be. He noticed that tomorrow night she has penciled in, in tiny letters "Elders, 8:30, at Jorgensen's." But the regular board meeting isn't until next week, and it's always at the church, not in one of the homes. No one notified him of any meetings. So he asked her about it when she came back, and she was a bit miffed that he had looked at her calendar. She said she'd just written down the wrong time and date in her book and hadn't erased it yet. But something strange is going on.

I can't imagine what it would be—we haven't had any disagreements with anyone, and nobody has indicated any dissatisfaction. I guess there's nothing wrong with the elders wanting to get together without us. After all, they were all friends long before we arrived. It's silly to be so paranoid. But the whole thing was a little odd.

On a bright note, Bennet took his first steps this morning! I was so happy for him. I wish we had a video camera or something, but I couldn't even find my 35-millimeter in time.

Phyllis

From:	The Millards <jstcea4jesus@familymail.net>
To:	"Green Eggs and Ham"
Subject:	**Bennet...**

...walking today, running by next Tuesday. Way to go, little guy!
Jocelyn

From:	P.Lorimer <phyllis.lorimer@joono.com>
To:	"Green Eggs and Ham"
Subject:	**Re: Bennet...**

<...walking today, running by next Tuesday.>
Hold your tongue, Ms. Millard! He gets into enough trouble as it is! :)
Hugs,
Phyllis

From:	Dulcie Huckleberry <dulcie@nebweb.net>
To:	"Green Eggs and Ham"
Subject:	**You are NOT going to believe this**

I just know you won't. I can hardly believe it myself, so why you would, I don't know. Why I'm even bothering to tell you, when it is so bizarrely unbelievable, is a mystery to me. I mean, you think you've heard some strange things? This tops it all.
Dulcie

From:	Zelia Muzuwa <zeemuzu@vivacious.com>
To:	"Green Eggs and Ham"
Subject:	**Re: You are NOT going to believe this**

Oh, come on, Dulcie. Spill already! Don't play these little games with me, girl. :)
Z

From:	Dulcie Huckleberry <dulcie@nebweb.net>
To:	"Green Eggs and Ham"
Subject:	**Re: You are NOT going to believe this**

Okay, okay. Well, I just got off the phone with Jeanine, my MIL. She up and announced that she and Morris have decided to get married at the Shoji Tabuchi Theater. On the *stage,* for crying out loud! And you'll never guess who is providing the music—the maestro himself. How that happened, I don't know. All Mom would say is, "Oh, sweetie, that's just the effect Morris has on people. He's *such* a dear." Ack! Pardon me while I go chug some Mylanta.

Tom says this is his mother's "defense mechanism" for dealing with anxiety. She does tend toward the theatrical anytime she's nervous. Tom thinks she's really scared about the idea of getting married again, so she is reacting by lowering her inhibitions and making it into a show. All I know is that we're all going to need counseling by the time this is over!

Oh, I didn't tell you the best part—they want to have their wedding photos taken in the theater bathrooms! Argh! Only in Branson can something like this happen....
Dulcie

From:	P.Lorimer <phyllis.lorimer@joono.com>
To:	"Green Eggs and Ham"
Subject:	**Bathroom wedding photos?**

I don't understand. Why would anyone want their wedding photos taken in a bathroom?
Phyllis

From:	Brenna L. <saywhat@writeme.com>
To:	"Green Eggs and Ham"
Subject:	**Not just ANY bathroom...**

Hey, Phyllis,
You obviously have never been to Branson. :) The Shoji bathrooms are legendary. Completely outrageous. I'm talking black onyx, marble, gold-leaf, stained glass, chandeliers, lion's head sinks, you name it. The women's restroom has a fountain and a fireplace. The men's has black leather chairs and a hand-carved pool table in it! People stop at the theater just to go peek in the bathrooms. It's crazy. But I never heard of anyone having their wedding photos taken there....
Brenna

From:	The Millards <jstcea4jesus@familymail.net>
To:	"Green Eggs and Ham"
Subject:	**Re: Not just ANY bathroom...**

We visited there a couple of years ago. The ladies' room has an orchid on every sink, and a maid who dispenses hand lotion to you as you go out. Is your MIL going to let the maid be in the shoot, too? It would be appropriate, you know... having a *bride's maid* in the photos....
Jocelyn

From:	Zelia Muzuwa <zeemuzu@vivacious.com>
To:	"Green Eggs and Ham"
Subject:	Re: Not just ANY bathroom...

<It would be appropriate, you know...having a *bride's maid* in the photos...>
GROAN! Boo hiss! A pun, my father always says, is the lowest form of humor.

Seriously, though, Dulcie, she's going to have her wedding pictures in the bathroom?
Z

From:	Dulcie Huckleberry <dulcie@nebweb.net>
To:	"Green Eggs and Ham"
Subject:	Wedding Branson Style

Yep. I don't know what's worse—that, or her idea of having Morris, dressed in a white tuxedo, ride down the aisle and onto the stage on a white horse swathed in marabou and sequins to "Ride of the Valkyries." She says it's more biblical to have the groom travel down the aisle because in Bible times, the bride always waited for the groom to come get her. So if she actually gets her way on that, we'll have the normal processional, and then we'll all wait onstage while poor Morris appears on his noble steed.

Evidently, Shoji is letting them use all the theatrical lighting, and most of the musicians have offered to play, as well, as their gift to the happy couple. It's going to be a show you won't want to miss. Or maybe you will... *sigh* Why can't I have *normal* relatives? At least I will look a little less like a giant wad of buble gum in my dress. I am beginning to discover my inner drinking straw....

Dulcie

From:	P.Lorimer <phyllis.lorimer@joono.com>
To:	"Green Eggs and Ham"
Subject:	Re: Wedding Branson Style

Hi, Dulcie! I was going to comment on the theological error of your mother expecting her fiancé to ride down the aisle on a white horse. But then I started thinking, "Oh, wait a moment, she's just exaggerating for emphasis." So, I'm *not* going to say anything, except that the picture you painted in my mind made me laugh. See? I am learning to have a sense of humor!

Phyllis

From:	Dulcie Huckleberry <dulcie@nebweb.net>
To:	"Green Eggs and Ham"
Subject:	Re: Wedding Branson Style

<But then, I got to thinking, "Oh, wait, she's just exaggerating for emphasis.">

Alas, Phyllis, my friend...this time I was being *totally* serious. She really intends to do just that.
Dulcie

From:	P.Lorimer <phyllis.lorimer@joono.com>
To:	"Green Eggs and Ham"
Subject:	Re: Wedding Branson Style

Oh, dear. I'm so sorry to hear that. My deepest sympathies.
Phyllis

From:	Zelia Muzuwa <zeemuzu@vivacious.com>
To:	Dulcie Huckleberry <dulcie@nebweb.net>
Subject:	Re: Wedding Branson Style

Hey, Dulcie! This sounds like fun! Any chance you could arrange a bus tour for us? :)
Z

From:	The Millards <jstcea4jesus@familymail.net>
To:	"Green Eggs and Ham"
Subject:	Re: Wedding Branson Style

Definitely can't have a Branson-style wedding without a bus tour!

From:	Dulcie Huckleberry <dulcie@nebweb.net>
To:	"Green Eggs and Ham"
Subject:	**You guys...**

...this isn't funny! It's humiliating! She just sent me an e-mail saying that Shoji is so excited about the wedding that he wants to make it into a videotape to sell in their gift shop! This is awful. What's next? Yakov Smirnoff officiating the ceremony?

Dulcie

From:	J. Huckleberry <ilovebranson@branson.com>
To:	Dulcie Huckleberry <dulcie@nebweb.net>
Subject:	**Wedding question**

Dulcie dear,

I just had the most wonderful idea! Since this wedding event is becoming rather large, I could use some help. You are so organized and efficient, and with your artistic eye for decorating, I think you would be just the person. I was wondering if I could count on you to be my wedding coordinator.

I know you're also going to be in the ceremony, as well as taking care of McKenzie, but this wouldn't be so much work. Just decorating the theater and the bathrooms, directing the rehearsal, cueing the processional, that sort of thing. Please? It would mean so much to me to know I have someone dependable taking care of those little details for me.

Thanks, sweetie,

Jeanine

From:	Dulcie Huckleberry <dulcie@nebweb.net>
To:	J. Huckleberry <ilovebranson@branson.com>
Subject:	**Re: Wedding question**

I don't know, Mom. That sounds like a huge job. Wouldn't it be better to ask someone in connection with the theater? I'd have no idea where anything was or what the rules were. And I must have you fooled—I'm neither organized or efficient. :)
Dulcie

From:	J. Huckleberry <ilovebranson@branson.com>
To:	Dulcie Huckleberry <dulcie@nebweb.net>
Subject:	**Re: Wedding question**

Of course the house manager will be helping you with whatever you need. I've already set that up. You'll be just fine. Don't worry about a thing.
Love,
Mom

From:	Dulcie Huckleberry <dulcie@nebweb.net>
To:	J. Huckleberry <ilovebranson@branson.com>
Subject:	**Re: Wedding question**

Mom, I really don't think this is a good idea. What am I supposed to do with the girls while I'm setting everything up? And during the rehearsal?
Dulcie

From:	J. Huckleberry <ilovebranson@branson.com>
To:	Dulcie Huckleberry <dulcie@nebweb.net>
Subject:	**Re: Wedding question**

Dulcie dear, don't worry. I have that all taken care of. You re-member Diana, Tom's cousin? Well, she's coming and she said she'd be *delighted* to take care of your children while you're busy.

I'll send you a schedule of everything in a few weeks. We have to have the ceremony early enough on Saturday morn-ing so that they can set up for the matinee show. And then, I just confirmed the booking for White Water for our re-ception! Won't a water theme park for a reception be fun? We can all run around in our bathing suits and play, if it's warm enough. I'm going to have a special bridal swimsuit made. Would you and Becky like bridesmaid swimsuits, too?

Oh, and one more thing—for the bridal processional, since Morris is coming in on a horse, I thought it would be fun to do something a little different for us gals. So instead of walking down the aisle, we're going to be let down from the ceiling! You and Becky will have beautiful sparkling stars, and I'm going to have a crescent moon twined with flow-ers. Unique, don't you think?

Gotta go—meeting with the photographer later this af-ternoon! TTFN (that means "Ta-Ta For Now," like Tigger, get it?).

Mom

From:	Dulcie Huckleberry <dulcie@nebweb.net>
To:	"Green Eggs and Ham"
Subject:	**I've been trapped—**

—into being my MIL's wedding coordinator! And it's going to be a nightmare. I *should* just give up and sell you all tickets. At least I'd make some money off my utter degradation and humiliation. Did I tell you she decided that Becky and I will be lowered onto the stage from sparkly *stars?* What if I break the cable? I'd just die of embarrassment....
Dulcie

From:	VIM <vivalaveronica@marcelloportraits.com>
To:	Rosalyn Ebberly <prov31woman@home.com>
Subject:	**Easter is such a pain**

<Now that you're a "mother," you really should take their religious upbringing more seriously. Children who don't attend church are 60% more likely to end up in jail, you know. And with yours already having so much family upheaval, they're surely at a higher risk as it is.>
Ros, darlin', I *am* a Mother—no quotes necessary! As far as religion, well, Frank got it in his head that we need to go to church on Easter Sunday. But there's a big egg hunt for the kids that morning, and I don't want to waste a perfectly good morning sitting in church just to appease his conscience. I know I won't get any sympathy from you, since you think warming a pew and listening to a sermon is the most fun a person could possibly have, but since you asked

what our plans are, I guess you can put up with my griping. :) I don't see why we even celebrate Easter—church,
eggs, bunnies. It's ridiculous. But the kids love their Easter
baskets, so I guess as long as *somebody* is having fun... There
ya go.
VIM

From:	Rosalyn Ebberly <prov31woman@home.com>
To:	SAHM I Am <sahmiam@loophole.com>
Subject:	[SAHM I AM] TOTW March 21: Keeping Holy Week Holy

Beloved Believers,
Is there any time of year that is as sacred and wonderful as
Holy Week? The blessed week we set aside to remember
our Lord's great sacrifice for us. The world has tried its best
to turn this wonderful celebration into a carnal, material-
istic excuse to consume chocolate bunnies, but I know that
all of you strive to keep the focus on our resurrected Sav-
ior.

Let's talk about the special things you do in your family
to commemorate this highest of all holidays.

We make resurrection cookies. I've attached the recipe and
instructions/symbolism to this e-mail. Every ingredient and
even the order of making the cookies is all symbolic of the
events of the crucifixion and resurrection. My children love
making them every year, and they are an easy and wonderful treat.

May you each be blessed by His resurrection,
Rosalyn Ebberly
SAHM I Am Loop Moderator

"She looks well to the ways of her household, and does not eat the bread of idleness."
Proverbs 31:27 (NASB)

From:	Brenna L. <saywhat@writeme.com>
To:	"Green Eggs and Ham"
Subject:	**Guess what???**

Sometimes God speaks through little kids! Madeline came home from school today, said hello to me, and went straight to Darren, who'd just come in for a mid-afternoon snack. (The guy eats more than our cattle!) She looked up at him with her big brown eyes and said, "Guess what, Daddy?"

He squatted down, elbows on knees, and said, "What, Squirt?"

"We read a really cool story in school today."

"Yeah?"

"Uh-huh. It was about a family who adopted a new kid. Adoption is when you make a kid part of your family even though they were born in another family."

I didn't even dare look at Darren's face. I figured he'd accuse me of setting him up for this. He didn't say anything for a second, and then asked, "So what'd you like about it?" His voice sounded sort of tense.

Madeline didn't notice. "Well, I was thinking on the bus about it. And it's sort of like God, you know?"

"God? In what way, Squirt?"

"Well, you know, like how God made us part of His family—when we're born again. That's what they say at church. So, are we adopted, Daddy? Are we?"

I could hear Darren blow out his breath, like he'd just put a newborn calf on his back. "I guess so, Squirt."

She ran off squealing and jumping. "Yay! We're adopted! We're adopted!" Then she ran back to Darren. "We should adopt some kids, you know, Daddy. A whole bunch. Then maybe God can adopt them, too." Then she was off again, singing some made-up song about how God adopts everybody. Funky theology aside, it was pretty cute. :)

Darren stood up and went back outside without saying anything. But now this evening, he's still really quiet, and he has that look on his face that he always gets when something is eating at him.

So pray, please. I think God might be doing something here.

Brenna

From:	Zelia Muzuwa <zeemuzu@vivacious.com>
To:	"Green Eggs and Ham"
Subject:	**Re: Guess what???**

Oh my goodness, Brenna, that made me bawl my eyes out! I'm going to print out the e-mail and tape it up by our desk. You don't mind, do you? Tristan is working late tonight, but I'm going to show it to him when he gets home. He's worked late almost every evening the past two weeks. I hate tax season!

We have our home visit coming up in two weeks—it's the last step before our social worker writes the home-study report. I can't believe it! It feels like we're moving along so quickly, until I look at how far we have to go. But it's an incredible adventure. I'm going to pray for your family, Brenna, that you will adopt a "whole bunch of kids." I haven't even completed one adoption yet, and I think I'm already hooked.

Z

From:	Dulcie Huckleberry <dulcie@nebweb.net>
To:	"Green Eggs and Ham"
Subject:	Re: Guess what???

Yes! Yes! Yes! Madeline got it! She understands! What a smart little cookie. I wish everyone was as astute as her. Everyone in God's family got there by adoption. Why can't more people understand this? Wow, it's just amazing she figured that out all by herself. I think the Lord must be speaking to your little girl, Bren.

Keep me up-to-date on what happens, okay?

Dulcie

From:	The Millards <jstcea4jesus@familymail.net>
To:	"Green Eggs and Ham"
Subject:	Tyler, again

It's been an awful week, and it's only Wednesday. Just when we thought Tyler was really improving, he got worse again. He's so stiff and sore in the morning that he doesn't even want to get out of bed. And he won't hardly eat anything! The doctors say it's a "flare." We were hoping for a remission, but I guess maybe it's too soon to expect anything like that. So they prescribed him stronger medication to control the pain, and the physical therapist is going to give him some more exercises to do.

I *hate* the exercises! Especially when Tyler's not doing so well. He cries and cries because it hurts. So I cry, right along with him. It makes me so angry sometimes—how could God let something like this happen to a little kid? We keep having him prayed for at church. I know in my head that God does love Tyler, and us, but my heart is having a hard time believing it. I don't want to get bitter!

It seems like our whole life is starting to revolve around Tyler's arthritis. Medication schedule, exercises, waiting on him when he's too tired or in too much pain to move off the couch, encouraging him to not get depressed. Nine-year-olds should not be dealing with depression!

I'm tired. And discouraged. I feel like I'm ignoring the other kids, and Shane and I haven't spent much time together, either. My entire life feels out of control, and I don't know how to regain control. None of us are really in a mood to celebrate Easter this week. I thought part of the purpose of Christ's death was to "heal our diseases." So why not Tyler's? I'm going to squeeze in a nap.

Jocelyn

P.S. Just so you know, I decided to go "no-mail" on SAHM I Am for a while. I just can't keep up, and I can't handle Rosalyn's attitude right now. I know I'll get mad and take it out on the loop. But I want you all to stay in touch, please!

From:	Dulcie Huckleberry <dulcie@nebweb.net>
To:	The Millards <jstcea4jesus@familymail.net>
Subject:	Re: Tyler, again

Oh, Jocelyn! I wish there was something I could do to help you. I will pray, though. You sound as discouraged as I was when I was pregnant with the twins and puking every day. I felt so guilty for ignoring poor McKenzie, and I was mad at God for making pregnancy so horrible. And some days, I was even mad at the twins for being so much trouble. Plus, you have the additional pain of seeing your son hurting. My heart aches for you! Please know you can always vent on me, and I'll still love you—just like Jesus does. He really does. I don't understand why He lets things like this happen, but I do know He cries when we cry. Just like you did with Tyler—'cause you're a loving parent.

Love,
Dulcie

From:	P.Lorimer <phyllis.lorimer@joono.com>
To:	"Green Eggs and Ham"
Subject:	Our..."church"

It's 11:45 p.m. on Thursday. I've been crying for about three hours now, and I'm exhausted. I'd like to go to bed, but there's too much to do. We have to pack up and get ready to move out on Monday. They (the oh-so-Godly "elders") have *fired* my husband and demanded we vacate the parsonage by midnight Monday. They came over unannounced this evening to deliver the news.

On what charge? "Willful deception." About Julia. Which is ridiculous because we never deceived anybody! The issue of Julia's birth came up in our talk with the departing pastor during Jonathan's interview. We explained it, and the pastor was okay with it and told us he would let the elders know. They claim he never mentioned it to them, so I have no idea what really happened. All I know is that we're being dismissed and they are using this as the excuse. Apparently, they figured it out when the secretary went to compile our anniversary and birthday dates to send us cards.

I knew it! I just knew somebody, sometime was going to condemn us for what we did.

They have the nerve to stand in our living room and give us the news, right in front of Julia! Then, they tell Jonathan he is still expected to preach on Good Friday and Easter Sunday, where he will then announce his resignation. I was so proud of Jonathan. He stood nose to nose with them and said, "After you barge into our home and humiliate us, you expect me to still do the Easter services? I don't think so, gentlemen." And he showed them the door and locked it behind them.

But I can tell he is just crushed. He's such a good pastor, and he's been so conscientious. All that, and he gets fired for this! I'm so angry, I'd like to physically hurt them. I never knew I had such a violent streak. I know I'll have to repent for that, but I can't honestly say I feel repentant at the moment. I'm just so mad! And hurt. This is the type of thing that made me worried about being a pastor's wife to begin with.

We don't know what we're going to do. I'm not welcome at Jonathan's parents' house, and my mom and dad don't have

the space for our whole family and our stuff. My brother lives in a tiny apartment in New Jersey, with his girlfriend. Jonathan's two sisters are missionaries in Pakistan. Monday, we're going to be homeless and unemployed. I should be scared, but I'm too overwhelmed to feel even one more emotion. Back to packing,
Phyllis

From:	Dulcie Huckleberry <dulcie@nebweb.net>
To:	P.Lorimer <phyllis.lorimer@joono.com>
Subject:	**Re: Our..."church"**

Phyllis,
I can't believe they did that to you! That's horrible. I'm so, so sorry. You can come stay with us, if you want. We don't have a huge house or anything, but we have a guest room and a mostly finished basement. And you could put your things in the basement and the garage—we don't keep too much in the garage. I bet McKenzie and Julia would have a lot of fun playing together. Please don't feel hopeless. I know God hasn't abandoned you.
Love,
Dulcie

From:	Zelia Muzuwa <zeemuzu@vivacious.com>
To:	P.Lorimer <phyllis.lorimer@joono.com>
Subject:	**Re: Our..."church"**

Boy, that's about enough to make me embarrassed to be labeled a Christian! No wonder non-Christians aren't exactly flocking to our churches. Makes me sick!

Listen, honey, you just come on over to Baltimore. We have an apartment over our garage that we're just using for storage. It's supposed to be an art studio for me—like I ever have time for that! Anyway, it's just one bedroom, and a living-kitchen area, but I could look around and find a daybed/trundle thing for the kids to sleep on. Don't worry about a thing, okay?

Love,

Z

From:	The Millards <jstcea4jesus@familymail.net>
To:	P.Lorimer <phyllis.lorimer@joono.com>
Subject:	**Re: Our..."church"**

Ooh, that makes me so mad for you, Phyllis! Shame on them! I can't imagine how frightening that would be. Why don't you come to Colorado for a nice visit in the mountains? You can have Shane's and my master suite—we'll bunk in the basement or move Audra into Cassia and Evelyn's room and take that one. The suite is almost like a mini apartment—bathroom, bedroom, sitting room (with fireplace, I might add), private deck. The only thing would be the kitchen, but you could just eat with us if you want.

You are going to need time to relax and get back on your feet after this blow. I can't think of a prettier place to do it than Colorado Springs. What do you say?

Love,

Jocelyn

From:	Brenna L. <saywhat@writeme.com>
To:	P.Lorimer <phyllis.lorimer@joono.com>
Subject:	**Re: Our..."church"**

Oh, that's low and mean! But somehow it doesn't surprise me, after how some "Christians" treated me after I had Madeline. I'm angry right along with you!

Hey, here's an idea—why don't you come out to the farm for a while? I can guarantee you will be *miles* away from the nearest church (from the nearest anything, for that matter!) :) Plus, Darren's folks have an extra house tucked over in one corner of the homestead. It's tiny—a little cottage built back in 1882, the first frame house on the farm. But a while back, Darren's parents got the idea of using it as a hunting-fishing cabin and making a bit of money off it. So it's all fixed up real nice, has three bedrooms (counting the attic), bathroom, living room, kitchen, and pantry/washroom. I already phoned Mom Lindberg and she was more than happy to let your family stay there for free, as long as you need to. She says to tell you she's very sorry to hear about what happened. Grandpa Holmes (her dad) was a Baptist preacher, so she knows all about growing up in a ministry family.

I am praying that Jesus sends you at least a little encouragement today.

Many hugs!

Brenna

From:	Zelia Muzuwa <zeemuzu@vivacious.com>
To:	"Green Eggs and Ham"
Subject:	**prayer for tyler**

Jocelyn,

Brenna and I just wanted you to know that we have organized a prayer vigil for Tyler today (Good Friday). Starting at noon for the next twenty-four hours, members of SAHM I Am are going to be taking turns praying for your son. We love you! (And just so you know, this was actually Rosalyn and Connie's idea. I sent in a prayer request for you to the list, and they suggested putting this together.)

Love,

Z

From:	P.Lorimer <phyllis.lorimer@joono.com>
To:	"Green Eggs and Ham"
Subject:	**Humbled...**

...by your love. I hardly know what to say. I didn't read your e-mails until this morning (Saturday). Friday, I spent the whole day packing and grieving. And just as I felt myself slipping back into my old hatred of organized religion, just as the bitterness started creeping through my heart, the Lord used you, my dear friends, to show me what His Body is really like. And it's so incredibly beautiful. We are absolutely amazed—did you realize, did you plan it out that each one of you offered your home to us? Or was that just a Holy Spirit "coincidence"? :) "Thank you" seems ridiculously inadequate for the gratitude Jonathan and I both feel toward you sweet, sweet women. Your kindness lifted our hearts and made the pain lessen. We love you all so very much.

After talking it over, we both felt that we should accept Brenna and Darren's offer of staying at their farm. Since they have an extra house, it seemed to make the most sense and be the least disruptive to any of your families. But I wish we were able to take each of you up on your generous hospitality. It completely blew us away. We'll never, ever forget it. You are so precious! I'm almost glad, now, that God let this happen to us, so we could experience this awesome outpouring of love. We've learned that in God's family, we're never homeless. In fact, we don't have just one home—we have four! Many, many blessings to each of you,
Phyllis

From:	Zelia Muzuwa <zeemuzu@vivacious.com>
To:	"Green Eggs and Ham"
Subject:	**Re: Humbled...**

Aw, man! I can't believe the Okie farm won out against Baltimore! :) I'll have to talk to Tristan about putting a cottage in the corner of our backyard. Of course, it would have to be a playhouse-size cottage. You lucky thing, Brenna! You and Phyllis will be the first ones out of all of us to meet in person!

Actually, I'm just so thrilled that you have a place to go now, Phyllis. We didn't plan it out that way, so it must be God. Love and hugs!
Z

From:	Brenna L. <saywhat@writeme.com>
To:	"Green Eggs and Ham"
Subject:	Re: Humbled...

Hah! Don't you know country girls always win? Even trans-planted city-to-country ones! But I'm just so glad we were able to help. Phyllis, send me your phone number so I can call you and work out all the arrangements. I'm not giving you my number, because I don't want you paying for the long-distance call.

On another topic...well, sort of related, now. When I told Darren just a while ago that Phyllis and family had accepted our offer, he was really excited. He said it had been a long time since he'd done something that felt so good. So we were talking about hospitality and Christian love. He told me he really misses having a regular church home. We go to church, but it's so far away, we don't really feel at home there. And since we aren't very active, we don't really know anybody in the church. He says he sometimes feels jealous that I have so many Internet friends, and he hardly has any friends at all. He was also really impressed that all of us offered our homes to Phyllis.

Then he started telling me how he always feels closed up inside, like he can't let anyone past a certain point. Except me, of course. He got really down on himself for being so reserved and standoffish. He was blaming himself for not hav-ing any friends. And then he brought up our conversation about his infertility.

"You know," he said, "I didn't realize I was such a proud person. Here I am, refusing to consider opening our home to a child, and you and your friends are willing to share your homes with an entire family!"

He hung his head, almost looking more pitiful than I could bear. Then he smiled up at me. "Why don't you tell me what you've found out about adoption, okay?"

"What do mean, 'what I've found out'?"

"Oh, come on, Brenna. I might be a dumb farmer, but I can figure out that you've been doing a whole lot of research-ing on the Internet. That's just how you are when you want something. So tell me whatcha got."

Isn't that amazing? And, Phyllis, it happened because of you! It happened because of all of you! If we adopt, we're going to have to name him or her "Phyllis Dulcie Zelia Joc-elyn Lindberg" after you all. He's out doing chores right now, but tonight, after supper, we're going to have a looong talk. God is just too good!

Brenna

From:	The Millards <jstcea4jesus@familymail.net>
To:	SAHM I Am <sahmiam@loophole.com>
Subject:	**[SAHM I AM] HAPPY EASTER**

Ladies,

I've been trying to write this e-mail all morning. But it's re-ally difficult to write when there are tears in your eyes. Thank you for praying on Friday. Thank you for the notes you sent. Thank you for the priceless gift you've given my son. Thank you for loving us so much. I don't deserve any of this. Espe-cially when I let my son's pain rock my faith the way it did this week. God's mercy is so great.

Tyler was in terrible pain yesterday. Couldn't even get out of bed. And I am ashamed to admit it, but I nearly gave up. I knew you all had been praying on Friday, and then for him to be a little *worse* on Saturday made me furious at God. It was Tyler himself, though, that brought me to my knees. He said, "Mom, you shouldn't be blaming God. Can you imagine how bad it would be without Him? Besides, He told me something this morning. He said that someday, He wants me to be a doctor and help other kids that are hurting. And so this way, I can understand what they're going through better, and I'll be a better doctor. So now, it all makes sense."

I just sat there with my mouth open. I never knew such wisdom could come from a child! He watched me, like he was worried I'd be mad at him or something. I gave him the best hug I could without hurting him, and then I started crying.

"Don't cry, Mom," he said. "I guess next time something bad happens, we won't have to get mad at God or ask Him why. He has it all figured out."

Oh, that pierced my heart. I spent the next several hours in my room, doing some major repenting and praying to God. But after that, I felt so much peace.

And this morning, when Tyler woke up, he wasn't stiff at all! He got right out of bed and was getting dressed on his own when I peeked in on him. He even scolded me for catching him in his undies! We went to church, and he ran around the parking lot with the other boys like it was nothing! I about fainted. Shane and I haven't been able to talk or think about anything else all day long. I don't know if the "flare" is over, if the arthritis is in remission, or if Tyler is completely healed—only time will tell. But for now, he seems just fine.

And now my tears have started up again, so I'm going to have to go cry some more. But they are wonderful tears of joy and gratitude. To God, first of all, and then to all of you.

You really were "Jesus with skin on" to us this weekend. And He used each of you to touch our family in a profound way.

I love you! Happy Resurrection Day, indeed!
Jocelyn

From:	VIM <vivalaveronica@marcelloportraits.com>
To:	Rosalyn Ebberly <prov31woman@home.com>
Subject:	**Your birthday**

Howdy Sis!
I think Mama will be calling you later today, but I wanted to give you a heads-up. She and Daddy are fixing to come down to Houston for Frank's photography show at the end of the month instead of going to Hibiscus for your birthday. It's Frank's first exhibit, and it's really important to him, so they decided it was a higher priority this year. I hope y'all understand. You can always have a birthday again next year, but a first show only happens once. I just wanted you to know so you don't get your plans all cattywhompus when Mama calls. We'll make it up to you later, okay? There ya go.
Love,
Veronica

From:	Rosalyn Ebberly <prov31woman@home.com>
To:	SAHM I Am <sahmiam@loophole.com>
Subject:	**[SAHM I AM] TOTW April 4: Ordering Our Priorities**

Women of integrity,

Don't you just love the arrival of spring? I know in only a few weeks, Hibiscus is going to live up to its flowery name and be awash with color and fragrance. But with the arrival of spring comes a busy whirl of activity. So before the roller coaster begins its descent, let's take a moment and discuss our PRIORITIES.

As SAHMs, it's tempting for many of you to become distracted by all the things that we fill our lives with. MOPS, Bible study, play groups, lunch dates, church events—all these compete for our time and attention. And then there are the time-wasters: watching TV, surfing the Internet, reading novels, shopping and so on, that cut even further into our already short days.

We must always remind ourselves what is most important. I do this by making a list and posting it by my bed so that it's one of the first things I see in the morning. It helps me focus on what I SHOULD be doing each day, and not get distracted by anything else. My priorities are, in order of importance: God, Chad, the children, household management, church, and lastly, friends. Not that you all aren't important to me—you're on the list, after all! But I have to keep you in the proper place in my life, not allowing you to become more important than the other items. If I had to choose between you and the rest of my list, any other thing would win first. That's just the way it has to be.

You, too, can be this disciplined if you work at it. The first step is to make your list of priorities. Next, order it according to CURRENT importance in your life. Put the least important item (like all of you) at the bottom. God SHOULD be at the top, but don't just put Him there because it's the right thing to do. At this stage, you order your list according to what is actually true in your life right now. I doubt many of you will have God at the top of your list, because if you did, you wouldn't be spending so much time e-mailing one another! :)

Then you can create a second list with the order your priorities SHOULD be in. This is the time to put God at the top, and Friends at the bottom (or somewhere down there). You'll likely have things from the first list that won't even make it to the second list—you don't REALLY have time in your life to make EVERYTHING a priority.

Notice on my list what was NOT there: Myself! That's right—in the spirit of humility and unselfishness, I do not make myself a priority. That means that I care very little about my own hobbies, accomplishments, dreams or desires. My life is poured out in completely selfless service to others. And that's what all of YOU should aspire to, as well! It's the most satisfying, fulfilling sensation in the entire world—to be NOTHING.

Totally yours,

Rosalyn

> "She looks well to the ways of her household, and does not eat the bread of idleness."
> Proverbs 31:27 (NASB)

From:	Brenna L. <saywhat@writeme.com>
To:	"Green Eggs and Ham"
Subject:	Re: [SAHM I AM] TOTW April 4: Ordering Our Priorities

Good old Rosalyn—she always knows how to make us feel great about ourselves.

Brenna (whose current priority for the day is mopping the floor! It's been raining, and I really am starting to think the mud is alive and sneaking into my kitchen and oozing itself all over my clean floor in shapes that look incredibly like my husband's boot-prints! Grrrr...)

From:	P.Lorimer <phyllis.lorimer@joono.com>
To:	"Green Eggs and Ham"
Subject:	Re: [SAHM I AM] TOTW April 4: Ordering Our Priorities

Hello girls!

I just ran over to Brenna's house to check my e-mail (no Internet access at the cottage) and I can attest to the creeping mud issue in her kitchen—except I'm afraid that now the mud is forming itself into shapes that look like *my* shoes, too! The nerve...

I am really enjoying Oklahoma and farm life. So is Jonathan. I hadn't realized how near to burnout he was in Wisconsin until we got here and started settling in. He is still sleeping 12 to 14 hours a day. At first, I was worried he was depressed. But now, it appears it's just his way of recovering from what happened. He isn't talking to me much about how he's feeling, but I'm hoping we'll have some time to check out Brenna's camping pasture. She and Darren offered to babysit the children some night after it dries out a bit.

What amazes me most is how quiet it is here. I thought small-town life was quiet, but this is silence on an entirely new level. You can stand outside on a still day and almost hear your heart beating. I spent most of the afternoon yesterday while Bennet and Julia were napping, sitting on a "big, round bale" in the field near the house just listening to the quiet and letting peace seep into my very bones. It was a balm to my spirit.

We haven't even discussed Jonathan's job situation yet. I don't think he's ready to work on it at the moment. But the Lindbergs aren't letting us pay any of the bills, despite our protests, not even groceries. And the car was (thankfully) paid for. So our only real concern is health insurance. We really should get the children on Medicaid, and just pray neither Jonathan nor I get sick or injured. But other than that small worry, we are loving it here.

Blessings,

Phyllis

From:	Brenna L. \<saywhat@writeme.com\>
To:	"Green Eggs and Ham"
Subject:	**Phyllis**

I hate to sound like I'm rubbing it in, gals, but I *love* having Phyllis here! You should have seen us when they pulled up in the drive. She got out of the car and I ran out of our house, and we squealed and gave each other a hug. Our poor guys were standing behind us looking at each other, like, "Hi, I don't know you, so I'm not going to hug you."

And then, Phyllis and I were all, like, "You don't look *any-thing* like I expected!" For some reason I thought she'd be tall, with short blond hair, sort of a squareish face, and blue eyes. But Phyllis has this elegant, oval face and long, straight brown hair and gorgeous brown eyes. When she wears her hair up, you'd swear she was a ballerina, she's so graceful looking. (She's looking over my shoulder now, and just slapped me on the arm, saying, "Oh, please!") :)

Hi, girls, this is Phyllis writing now. Brenna exaggerates. I'm hardly graceful. She had me fooled, too. I was expecting she'd be really short, petite, with glossy light brown hair cut in a pageboy. But she's taller than I imagined, willowy (e.g., zero body fat, which I'm trying not to be envious about), with curly hair that is long and dark brown, and a sparkly smile that lights up her whole face. No wonder Darren was swept off his feet when he met her! :)

Okay, Brenna's back—zero body fat, whatever! Anyway, as you can tell, we're having fun getting to know each other in person. We were thinking that sometime, maybe next year, we should all try to get together somehow. Like a Green Eggs and Ham retreat somewhere. Wouldn't that be fun? We could leave the kiddos with our DHs and have a girls-only weekend. :) Hmm, I'll be fantasizing about that for the rest of the day!

Okay, I'd really better go mop that floor…the mud is launching an invasion on my house.

Brenna

From:	Dulcie Huckleberry <dulcie@nebweb.net>
To:	"Green Eggs and Ham"
Subject:	**Dress Measurements!!!**

Whoo-hoo, girls! I just got Tom to help me take my measurements to send to Jeanine so she can get my dress for the wedding. (He enjoyed "helping" me way too much!) But I'm dancing around the house, chanting,

I AM DOWN TWO SI—ZES!

I AM DOWN TWO SI—ZES!

I think Tom thinks I've lost my mind. But he doesn't realize how hard I've worked! Yippee!!! Lower me from a star, Jeanine! Bring on the drinking straw dress! I'm ready! Lithely yours (well, okay, maybe not quite lithe, yet, but definitely closer…),

Dulcie

From:	The Millards <jstcea4jesus@familymail.net>
To:	"Green Eggs and Ham"
Subject:	**Re: Dress Measurements!!**

Way to go, Dulcie! Doesn't it feel great?

By the way, how do you like having Tom home?

Jocelyn

From:	Dulcie Huckleberry <dulcie@nebweb.net>
To:	"Green Eggs and Ham"
Subject:	**How do I like Tom being home?**

You know, Jocelyn, that's a very interesting question. He's been home about a week now—with 75% bench pay, which is pretty good. It looks like he will have an Omaha assignment in about two weeks, so this is a vacation for him. And I thought I'd be ecstatic.

Can you hear the "but" in that? :) Quite honestly, it's not exactly like I'd expected it to be. I love Tom—you all know that. But having him around all the time is...bugging me. That's so awful to say. He's wonderful about trying to help, but I think I actually get more accomplished without him here. Like this morning—he offered to get the twins up and dressed for me. I thought that would be great. But I discovered something. My husband cannot put on a diaper right to save his life. And we don't even use cloth diapers! All he has to do is position the silly thing and bring the tapes up and around. But, I kid you not, both Haley's and Aidan's diapers were sliding off their little bottoms by the time he brought them downstairs for breakfast! I've never seen such a pathetic diapering attempt! Aidan's was so loose, she leaked, and I had to find her a new outfit.

Oh, speaking of outfits! I didn't know Tom was so clothing challenged! He put poor Haley into bright red pants with a pink-and-blue-striped top that was about two sizes too small. It wasn't even in her dresser—it had gotten shoved into the closet and McKenzie found it. But it was the most hideous getup I've ever seen! And when I protested about it, he looked completely puzzled.

"What's wrong with it? Red and pink are sort of the same, aren't they?"

ARGH! By the time I re-changed their diapers and got them dressed appropriately, I could have had all three of them dressed and done with breakfast.

And don't even get me started about the evenings. (But since I am started, let me tell you about it.) I must have forgotten what it was like having him home. I keep tripping over him, or his stuff. I didn't think he had that many belongings in the hotel at KC—maybe they propagated during the trip to our house. I always thought Tom was a neat freak and I was the messy one. Now…I'm not sure.

So he sits around watching TV or surfing the Internet in the evenings. Oh, and that's another thing—I don't like sharing my computer! When he's on a job, he gets to borrow a company laptop, but since he's home right now, no laptop. And he takes up all my e-mailing time reading programming news and looking at all the latest, greatest computer developments.

I hate to sound hard-to-please, and I do like having him home. But it's almost like having another child around, if you know what I mean. Another person to supervise, another mouth to feed, another body to clean up after. And his constant attempts to "help" remind me of McKenzie. I think I can teach him how to do some of the chores, given enough time. Handyman he is not.

Boy, do I sound ungrateful or what? I'm sorry. Don't mean to vent to all of you, especially when you've put up with my griping about him being gone. :) Just take it as a lesson, girls—be careful what you wish for. You just might get it. Dulcie

From:	The Millards <jstcea4jesus@familymail.net>
To:	Dulcie Huckleberry <dulcie@nebweb.net>
Subject:	**Re: How do I like Tom being home?**

Dulcie, you're so funny! Don't you know Tom's just being a man? :) Shane is useless at choosing clothes for any of the kids. In fact, I have to help him pick out his own outfits. He has finally figured out how to diaper decently. But it did take a while.

Enjoy your man. Enjoy having him home. Forget the inconveniences and just concentrate on the perks—cuddle time, free babysitting, an adult to talk to and so on. You'll get used to the new routine soon.

Love,
Jocelyn

From:	Brenna L. <saywhat@writeme.com>
To:	"Green Eggs and Ham"
Subject:	Re: How do I like Tom being home?

Hey, Dulcie! Husbands take up a lot of room, don't they. :) Darren has dinosaur-size feet and great big hands. I never let him anywhere near anything breakable! And I'm constantly tucking my toes out of the way so they don't get squashed. But I honestly believe—in spite of the extra work involved—that having a husband is far superior to having a cat.

Hugs,
Brenna

From:	P.Lorimer <phyllis.lorimer@joono.com>
To:	"Green Eggs and Ham"
Subject:	Re: How do I like Tom being home?

Jonathan just put a stained dress of Julia's through the wash on hot and the dryer on high. I told him he might as well have put the entire thing in the oven and baked it at four hundred and fifty degrees. That stain is *never* coming out—and it was one of my favorite outfits for her! Does that count toward our emerging list of ways that husbands are…inconvenient? Sorry, I'm just a tad irritated. How many times have I told him to check for stains and treat them *before* putting them in the wash?

Big sigh,

Phyllis

From:	Zelia Muzuwa <zeemuzu@vivacious.com>
To:	"Green Eggs and Ham"
Subject:	**Re: How do I like Tom being home?**

<How many times have I told him to check for stains and treat them *before* putting them in the wash?>

Oh, Phyllis, I'm sorry. I really am. But I've been saving up this Shakespeare quote, just waiting for a time like this to share it:

"Prithee, honey-sweet husband, let me bring thee to Staines."

Gotta love the Bard!

From:	Brenna L. <saywhat@writeme.com>
To:	"Green Eggs and Ham"
Subject:	**Zelia's Bard**

<"Prithee, honey-sweet husband, let me bring thee to Staines.">

Okay, Z, out with it—tell us the truth. You had to have made that one up! Where do you find these quotes, anyway?

Brenna

From:	Zelia Muzuwa \<zeemuzu@vivacious.com>
To:	"Green Eggs and Ham"
Subject:	**Re: Zelia's Bard**

Did not! Act 2, scene 3 of *The Life of King Henry the Fifth.* You can look for yourself—Shakespeare is on the Internet, my friend.

From:	Brenna L. \<saywhat@writeme.com>
To:	"Green Eggs and Ham"
Subject:	**Re: Zelia's Bard**

Oh, *The Life of King Henry the Fifth*…of course! I should have known. I love that play! I want to read it again—it's been a whole three months since I last read it. But it's going to have to wait. I'm right in the middle of *The Brothers Karamozov,* and after that, I've promised this will be the year I finally read *Crime and Punishment.*

"Literarily" yours,

Brenna

From:	The Millards <jstcea4jesus@familymail.net>
To:	"Green Eggs and Ham"
Subject:	**Re: Zelia's Bard**

What happened to you, Brenna? You take a Rosalyn pill this morning or something? :)

From:	Dulcie Huckleberry <dulcie@nebweb.net>
To:	"Green Eggs and Ham"
Subject:	**I screwed up...**

I asked Tom to set up filters on my e-mail program yesterday, so that everyone's e-mails would go to their own folders. He saw the ones to our Green Eggs alias with "How do I like Tom being home?" in the subject line, and was curious what I'd written. So he checked my "Sent Mail" and read what I wrote, about how frustrated I was.

He's furious, and hurt. I tried to apologize, but he won't listen. All the stuff about the Christmas party that we never talked about came back up. To make a long story short, he says that since I don't want him around anyway, he's going to take that remote job after all. And he does mean *remote*.

It's the Alaska job. For a year. He leaves Monday.
Dulcie

From:	Rosalyn Ebberly <prov31woman@home.com>
To:	SAHM I Am <sahmiam@loophole.com>
Subject:	[SAHM I AM] TOTW April 18: Making Room in Your Life for God

Holy Housewives,

Here is a topic near and dear to my heart—DAILY QUIET TIME. That blessed and sacred hour of prayer. The communion! The fellowship with God! Let's share our wondrous experiences of walking with God in our devotional time.

I always have my quiet time in the early mornings. It's more Scriptural that way, and it's like tithing the first part of my day right to the Lord. I have a study guide, which takes about forty-five to sixty minutes per lesson. Then I spend another half hour memorizing Scripture. After that, I take another hour to pray through my entire prayer list, beginning with the president of the United States, and ending with specific petitions for each missionary our church supports. My husband and children take up a large portion of the time in between.

It's common to hear SAHMs protest, "But I'm too busy! I don't have time to spend two and a half or three hours in quiet time." My response is always "Well, I'M too busy NOT to spend three hours with God!"

So, what about the rest of you? Are you "too busy" to spend time with God? Or too busy NOT to?

Devoted to Him,

Rosalyn

"She looks well to the ways of her household, and does not eat the bread of idleness."
Proverbs 31:27 (NASB)

From:	Zelia Muzuwa <zeemuzu@vivacious.com>
To:	"Green Eggs and Ham"
Subject:	totw...*sigh*

I never enjoy discussions about quiet time. They always make me feel guilty. Yes, you all are witness to this sad but true fact—my weakness where Rosalyn is concerned is when she brings up daily devotions. I can ignore housecleaning, or discipline, or organic cheeseball recipes and all the other inane topics she moralizes ad nauseum about. But she mentions devotional time with God, and I suddenly feel like I'm 10 years old again, with the pastor looking down at me from his pulpit, shaking his finger in my face and telling me what a bad Christian I am.

It's not that I don't love God. but I can't seem to sit down and concentrate on studying the Bible for longer than...well, five minutes. And I get lost and frustrated with long prayer lists. I hate memorizing, and I especially hate getting up early in the morning. So quiet time, for me, is just another unpleasant chore I have to do. And I don't do it, because there are a million other things that are more urgent. Nobody will go hungry if I don't read the Bible every day. But if I don't make dinner...?

Then, I feel even more guilty because a "good" Christian would "hunger for the word." A "good" Christian would *long* to spend time "on their face in prayer." A "good" Christian would "hide God's word in their heart." I want to be a good Christian, but it seems sometimes like a little too much effort.

Z

From:	P.Lorimer <phyllis.lorimer@joono.com>
To:	"Green Eggs and Ham"
Subject:	**Re: totw...*sigh***

Zelia,

I used to feel the same way! But when I was in graduate school, I finally "got it." We are *not* supposed to have "quiet time." Not at all! We are supposed to have a love relationship with the God of the universe, who adores each of us as individuals. Do you force yourself to spend a certain block of time with Tristan every day, where you engage in intense study of something somebody else wrote about what he said? Where you deliberately work at memorizing a letter he wrote you? Where you rattle off a honey-do list of needs you or other people have? How fun would that be for either one of you?

I would imagine when you spend time with your husband, you laugh and talk together, show affection and listen to each other. It's not "quiet" at all!

Don't you think God would rather have that sort of a natural, spontaneous relationship with you, instead of some regimented, formulaic ritual? :)

Phyllis

From:	Zelia Muzuwa <zeemuzu@vivacious.com>
To:	"Green Eggs and Ham"
Subject:	**Re: totw...*sigh***

You know what, girl? Sometimes you've got more wisdom in your pinky than a whole convention of pastors will ever have! Thank you. I'll be thinking about what you said.

From:	Dulcie Huckleberry <dulcie@nebweb.net>
To:	Jordan and Becky <schwartz@ozarkmail.net>
Subject:	**Heard from Tom?**

Dear Becky,

Has Tom e-mailed you or called you? He's done neither with me. And I couldn't bring myself to admit that to Mom, because then she'd know how awful things are with us right now. So I was hoping you'd heard from him. He left a week ago today, and I'm just miserable. Please believe me, I never meant to hurt him so bad. I'm still not sure what I did that was so wrong. I was just teasing around with some of my friends. You know how girls talk about their husbands some-times... I was a lot nicer than some women are about their DHs!

Anyway, if you're not mad at me, too, for chasing your brother off to Alaska two months before the wedding, please tell me if you know how he's doing. I dropped him off at the airport, and he didn't even want us to come in and wait with him. Just said he'd see me at the wedding. No kiss, nothing. Any advice would be hugely appreciated.

Your sister,

Dulcie

From:	Jordan and Becky <schwartz@ozarkmail.net>
To:	Dulcie Huckleberry <dulcie@nebweb.net>
Subject:	My brother

Hi Dulcie,

Why is it that both of you seem to have appointed me as your personal marriage counselor? What do I know? I'm just his kid sister! :)

But, to answer your question, he did call the other evening, and it sounds like he arrived okay and is getting settled. Miserable, but settled. Also sounds to me like he's starting to cool down and realize he made a very stupid decision! And now you're both stuck with it.

Trust me, this has all been *very* educational for Jordan and me. We are taking pages and pages of notes—we call it our "Let's Learn from Tom and Dulcie's Screwups Notebook." So, thanks to you, we should have an *awesome* marriage! :)

Okay, I'll be nice now. You wanted my advice on Tom? You want to know why he got so upset about whatever was in that e-mail? Think about it, Dulcie. He grew up with an alcoholic dad that was always telling him how useless he was, how he couldn't do anything right. A dad that up and split when Tom was 13 and I was 11. We didn't hear from him again—got an obituary notice about ten years ago that he died of liver sclerosis. If you had that sort of experience as a kid, how sensitive would you be about someone you love saying you were in the way and didn't know how to do anything right? He's gotten to the point where the only thing he is confident in is his ability to program computers. Do you blame him for running away from the rest of it?

That's about the best I got for you. Sorry it isn't more.

Hugs,

Becky

From:	Dulcie Huckleberry <dulcie@nebweb.net>
To:	Jordan and Becky <schwartz@ozarkmail.net>
Subject:	**Re: My brother**

Oh, Becky! He never told me any of that. I never, *ever* would have joked about him if I'd known. All he would say about his dad was that he drank a lot and divorced your mom and died a while ago. I didn't know. Honest...I just didn't know.

Dulcie

From:	Jordan and Becky <schwartz@ozarkmail.net>
To:	Dulcie Huckleberry <dulcie@nebweb.net>
Subject:	**Re: My brother**

<He never told me any of that.>
Yeah, well, it's not exactly the sort of thing we like to put in our family Christmas letter or anything....

Give him another week or so. I bet he'll come around enough so you can talk to him.

Becky

From:	J. Huckleberry <ilovebranson@branson.com>
To:	Dulcie Huckleberry <dulcie@nebweb.net>
Subject:	**Flowers**

Darling,

You're so good with design. Look at the attached photos for me and tell me which color of amaryllis would look better in my bouquet. Do you like the fuchsia-striped ones, or the white ones with the red star in the center? Oh, maybe I should go multicolored and have one of all of them!

By the way, just for the record, I am not in favor of Tom going off to Alaska for a whole year. What was he thinking, leaving his family like that? It's bad enough for him to have been home only on weekends, but this is shameful! I'm sorry, dear. I thought I raised him better than that. You poor thing. I'm sure the salary is very attractive, but really, there's more to life than making money. I'll tell him so, too, at the wedding.

Well, I'm off to work. Have a great day, honey!

Jeanine

From:	Thomas Huckleberry <t.huckleberry@cortech.com>
To:	Dulcie Huckleberry <dulcie@nebweb.net>
Subject:	**Contact info**

Dulcie,

Did you get the voice mail I left last week with my new office and hotel contact info? I didn't get a reply, so I wanted to make sure you found it.

Anchorage is very pretty. A little smaller than Omaha. Chilly, too. Your mother wouldn't have to worry about her flowers trying to come up early here. Everyone seems nice so far.

Let me know if you got that voice mail, or if I need to e-mail you my info again.

Thanks,

Tom

From:	J. Huckleberry <ilovebranson@branson.com>
To:	Dulcie Huckleberry <dulcie@nebweb.net>
Subject:	**Music**

Dulcie dear,

Do you think it would be better to have the whole band or just Shoji play "Ride of the Valkyries" for Morris's processional? Shoji offered, but I have never heard a violin version before. Would it sound weird, do you think?

Jeanine

From:	Zelia Muzuwa <zeemuzu@vivacious.com>
To:	Dulcie Huckleberry <dulcie@nebweb.net>
Subject:	**Adoption reference**

Dulcie,

Would you be willing to write a reference for us for the adoption? I know we've never met in person, but you know me probably better than anyone else, except Tristan. Our case worker said it would be okay. If you'd like to do this, let me know and I'll send you the information sheet on what you have to include in the letter.

I'm really jazzed—tomorrow is our home visit! But I'm nervous, too. I've cleaned the entire house, top to bottom. Tristan probably would have all sorts of fun teasing me about how suddenly obsessive I've become about picking up. But he's still trying to recover from tax day.

I hope you're doing okay. You've been a bit quiet this week.

Hugs,

Z

From:	Brenna L. <saywhat@writeme.com>
To:	Dulcie Huckleberry <dulcie@nebweb.net>
Subject:	**Question about your parents**

Hi Dulcie!

I have sort of an awkward question to ask you about when you were adopted. Did your parents ever feel sad or anything because they missed out on being pregnant with you? I guess it was probably different for them since they'd had children already....

See, Darren told me last night that he doesn't mind the idea of adoption so much. Ever since Madeline made that comment to him about all of us being adopted by God, he's decided adoption is pretty cool. But he's feeling really sad about not being able to go through a pregnancy with me. He said he keeps looking at all my baby pictures from Madeline, and when I was pregnant with her, and the ultrasound picture and all that. And he told me he really wants to do all that stuff with me, since I had to go through it alone the last time. (Well, my mom was with me, but it's not the same as having a husband.) He got really sad, and even looked like he was going to cry—which he *never* does.

So that's why I was asking. I hope it doesn't offend you or bother you at all. I'm not trying to be nosey. I just wondered if that feeling of disappointment ever goes away.

Thanks for being such a good friend.

Brenna

From:	J. Huckleberry <ilovebranson@branson.com>
To:	Dulcie Huckleberry <dulcie@nebweb.net>
Subject:	**Wedding Favors!**

I almost forgot! What do you think we should do about wedding favors? I haven't ordered any yet, and if I don't this week, I'm afraid they might not arrive in time. I was thinking it would be nice to make them a Branson souvenir/Wedding favor combination. I saw the cutest miniature cedar rolling pins in a gift store on the strip the other day—they had "Ozark Husband Tamer" carved on them. I think there'd be enough room on the opposite side to put our name and wedding date. That would be for the ladies. The men could have corncob bubble pipes with our names and date on it. Wouldn't that be just so cute?

Gotta run! TTFN!

Jeanine

From:	Dulcie Huckleberry <dulcie@nebweb.net>
To:	"Green Eggs and Ham"
Subject:	**Busy Day!**

Hi everyone!

I've had a whirlwind day! I scheduled a dentist appointment for McKenzie this morning, and then we all went to the store to buy shoes for the twins, who seem to be having another growth spurt. We ate lunch out, and then I figured I really should stop at Jiffy Lube and get the oil changed in the car, since it was long overdue. While the car was being worked on, we walked over to our hair salon and got all four of us trimmed up. After that, I went grocery shopping, and then the girls were getting really fussy, so I took them home and put them down for a nap. Spent all afternoon doing bills, then laundry. Since I was working on clothes anyway, I decided to sort out the spring and summer clothes the girls will need and get them washed and put away. Fixed supper, put on a movie for the kids, and ran next door to feed the neighbor's cat for her while she's visiting her niece in Ohio. Came back and read a story to the girls and put them to bed.

I have a ton of e-mails! And I still have to marinate some chicken for a slow-cooker recipe tomorrow. So if any of you wrote me, I'll try to answer right away. I just feel like I'm chasing my shadow today! But I did get everything done that I wanted to, which is a good feeling.

Have a good evening.

Dulcie

From:	Dulcie Huckleberry <dulcie@nebweb.net>
To:	Brenna L. <saywhat@writeme.com>
Subject:	**Re: Flowers**

I'd suggest the pink ones. They'll match our dresses better. Don't do multiple colors. Simple is best.

I think Tom felt like he didn't have any choice. Don't get upset at him. We'll manage.
Dulcie

From:	Dulcie Huckleberry <dulcie@nebweb.net>
To:	Zelia Muzuwa <zeemuzu@vivacious.com>
Subject:	**Re: Music**

Considering "Ride of the Valkyries" is already an unusual choice for processional music, I'd suggest letting the band play it so it will sound more traditional. You don't want Shoji up-staging you. *You're* the bride.
Dulcie

From:	Dulcie Huckleberry <dulcie@nebweb.net>
To:	Brenna L. <saywhat@writeme.com>
Subject:	**Re: Adoption reference**

I'd be happy to do a reference for you for the adoption! Just send me the information you have. Good luck on the home-study tomorrow!
Dulcie

From:	Dulcie Huckleberry <dulcie@nebweb.net>
To:	J. Huckleberry <ilovebranson@branson.com>
Subject:	**Re: Question about your parents**

I don't mind you asking at all! My parents have never mentioned how they felt about not being pregnant with me. But I can understand that Darren must be experiencing some very real grief. I wouldn't think that it will ever stop mattering completely, but I bet the pain won't be quite as intense once he goes through the adoption. It has a way of healing hearts, from what my parents have said.

Love,

Dulcie

From:	Dulcie Huckleberry <dulcie@nebweb.net>
To:	Thomas Huckleberry <t.huckleberry@cortech.com>
Subject:	**Re: Wedding Favors!!!**

How about some homemade Ozark fudge truffles or something? I think everyone would *really* appreciate that more than the rolling pins or corncob pipes.

Dulcie

From:	Thomas Huckleberry <t.huckleberry@cortech.com>
To:	Dulcie Huckleberry <dulcie@nebweb.net>
Subject:	**Huh?**

Dulcie,
You okay? I didn't say a word about wedding favors. I wanted to know if you got my voice mail last week.
Tom

From:	Dulcie Huckleberry <dulcie@nebweb.net>
To:	Thomas Huckleberry <t.huckleberry@cortech.com>
Subject:	**Re: Huh?**

Tom,
I didn't write you about wedding favors! That was your mother. How did you get it? And no, I forgot to check the voice mail. I'm sorry! I'll do it right now.
Dulcie

From:	Zelia Muzuwa <zeemuzu@vivacious.com>
To:	Dulcie Huckleberry <dulcie@nebweb.net>
Subject:	**Re: Music**

<Considering "Ride of the Valkyries" is already an unusual choice for processional music, I'd suggest letting the band play it so it will sound more traditional. You don't want Shoji upstaging you. *You're* the bride.>
Wow, Tristan is really going to flip when he hears about this! Bad enough, I'm getting married on the sly, but "Ride of the Valkyries"? You gotta be kidding me! Defense mechanisms aside, I didn't think she'd go through with it!

From:	Brenna L. <saywhat@writeme.com>
To:	Dulcie Huckleberry <dulcie@nebweb.net>
Subject:	**Re: Adoption reference**

<I'd be happy to do a reference for you for the adoption! Just send me the information you have. Good luck on the home-study tomorrow!>
That's just plain mean, Dulcie! Are you trying to make fun of us?
Brenna

From:	Dulcie Huckleberry <dulcie@nebweb.net>
To:	"Green Eggs and Ham"; Thomas Huckleberry <t.huckleberry@cortech.com>; J. Huckleberry <ilovebranson@branson.com>
Subject:	**Argh! Do-over!**

Have mercy on me and *delete* whatever e-mails I just sent! I beg you. No one got the right reply. I'm very sorry. Didn't mean to confuse, offend, concern or otherwise disturb your peace. Ignore the whole thing. But give me until tomorrow to sort it out, please. I must really need some sleep...
Dulcie

From:	VIM <vivalaveronica@marcelloportraits.com>
To:	Rosalyn Ebberly <prov31woman@home.com>
Subject:	**I can't keep up...**

Ros, I blew it! Ashley had her school awards ceremony on Friday, and I *totally* forgot. She was all worked up about it, and I feel like a complete heel. We have an important ad campaign due next week, and I've been frazzled trying to get everything done. Plus, Stanley had a cold, and Carmen was gone all week because of a death in her family. Frank has wedding photos scheduled every weekend from now through July, and Courtney's piano recital is on Sunday. I feel like all I've done this week is run around fussing at everybody like a grumpy possum.

I was excited to get this promotion, but I was more excited about becoming a mama. I love these kids like they were my own, and it makes me just plumb boo-hoo to think how I've let them down the past few months. It must be so easy for you—having all that time to devote to them. Playing with them the whole day, no pressures, no hassles. No wonder at all you chose to stay at home. If I had my druthers, I'd do it, too, but it's hard to imagine giving up my career. I'm good at it. At home, I'm afraid I'd be bored as a dog that can't dig. I'm not like you—I *need* to accomplish something with my life. There has got to be a way to make this work.

Mama told me this morning that she and Daddy are real proud of what a great mother you are. I only wish they were that impressed with my mothering skills, too, but I don't think my track record this week has been very admirable. So there ya go. Any suggestions?

Ronnie

From:	Rosalyn Ebberly <prov31woman@home.com>
To:	SAHM I Am <sahmiam@loophole.com>
Subject:	[SAHM I AM] TOTW May 2: Balancing Our Many Hats

Flexible Females,

Have you ever had this experience? Someone asks you "So what do you DO?" What do you say? "I'm a stay-at-home mom." And they raise their eyebrows and say, "WOW! That's just wonderful! I could NEVER do that. I'd go crazy. Don't you get bored? How do you stand being around CHILDREN all day long?" (That last question particularly amuses me when it comes from an elementary school teacher.)

I've often thought about taking a poll. How many of you SAHMs are bored at home? What? No hands popping up in the air? You say it's quite the opposite? You have more to do than would be possible to accomplish in an entire lifetime? Ah, I thought so.

Perhaps, when people ask us the "What do you DO?" question, we should respond with a description of our various jobs, instead of with a job title. We could say, "I work in hospitality, early childhood education, counseling, nursing, nutrition, administration, transportation and food management. What do you DO?"

Ladies, we SAHMs wear numerous hats. If we aren't careful, they can easily slide right off our heads into a heap on the floor. Let's discuss ways this week to keep our hats in balance. How do you manage being an educator and chef, housekeeper and counselor? What other hats do you wear?

My own technique for maintaining balance is to keep my POSTURE:

P—Positive Attitude. I always try to find the best in every situation and see the best in every person.

O—Objectivity. Never let biased opinions color your judgment. I certainly never do, and see how balanced and objective I am?

S—Spiritual Life. This is, of course, the most important one, but if I put it at the beginning, I'd have "SPO-TURE," which is not a word.

T—Training. Self-discipline, instruction and sound counsel from others who are more mature than yourself, like Connie or me.

U—Understanding. You have to know who you are and where you are going, and understand the way to get there. This could also be called "Focus" but there are no "Fs" in "POSTURE."

R—Relationships. As I clearly demonstrate, life is about relationships, not duties. Always be people-oriented, instead of task-oriented.

E—Eliminate all unnecessary hats; learn to say NO! (This is perhaps the easiest for me—I say no to so many activities, it's a wonder I have anything to do at all.)

I just know that if you remember to keep your "POS-TURE," all your hats will stay balanced. Comments, anyone?
Lovingly,
Rosalyn Ebberly
SAHM I Am Loop Moderator

"She looks well to the ways of her household, and does not eat the bread of idleness."
Proverbs 31:27 (NASB)

From:	Connie Lawson <clmo5@home.com>
To:	SAHM I Am <sahmiam@loophole.com>
Subject:	Re: [SAHM I AM] TOTW May 2: Balancing Our Many Hats

Oh, Rosalyn! This has got to be one of your best TOTWs! And it is so vital to learn to balance our "hats." (What a cute metaphor, Rosalyn. You have such a way with figurative language!) With five children around, plus DH Kurt, my life is too busy to spend time picking up fallen hats. Rosalyn's POSTURE acronym has helped me *so* much! I think she should write a book about it. She could call it *How to Improve Your POSTURE*. Wouldn't that be darling?

Well, I must rush. Time to don my "Taxi" hat—James and John have softball practice in a half hour.

Love,
Connie

From:	Dulcie Huckleberry <dulcie@nebweb.net>
To:	"Green Eggs and Ham"
Subject:	Connie and Rosalyn

Connie reminds me of the little yippy dog in the cartoons whose friend is the big bulldog Spike.

This is my friend Spike! (yip, yip) He's *so* big and strong! (pant, pant) He can beat up anybody! I'm just a little dog, but Spike—he's my friend! (yip, yip) If anybody tries to mess with me, Spike, here, takes care of them *good!* (pant, pant) Right, Spike? Huh? We're good pals, me and Spike. (yap, yap)
Dulcie

P.S. The weirdest thing happened today—I was scrubbing some pots, and so I took off my rings and set them on the counter by the sink. When I turned on the garbage disposal, my arm hit a glass and it fell over and knocked my rings into the drain, with the disposal on! One ring is history. My wedding ring has big scratches all over it and is all bent out of shape. I called Tom, and he said to talk to the jeweler. If it can't be repaired, he's going to take some time off around his mom's wedding so we can shop for a new ring. So I'm taking it in today. It just feels a little ominous— damaging your own wedding ring. Do you think it's symbolic?

From:	Zelia Muzuwa <zeemuzu@vivacious.com>
To:	"Green Eggs and Ham"
Subject:	Re: Connie and Rosalyn

Yeah, until the "giant mouse" arrives, and little dog ends up using Spike as a billy club to attack the "giant mouse" and Spike runs off howling and whimpering—then, little dog says, "See, Spike ain't scared of nobody! I want to be just like my friend Spike. Hey, Spike! … Spike? Where'd you go? Huh, Spike? SPIKE!" But poor, wussy Spike is already three counties over, hiding under some old lady's front porch. :)

Boy, I think maybe I watch too much TV….

And no, your damaged wedding ring is in no way symbolic. Mine's had a stone replaced, been resized with each pregnancy, and gotten stuck in an elevator door (long story…). Hope yours can be repaired without buying a new one.

Z

From:	The Millards <jstcea4jesus@familymail.net>
To:	"Green Eggs and Ham"
Subject:	**Speaking of watching TV...**

...Zelia, Ms. Ham, aren't you supposed to be working on an adoption? When do you find time to veg in front of the television? By the way, you never told us how your visit with the social worker went.

We decided to let Tyler join a swim team this summer. He's still feeling quite well—no soreness or stiffness, praise God! But we thought it might be best to avoid contact sports for a while anyway, to be on the safe side. And swimming is so good for the joints.

You know, Shane and I were talking about the whole thing with Tyler the other day. We realized we are so much closer to each other now than we were before Tyler's illness. We were both so busy before, and we were growing apart without even knowing it. I'm actually feeling thankful that God allowed this to happen before any permanent damage was done to our marriage. Don't we have a merciful God?
Peace,
Jocelyn

From:	Zelia Muzuwa <zeemuzu@vivacious.com>
To:	"Green Eggs and Ham"
Subject:	**Home study**

You mean, I never told you how the home visit went? I thought for sure I did....

Anyway, it was totally *not* what I had expected. Our social worker arrived a few minutes late, which left a few minutes extra for me and Tristan to fuss over the house. We had everything just perfect! Candles on the table, freshly vacuumed carpets, no dust anywhere. Tristan even alphabetized the salad dressings in the fridge. (Personally, I thought that might be going a bit far, but then I remembered who had insisted on climbing around on an extension ladder to wash the siding and polish all the windows, even on the second floor... *blushing*). At any rate, the house was cleaner than it's probably ever been in its eighty-year existence.

We'd brought Cosette and Seamus home from school early, and all the children were supposed to be in their rooms until we sent for them. Seconds before the social worker arrived, however, Griffith trotted downstairs and reached for one of the apples we had in a fruit bowl on the table. In doing so, he tipped over one of the taper candles. The next thing we knew, Griffith was screaming that the tablecloth was on fire.

Tristan grabbed a towel and was beating out the flames when the doorbell rang. I didn't know what to do, but it didn't seem like too good an idea to leave the poor woman standing outside, so I let her in and yelled something incoherent about the table being on fire, and left her standing in the foyer.

When she wandered by herself into the dining room, she was greeted by the sight of Tristan leaning disheveled against the wall, singed towel in hand, and me trying to comfort a sobbing Griffith. Seamus, in his desire to help, had grabbed a pitcher of water from the fridge and dumped it all over the table. Water had soaked the rug and there were puddles across the wood floor where he'd spilled coming from kitchen to dining room. He stood there, announcing for all to hear, "I did *not* make Griffith do this! It really wasn't my fault this time! I had nothing to do with it!"

Cosette seemed to be the only one to keep a clear head. She walked over to the social worker and, holding out her hand, said, "Hello! My name is Cosette. Don't mind us—it's always like this around here." (See, children really *do* listen to what you say!)

So much for a good first impression! The social worker asked if we were all okay and if she needed to come back at a different time. But I figured, "Hey, the damage is done. Might as well get the meeting over with, so she can go back to her office and mark 'LUNATICS' all over our files."

But after we got her settled in the living room and opened a few windows to air out the smoke and burned-fabric smell, she folded her hands across her notebook and said, "First thing...relax. I'm not here to find reasons why you can't adopt. I'm here so I can make a report on all the great reasons why you should."

Whew! And you know what? We had a lovely time! She'd already asked us most of the hard questions in our previous meetings at her office. This time, we just chatted and she got better acquainted with the kids. When we finally did take her on a tour of the house, she hardly glanced at the fridge, much less opened it! No white-glove test on the bookshelves, no peeking in the closets. Just walked through all the rooms with us exclaiming how beautiful our home was and how amazed she was about the wall murals in the kids' rooms—especially after she found out I'd painted them.

She's supposed to have the final report done this week, actually. I can hardly wait!

Z

From:	Thomas Huckleberry <t.huckleberry@cortech.com>
To:	Dulcie Huckleberry <dulcie@nebweb.net>
Subject:	**Ring shopping**

Dulcie,

Checked with my supervisors, and they really need me to stay through the 19th. So I'll be leaving on Friday morning, the 20th, and will just have enough time to get to the rehearsal that evening. (In fact, it's a good thing the rehearsal is after the evening performance, or I'd miss it entirely. As it is, I told Mom not to expect me for rehearsal dinner. Sorry about that.) I'm flying in to KC and renting a car to drive down to Branson. But that means I won't be able to come to Omaha first. So maybe we can postpone our ring shopping until the 22nd and just pick something up in Branson or Springfield. Hope that's okay. It's the best I could do.

Love,

Tom

From:	Dulcie Huckleberry <dulcie@nebweb.net>
To:	Thomas Huckleberry <t.huckleberry@cortech.com>
Subject:	**Re: Ring shopping**

"Pick something up"? You don't just "pick up" a wedding ring. You "pick up" a loaf of bread or a gallon of milk from the grocery store. You "pick up" a pizza or a rented video. You "pick up" a newspaper. You do *not*, however, "pick up" a WEDDING RING! You choose it with care and consideration and love—don't you remember? It's supposed to be *special!*

Five years in June—is this what I mean to you after only five years of marriage? Am I now a loaf of bread to you? Or a pizza? How could you be so callous?

Your "gallon of milk,"

Dulcie

From:	Thomas Huckleberry <t.huckleberry@cortech.com>
To:	Dulcie Huckleberry <dulcie@nebweb.net>
Subject:	**Re: Ring shopping**

Oh, come on, Dulcie! Don't even try this with me. You know perfectly well that's not what I meant. You are not equivalent to a piece of jewelry. And I don't think the person who tells all her friends what a lousy husband I am and who mocks the books I *allegedly* read should have the nerve to call me "callous."

And, yes, actually…I do remember shopping for your first ring. I remember every detail.

Tom

From:	Dulcie Huckleberry <dulcie@nebweb.net>
To:	P.Lorimer <phyllis.lorimer@joono.com>
Subject:	**What have I done?**

Phyllis dear, I couldn't write this to the other girls, but I was hoping you could give me advice. I got myself in a fix and I'm not sure what to do.

You see, this evening, since Tom isn't home, and since I was feeling sort of bored, I decided to go to a Bible study our church hosts on Wednesday nights. It was good to get out, and it was great to be able to talk on an adult level with so many people. I didn't know most of them—our church is getting so large, and I haven't been in the habit of doing anything there on Wednesdays. Anyway, I enjoyed the study, and afterward I was sitting around talking with a few of the people who were in my discussion group. One of them, in particular, was really nice. Very outgoing. Friendly. Mature. Interesting.

And...MALE. (*Gorgeous,* to boot!)

But there were several of us sitting around talking, like I said, so nothing of that nature crossed my mind. Then, after a few minutes, the others left. And it was just me. With him. We kept talking, about the study, about all the general sorts of things you talk about with someone you've only just met. After about fifteen minutes, I realized with a shock that I'd forgotten to pick up the girls from their classes! I jumped up, rambling apologies all over the place, expecting him to take the not-so-subtle hint to leave. But he stood up, too, and said, "You have three little ones? And you're all by yourself?"

I'm not always the brightest star in the sky, Phyllis, because I thought he was expressing surprise that I'd brought three kids *to church* by myself. So I nodded. "Uh-huh. All by myself."

He says, "Wow, I really admire that. It takes a lot of strength and energy, I bet."

I say, sort of confused why he's making such a big deal out of it, "Not really. It's just church."

He shakes his head. "No, all of it. You, shouldering the full parenting load yourself. How long has it been?"

Again, call me stupid. I still didn't get it. "Well, Tom left a few weeks ago, but he really hasn't been in the picture for the past year."

"So it's still really fresh for you, huh?" By now, he's looking at me with these great brown eyes, nearly brimming over with compassion. Melting my heart...

"Well," I babble, not noticing that somehow I am walking with him to the nursery, "I didn't like it, but I'm getting used to it now."

"I understand. I have two kids myself. But I left them with a babysitter this evening, for this very reason—so I wouldn't have to hurry to pick them up. Now I know why. God wanted me to help you with yours."

Isn't that just so sweet? And still, fool that I am, I was clueless. After I pick up McKenzie and apologize for being so late, this man kneels and shakes McKenzie's hand. "Hi," he says, "my name is Travis. What's yours?"

"McKenzie," she says, then asks, "Are you my mommy's friend?"

I must have looked startled at that, because he glances up at me and smiles this great smile that made me feel all warm inside.

"Well, I guess we have to ask her."

I didn't want to hurt his feelings or confuse McKenzie, so I said, "Of course he is."

He carries both twins all the way to my minivan and helps me load them up. Handles the car seats like a pro, I might add. Then, after I shut the door, he walks me around to my door. "Hey," he begins, "are you in the church directory?"

"Yep," I tell him with a little laugh. "The only Huckleberry listed!"

He grins this dangerously cute grin and tilts his head, "I've never called a Huckleberry before. I think I'll give it a try this week." Then he opens my door, helps me into the van and closes the door. With a tiny wave, he walks off.

And you know what?

IT TOOK ME FIFTEEN MINUTES INTO THE DRIVE HOME BEFORE IT DAWNED ON ME WHAT HAD JUST HAPPENED!

All of a sudden, I felt like I'd been in some trance and then jolted out of it. He was hitting on me the entire time, and I totally encouraged him! What have I done, Phyllis? The thing is…he made me feel really good. Even though I know it's bad, I haven't felt so much like a real person, like a woman, in months. I hate this! I hate living the life of a single mother while at the same time having the moral constraints of being married. It's the worst of both worlds. I have this little voice that's saying "I hope he calls." And then the rest of my brain is saying, "He had SOOOOO better not call!"

I am such a bad, bad, bad, bad person. What am I going to do?

Help me!

Dulcie

From:	P. Lorimer <phyllis.lorimer@joono.com>
To:	Dulcie Huckleberry <dulcie@nebweb.net>
Subject:	**Re: What have I done?**

Calm down, Dulcie. You've done nothing…yet. But there are a few things you're going to have to do. And I don't think you're going to like them.

First, you are going to face up to the fact that you were strongly tempted by this man. Second, you are going to call on the Lord to help you resist that temptation. Third, you are going to *flee!* This means, I'm sorry to say, that at least for the foreseeable future you will need to find a new church. I don't care how big your church is—it's not big enough to avoid temptation of that kind. And fleeing also means that if this man does call you, you are going to tell him you are very much married and had no intention of giving him the wrong impression. You apologize and you get off the phone. Understand? I will ask you about this later, to see if you followed up on it.

Next, you must talk to Tom. You must tell him that you need him to come home. Ask him to quit his job, if necessary, but his being in Alaska is *not* a good thing right now. You need him there in Omaha with you. Your other choice would be to move to Alaska to be with him. Actually, that's not a half-bad idea. It would address the need to *flee,* as well.

I can well imagine why you chose to share this with me. And let me tell you, Dulcie, I know what it's like. The consequences of giving in to temptation with someone I love and was free to marry has been devastating enough. Please take a moment and imagine how much greater the disaster will be if you, as a married woman, follow my path.

Thank you for trusting me. I trust you, too.
Phyllis

From:	Dulcie Huckleberry <dulcie@nebweb.net>
To:	Thomas Huckleberry <t.huckleberry@cortech.com>
Subject:	**An interesting little thing happened...**

...at church last night. You won't believe it, I'm sure. But I decided to go to Bible study, and afterward, this really hot guy is so totally into me that he spends twenty minutes chatting with me, walks me to the nursery, makes friends with McKenzie and then carries the twins to the van and puts them in their car seats for me. I somehow missed all the signals, until after he asked if I was in the church directory and mentioned that he'd like to call me. Isn't that a hoot? :)

Anyway, I just thought you'd like to know. Sort of a reminder as to why it might be a good idea to do some serious ring shopping with me down in Branson. You also might want to consider making time to come home every now and then on the weekends. Either that, or start looking for a Realtor up there in Anchorage. Because, sweetheart, I love you and I'm running away from this temptation as fast as I can. But it wouldn't be a bad idea for you to lend me a hand, if you get what I mean.

Love you,
Dulcie

From:	Thomas Huckleberry <t.huckleberry@cortech.com>
To:	Dulcie Huckleberry <dulcie@nebweb.net>
Subject:	**Re: An interesting little thing happened...**

Wow...Dulcie. I'm really not sure what to say. I think we need to talk. I know we need to. I'll tell my supervisors I need a few extra days off. I haven't bought the plane tickets yet—I'll try to get the whole week after the wedding off. Please, Dulcie, please don't give up on me.

Love,
Tom

From:	Dulcie Huckleberry <dulcie@nebweb.net>
To:	P.Lorimer <phyllis.lorimer@joono.com>
Subject:	**Re: What have I done?**

Phyllis,
Your e-mail hit me like a slap in the face. Thank you. My hands are shaking—I've been awake all night. I guess I somehow thought I was above being tempted. It's really embarrassing to think I was so easily targeted.

I've been really praying, and guess what was the only response? I got this picture in my mind of Travis, looking so handsome. And then it suddenly changed. Instead of thick, wavy hair, he was mostly bald. What little hair was left had a serious case of bed-head. And he was paunchy and wrinkled, and had a big nose.

I guess the point is that all guys (and me, too) will end up old and funny-looking. The thing is, I love the idea of growing old with Tom. I see the laugh lines around his eyes and I want to kiss them because they remind me of all the good times we've had together. And we can joke about how the girls have caused all our gray hair.

But when I looked at the picture in my mind of Travis as an old man, all I saw was…an old man. Not my soul mate, not my friend. Just a man who was kind to me once when I was lonely. Now, why would I throw away a marriage for that?

I thought you might like to know. Thank you again, dear friend, for your advice and love.

Love,
Dulcie

From:	Rosalyn Ebberly <prov31woman@home.com>
To:	SAHM I Am <sahmiam@loophole.com>
Subject:	[SAHM I AM] TOTW May 16: Making Family Memories

Magnificent Moms,
May…the season of graduations, the season of weddings, Memorial Day. Summer is just around the corner, and with it all those special times of family togetherness—vacations, gardening, trips to the zoo. It's a perfect time to discuss how to make family memories.

It's not enough to just sit back and let memories happen on their own! You have to work at it. Make them occur. And then do everything in your power to preserve them for future generations. This is, I dare to say, a sacred duty. For if you, the mother, are not the family historian, if you do not cherish these days, who will? (Certainly not our husbands, precious as they are!) They will slip through our fingers and vanish into the Sands of Time.

You must plan outings! You must take rolls and rolls of pictures! You must preserve them in scrapbooks—acid-free, lignin-free, and PVC-free archival-quality scrapbooks only, preferably strap-hinged. And, of course we mustn't forget, *you must journal in your scrapbooks!*

Now, granted, this is only *one* way of making and preserving memories. I'm sure you all have others, so feel free to share. None of them will be as successful as the plan I've outlined above, but I certainly won't be unsupportive of your efforts. So, please…tell me what you are thinking.

With fond memories,

Rosalyn Ebberly

SAHM I Am Loop Moderator

"She looks well to the ways of her household, and does not eat the bread of idleness."
Proverbs 31:27 (NASB)

From:	Dulcie Huckleberry <dulcie@nebweb.net>
To:	SAHM I Am <sahmiam@loophole.com>
Subject:	Re: [SAHM I AM] TOTW May 16: Making Family Memories

Hello everyone!

Well, I can tell you how *not* to make family memories—agreeing to coordinate your mother-in-law's wedding. I'm just popping in to say I'm going to have to go no-mail this week, so I can get ready to leave on Thursday. I'm driving down with my girls, and it's about a ten-hour trip. Plus, my MIL is calling me about five times a day right now to ask me things like if I have the phone number for the florist. (Why on earth would I have the florist's phone number? My MIL is supposed to have a friend in Branson handling the flowers!) Or e-mailing me with a whole bunch of salon photos. "Which hairstyle do you think would look best with my veil, darling?" Like 50-something-year-old women should even wear veils! I told her it didn't really matter since the hairstylist would just do her own thing anyway. That's what happened with *my* hair.

So, needless to say, I don't have time to keep up with e-mails. But I'll let everyone know how it went when I get home. I'm sure I'll have lots of good stories to tell....

Don't say anything interesting until I get back!

Dulcie

From:	P.Lorimer <phyllis.lorimer@joono.com>
To:	"Green Eggs and Ham"
Subject:	**Camping Trip**

Hi gals! (See, I'm even starting to write like the locals)
Jonathan and I finally were able to try out Brenna's camping pasture. We went last night and it was so wonderful. Brenna and Darren loaned us all their equipment, and Darren even took Jonathan out earlier in the day to help set it all up for us, which was absolutely cherubic of him as we know nothing about

camping. Then, Darren came back and picked me up. I was surprised—I assumed Jonathan would be with him. But Darren said Jonathan was taking care of a few things at the campsite.

It was my first time going out in the pasture. And since all of us, except Brenna, are city girls, let me describe this to you. When I say "pasture" I don't mean some little fenced-in patch by the house. I mean acres and acres of gently rolling land with no buildings or telephone poles in sight, and the sky spreading out over you for as far as you can see. The only nod to human presence was one lone oil well on the top of a modest crest in the distance. The tent was nestled against some trees lining a little creek (or "crik" as Brenna has instructed me is the proper pronunciation). The guys had set up a camping table and a couple of canvas chairs that looked like recliners. Darren had even set up his camp stove on a separate table. We had hoped to have a bonfire, but Darren and Brenna said it was too dry for that and there was a risk of starting a prairie fire.

After Darren dropped me off, Jonathan stepped out of the tent holding a bouquet of wildflowers for me. I thanked him, and his response nearly knocked me off my feet.

"This is just one of many bouquets I should have been giving to you all along."

It continued like that the entire evening. He fixed dinner for me (not too shabbily, either), served me at the little camping table as if I were dining in the finest restaurant. Actually, I doubt a restaurant could rival the ambience of open space so wide and yet so private, and the serenade of meadowlarks. Every time I thanked him, he said something like "I'm just making up for lost time" or "This is something long overdue." I was feeling so sorry for him, I finally stopped saying thank-you or commenting on anything. If he was doing all this simply out of guilt, I didn't really want to know.

Sorry if I'm getting a bit personal here, but after we were done eating, and he'd insisted on cleaning all the dishes himself, he spread a quilt on the ground and told me he was going to give me a massage. I asked him why, and he said, because of all the stress I'd been under the past couple of years. Stress I'd been under? I'm not the one who got fired. But he didn't explain to me. Simply asked me to lie down. And by the time he finished, I was so relaxed I had fallen asleep.

When I opened my eyes, it was dusk. A gorgeous, scarlet sunset burned the sky. Jonathan sat cross-legged on the quilt, just watching me, a gentle sort of smile on his face. He wrapped a blanket around me, and I sat up, not sure what he had planned next.

He had a set of papers beside him, and now he held them up. "You see this?" he asked. "It's a sermon. I'm going to give you a very special sermon. But I'm not preaching to you. I'm preaching to me. Will you listen?"

As if I'd say no! So he stood up, notes in hand, and paced a few steps away, looking suddenly every inch the pastor I've been used to seeing in the pulpit each Sunday for the past two years. It seemed a little out of place out here, as contradictory as the oil well up on that hill surrounded by all this natural beauty.

He preached the most beautiful sermon I'll ever hear in my life. About the gift of marriage, about the rarity of finding a woman of virtue, about how those who make ministry their god commit adultery as surely as if they had a mistress. About repentance, about respect and love and the meaning of becoming a servant to one's spouse. When he finished, it may sound silly, but he gave himself an altar call. He kneeled in front of me.

"I always tell people the altar is a place of sacrifice. Well, I'm sacrificing right now my ministry. If killing it is what it takes to truly minister to you and my children, then it has to die."

By this time I was weeping, and so was he. All these weeks—this is what he has been struggling with. This is why he couldn't talk to me about being fired. I'd agonized about how badly I wanted things to change, without knowing how to tell him. But God knew. And Jonathan eventually did, too. We held each other, and then later, he took me by the hand, and under the stars, we pledged our wedding vows to each other again.

It wouldn't be right for me to share what happened next, but the entire experience brought us to a whole new level of intimacy that I never dreamed possible. And I've never been so full of joy in my life.

Blessings,

Phyllis

From:	Brenna L. <saywhat@writeme.com>
To:	"Green Eggs and Ham"
Subject:	Re: Camping Trip

Well! I'm not sure Darren and I will ever think of our tent and our pasture in quite the same way again. Can't decide if that's a good thing or not. :)

Seriously, I'm thrilled for Phyllis and Jonathan. Phyllis was glowing when she returned Tuesday morning.

Dulcie, before you leave, give us a final dress update. How does it look? Do you like the "new you"?

Brenna

From:	Dulcie Huckleberry <dulcie@nebweb.net>
To:	"Green Eggs and Ham"
Subject:	**Dress Update**

The dress is foofy fuchsia and tattooed with a million sequins. It has big, poofy chiffon sleeves, a mermaid shape and chiffon ruffles that poke out of the bottom where the mermaid's fins should be. In short...it's *hideous.*

However...IT'S A SIZE 10! And it fits! This fact alone has endeared the homely rag to me for life. I, Dulcie Amanda Huckleberry, am officially a size ten.

As happy as this makes me, I did learn something, though. I have saddlebags! Waaaahhhhhh! I guess I never saw them before because they blended in with the general rotundness of my legs. And my stomach still has that slightly lumpy "I've had three children in two pregnancies" look to it. The moral of my story? There's more to being content with myself than fitting into a certain clothing size. *sigh* So, in regard to Dulcie's Quest for a Positive Self-Image...the saga continues.
Dulcie

From:	The Millards <jstcea4jesus@familymail.net>
To:	"Green Eggs and Ham"
Subject:	**Re: Dress Update**

<The moral of my story? There's more to being content with myself than fitting into a certain clothing size.>
Well, duh, Dulcie! I could have told you that. :) But I'm glad your diet was successful for you. Congratulations. Enjoy

wearing your....attention-getting dress. Did you take your MIL up on her offer of a bridesmaid swimsuit, too? That idea just cracked me up. I want pictures of the dress and the swimsuit—with you in them! Better yet, do a scrapbook like Rosalyn suggested. It's your "sacred duty" after all....
Jocelyn

From:	Dulcie Huckleberry <dulcie@nebweb.net>
To:	"Green Eggs and Ham"
Subject:	**Re: Dress Update**

Silly people, why should I make a calendar or scrapbook, when you'll be able to purchase the stinking video from the Shoji Tabuchi Gift Shop? (And pictures of me in a swimsuit? Don't hold your breath.)

Gotta go finish packing! I will give you as many updates as I can, but the schedule is going to be insane. At least I can use Tom's laptop once he gets to the hotel. I wasn't sure he would room with me. Then, when he said he was planning to, I made the mistake of acting all excited about it. His response? "Well, it would be kind of stupid to pay for two hotel rooms, don't you think?" Ugh! Boys are so dumb sometimes! :)
Dulcie

From:	VIM <vivalaveronica@marcelloportraits.com>
To:	SAHM I Am <sahmiam@loophole.com>
Subject:	**[SAHM I AM] New SAHM Intro**

A big howdy from a brand-new stay-at-home mama in Houston, TX! I just got married this year and now have three stepchildren. It's a lot more difficult than I thought to be a mom and a career woman. So, even though I had a successful, award-winning marketing career, I've quit my job and am fixing to stay home with my children from now on. There's a certain someone special on this loop who inspired me to take this step, and I know she will be absolutely flabbergasted to read this e-mail—but I've always loved surprises. LOL! :)

I'm as nervous as a long-tailed cat in a roomful of rocking chairs about doing the SAHM thing—I never did feel so lonely as this morning when I waved goodbye to my sweet husband and it was just me and little Stanley. How on EARTH do you all fill your blessed days? I know I'll need lots of help and advice, so lay it on me!

Just a big greenhorn from Texas when it comes to SAHM-ing,

Veronica Marcello

From:	LOOPHOLE GROUPS NOTIFICATION
To:	VIM <vivalaveronica@marcelloportraits.com>
Subject:	**UNSUBSCRIPTION FROM SAHM I AM**

This notice is to inform you that you have been unsubscribed from the SAHM I Am e-mail loop by the moderator. If you have questions or feel this action is in error, please contact sahmiam-moderator@loophole.com.

Sincerely,

Loopy! Loophole Administration

From:	Connie Lawson <clmo5@home.com>
To:	Rosalyn Ebberly <prov31woman@home.com>
Subject:	**Veronica Marcello**

Rosalyn,
I got an e-mail this evening from the new SAHM I Am member, Veronica Marcello, who was very upset because she had been unsubscribed from the loop. I checked the loop activity and found that you were the one who removed her. Why? I thought we had agreed to talk to each other before kicking anyone off the loop. What were you thinking? She sounds like she's practically in tears over it, poor thing. Please put her back on the loop immediately.
Love,
Connie

From:	Rosalyn Ebberly <prov31woman@home.com>
To:	Connie Lawson <clmo5@home.com>
Subject:	**Re: Veronica Marcello**

Connie, she's my *sister.* Need I say more?

"She looks well to the ways of her household, and does not eat the bread of idleness."
Proverbs 31:27 (NASB)

From:	Connie Lawson <clmo5@home.com>
To:	Rosalyn Ebberly <prov31woman@home.com>
Subject:	**Re: Veronica Marcello**

<Connie, she's my *sister.* Need I say more?>
Yes, actually. I know you two haven't always gotten along, but
that's no reason to ban her from our group. We're open to
any SAHM who needs us—you know that.

From:	Rosalyn Ebberly <prov31woman@home.com>
To:	Connie Lawson <clmo5@home.com>
Subject:	**MORE**

Getting along has nothing to do with it! I can't take any
more! It's bad enough that my parents blatantly favor her—
always have from the moment she was born—that everyone
admires her and her "astonishing" accomplishments. They
don't even care that she can barely remember college because
she partied all the time, and STILL managed to stay in the
honors program, that she had a new boyfriend every three
weeks, that she lied on her résumé to get her first job after
graduating. Meanwhile, I became a Christian, was a virgin
when I got married, worked hard to finish college with a B
average and help my husband get his degree, have given birth
to three children, gave up any chance of my own career to
raise them and have had important successes of my own.

My parents don't give a hoot that my quilts and cooking
win awards, that I have a special mentoring ministry for
young women at church, that I have published articles in
family magazines. All they care about is Veronica. And now
that she is married to this exotic Italian photographer with
his three gorgeous children and palatial house—*with* housekeeper, I might add—they don't give me or my children the
time of day! They skipped my birthday last week to go to
Houston for Frank's debut photography exhibit. They ignore
my kids and insult my husband.

Oh, and Ronnie—she's such a sham! When she moved to Houston, she decided having a Southern accent would be cute, so now her e-mails are all sprinkled with "y'alls" and "bless your hearts" and "well, aren't you *cute*" (which really means you're an idiot), the incessant "there ya go" (whatever that means) and other linguistic flotsam and jetsam from Hicksville, Texas. Good grief, we were born and raised in Chicago! There's not a drop of Texan blood in her. She just does it for attention.

I can live with all that—goodness knows, I've managed to for most of my life.

But now she's gone and horned in on my territory! Domestic life was the one area in which I excelled, in which she had no part. It was my one chance to try to make my parents proud of me. And now she wants to be on *my* e-mail loop! How dare she quit her job? How dare she try to live my life as well as hers? She did this on purpose. She can't stand not being the best in everything. And now Mom and Dad are calling her a hero, just because she's decided to stay at home. In my seven years of SAHM-hood, have they ever once said I was a hero? *No!* They've called me unambitious, boring and a disappointment. But never a *hero.* I'm sick of it.

So, here's the deal, Connie. You're right—we can't turn down people who need the loop. And if she really was dumb enough to quit her job, she's going to need it. She doesn't have a clue what being a SAHM will mean for her. But I refuse to stick around and listen to her little jabs, subtle put-downs and reminders that I am and always will be second best in my family. I don't need more of that than I already have.

I am officially resigning as Loop Moderator and as a member of SAHM I Am. You don't really need me anyway, and it will just be easier for everyone this way. In fact, make Veronica the new moderator—you can make all her questions the topics of the week.

Goodbye,

Rosalyn

"She looks well to the ways of her household, and does not eat the bread of idleness."
Proverbs 31:27 (NASB)

From:	Dulcie Huckleberry <dulcie@nebweb.net>
To:	"Green Eggs and Ham"
Subject:	**Report From Branson #1**

Dulcie Huckleberry, reporting live from Branson, MO, Thursday, May 19, where I have just arrived at my hotel, and have met Tom's cousin Diana who will be minding my children for the majority of the weekend.

"Minding the children" is a good way to put it, too, since I doubt it will be the other way around—children minding *her*. She's barely 20, barely dressed and barely endowed with common sense. If we can survive the weekend without the kids talking her into letting them overdose on TV cartoons and candy, I'll consider it a success. But to be fair, I don't think they'll be in any real danger, except perhaps from tooth decay. And to think, Brenna, by the time you were her age, you had a daughter McKenzie's age! Wow!

Anyway, she's going to watch the kids all day tomorrow so I can run errands with Jeanine and Becky. Then comes the evening rehearsal dinner, followed by the rehearsal at 11 p.m.— and that's *if* by some miracle we start on time. But we had to wait until after the evening show lets out. I've given strict instructions that McKenzie is to have an early supper and go to bed at 5 tomorrow, so that we can keep her out that late. I hope Jeanine realizes what this shows about how much I love her!
More later,
Dulcie

From:	Dulcie Huckleberry <dulcie@nebweb.net>
To:	"Green Eggs and Ham"
Subject:	Branson Report #2

★GREAT BIG YAWN★ Good morning, ladies…it's 4 a.m. Saturday morning. I thought about e-mailing Rosalyn, just to brag about how I'm actually awake already, but I'm too sleepy to be catty this time. I've been up all night, decorating the theater. I sent Jeanine home at midnight, after the rehearsal. I figured it would be better for the bridesmaids to look like leftover mac'n'cheese than the bride herself. We finally finished at 3:30 a.m., but I didn't figure it would do me any good to go to sleep—just make it harder to wake up later.

Overall, the rehearsal went fairly well—if you don't count the fact that the horse never showed up. Who knew animals could double-book, too? So we're going to have to wing the processional today. Actually, me and Jeanine and Becky will be "winging." I guess Morris and his horse will have to "hoof" it. Okay, bad pun, I know…what do you expect on zero sleep?

Speaking of winging, I've never had to be lowered from a ceiling before. It involved climbing a catwalk above the stage and entrusting my life to a flimsy, cheesy-looking star, controlled by a stagehand who looks about 13 and thought it was really funny to let out the cable too fast and watch us cling to the star, shrieking and screeching. Well, that was bad enough, but then, while I was answering a question about the placement of the candelabras, he coaxed McKenzie into the star and did it to her! She started screaming! When I saw her, high over my head, terrified out of her mind, my temper got the better of me. After McKenzie returned to earth and I consoled her, I marched across the stage, grabbed the stagehand by the ear and gave a good, motherly twist, immensely enjoying his howl of pain. "You ever do something like that to my child again, young man, and I will tear your ear clean off. Understand?"

"Yes, ma'am," he sputtered.

I let go his ear, and stalked off. Everyone else backed out of my way. You just don't mess with a mommy!

You guys, Im getting so tired…at least I cna take a nap this afternoon btweeeen the wedding in the morning adn the reception in evening. Wow, did you kow that if you stare at a computer screen for five minutes and then look away, youcan see littl splotches that look remarkably like oascar the grouch?

After the rehersl i had to help decorate the theater. Jeanine paid to have an enetire set constrecuted to look like a church, copmlete witn shtained glas windows and a big cross. If she wanntde to make it lok like her widding ina chruch, why didnt she just hae the wjdding in a church? Pardon my tpos, i'm to tird to fxi them. and then we had to ty big pew bows to the asle seats—bows that ligt up and emit bubbles from the flowerz, Anueods,chy, cssssssssssyyy-yyy4,src..zzzzzzzzzzzzzzzzzzzzzzzzzzzzzzz

From:	Dulcie Huckleberry <dulcie@nebweb.net>
To:	"Green Eggs and Ham"
Subject:	**Branson Report #3**

Hey, girls, I'm so sorry about my early-morning post! I fell asleep at the computer, and must have pushed "Send" when my head hit the keyboard. I woke up to find it was 8:07—and I was supposed to be at the theater by 8:30! So I went banging around the hotel room, waking up Tom and the girls, who didn't have to be awake for another forty minutes. After the world's quickest shower, and blow-drying my hair, I managed to grab my dress and supplies and get over to the theater by 9.

I'll spare you the details of getting ready—the hairdresser who griped about how difficult my hair was to work with, how Tom forgot to bring McKenzie's dress with them to the theater, how tense things were between me and Tom... Well, perhaps I shouldn't spare *that* detail. Things between Tom and me were tense—*really* tense. Last night, when he arrived at the theater for rehearsal, I was in the middle of trying to line up the wedding party on the stage. Jeanine had her ideas, Morris had his, I had mine, the pastor had his. Mine were the only not-ridiculous ones, so I was already stressed. I looked out across the empty theater and saw Tom at the back. For a moment our eyes met, and both of us froze. I stopped talking mid-sentence, and everyone suddenly got all awkward and busy. Evidently Jeanine had been spreading tales about the two of us...

Anyway, we haven't really had a chance to do more than say "hi," "bye," and "you better run back to the hotel and grab Mac's dress," and "yes, dear." Like I said... tense.

Okay, back to the wedding... So finally, I was dressed, and so was McKenzie. The set was staged, the costumes were peopled, and I hurried backstage to climb up to the catwalk to prepare for my descent.

Do you know how impossible it is to climb a catwalk in a mermaid dress and spiked heels? Guess this is why actors do dress rehearsals *in costume*. There was absolutely no way for Becky and me to raise our feet high enough to reach the ladder rungs without just pulling our dresses past our waists and climbing in our never-minds. So here I was, minutes before the start of the processional (or descentional, rather), halfway up a ladder, with all the backstage guys gawking. Becky shimmied up pretty quick, but I snagged part of the dress on the ladder. Since it was all bunched up around my middle, I couldn't see where it was stuck. Becky was now frantically motioning to me to hurry, but all I could do was shake my head and point to my dress, mouthing, *I'm stuck!*

By this time, the people below must have figured out my dilemma. They cued the musicians to continue the prelude, while Jeanine sat up in the catwalk on her moon, looking pale and faint. It should have occurred to me, I suppose, to wonder how she got up there. Turns out she had the good sense, before they opened the theater, to have the moon lowered. She climbed up and got a free ride. Grrrrr… She is the bride. She is the bride. She is the bride….

Anyway, back to me stuck on the ladder. I was starting to wonder if my arms were going to fall off, or if it might be more comfortable to simply kick my shoes off rather than stand on the ladder in heels. The thought of nailing the manic stagehand from last night with one of the spiked heels did appeal to me. Suddenly, I heard and felt someone below me on the ladder.

It was Tom, climbing the opposite side. When he reached the rung I was on, he slid his feet between mine. We were smashed together real close, with only the ladder between us. "I hear you're stuck," he said. I nodded at him. He wound his hand under a rung, into the folds of my dress, feeling along me and the ladder until he found where I was snagged. Then, he hooked one arm around the ladder so he could use both hands to free me.

Maybe it was being thirty feet off the ground, clinging to a ladder, with my husband's hands fussing with my dress…but I had the most amazing case of butterflies I've had in years! I was having trouble breathing, and all I could think about was how close we were and the scent of his cologne. "You look great," I whispered to him.

He gave me this big grin and glanced pointedly down at my still-exposed legs. "Thanks. So do you."

Alas, he freed my dress too soon, and clambered back down the ladder while I resumed my climb up.

After that, things progressed as planned, mostly. McKenzie did look like a fairy princess—in an overdone toy-dress-upkit sort of way, but cute nonetheless. When she reached the front of the theater and climbed the steps to the stage, having scattered rose petals down the aisle, she turned to watch Morris on the horse, and the moment that dumb horse stepped on one of her rose petals, McKenzie started wailing, "The horsey is squishing my *flowers!*" As the audience laughed, I tried to quiet her. But she would have none of it. "Bad horse! Naughty horse! You're gonna get a spanking!" Her voice sailed right over "Ride of the Valkyries" as if it were "Brahm's Lullaby."

By now, we'd lost control of both the audience and the flower girl. I didn't know what to do—try to calm her down or take her backstage. Tom's great-aunt sitting in the front row solved the problem for me. She offered McKenzie a chocolate kiss, which promptly shut off the tears and made the woman my hero for life. McKenzie's chomping on the chocolate drop left her with a brown smear around her mouth and a little stain on her dress, which belied the idea that she was "mature for her age"—but I can live with that.
Dulcie

From:	Connie Lawson <clmo5@home.com>
To:	SAHM I Am <sahmiam@loophole.com>
Subject:	**[SAHM I AM] TOTW May 23: Resolving Conflicts**

My SAHM Girls,
Rosalyn's topic this week was supposed to be about resolving conflicts. But it seems that she has her own to deal with. And she needs our help.

For three years, Rosalyn has always been there for us—ready with helpful advice, encouragement and inspirational

stories. She's never complained or griped about her own cir-
cumstances but has given to us from her heart.

But now, due to family issues, she has grown discouraged
and weary. So dispirited, in fact, that she has resigned from
the loop, convinced we no longer need her. But is that true?
Can we really imagine a SAHM I Am loop without the
pleasant wisdom of our sister Rosalyn? I can't!

So I am asking all of you, even you lurkers out there, that
for this week's topic we not have a discussion. Instead, let's
send personal notes of encouragement and love to dear, dear
Rosalyn, and ask her to rejoin the loop. She needs a ton of
cyber-hugs, and I know you ladies will come through for her,
just as we have for all of you at one time or another. E-mail
her at her private address: prov31woman@home.com.
God bless you all!
Connie Lawson
SAHM I Am Loop Mom

From:	P.Lorimer <phyllis.lorimer@joono.com>
To:	"Green Eggs and Ham"
Subject:	**Where's Dulcie?**

Wasn't she supposed to be home Sunday evening? I haven't
heard a word from her since she sent her last Branson report.
(Wasn't that hysterical? Jonathan and I went over to Brenna
and Darren's and had an e-mail-reading party, complete with
popcorn and soda. It was better than a movie!)

By the way, Jonathan is applying to a church in upstate
New York. We don't know if anything will come of it, but
we feel ready to return to the ministry. Now that we have
things worked out between us, I'm actually excited about being a pastor's wife. But I'm also excited because this city has

a university with a great PhD program in history. And Jonathan is absolutely 100% committed to my getting a doctorate. Now, Lord, please grant me patience....

Love,

Phyllis

From:	The Millards <jstcea4jesus@familymail.net>
To:	Rosalyn Ebberly <prov31woman@home.com>
Subject:	**On Behalf of the Green Eggs and Ham...**

Dear Rosalyn,

Zelia, Phyllis, Dulcie, Brenna and I want to encourage you to come back to the SAHM I Am loop. I e-mailed Connie after she announced your decision to the loop, and since I've known you both for so long, she felt it would be okay to tell me the whole story about you and your sister. I explained it to the other four girls, and we just want you to know we are really sorry that you've been carrying around this pain for so long all alone. If we had known, we could have been praying for you and encouraging you. Please rejoin the loop so we can support you like we are supposed to. But if you return, you have to start being more honest with everyone—otherwise it defeats the purpose of belonging to a group like SAHM. I hope you'll come back, and that you and Veronica can start a new, positive phase in your relationship.

Much love,

Jocelyn

From:	Zelia Muzuwa <zeemuzu@vivacious.com>
To:	"Green Eggs and Ham"
Subject:	**Re: Where's Dulcie?**

I haven't heard from her, maybe she and Tom decided to get stuck on the ladder again after the ceremony...they certainly sounded quite cozy up there... :)

From:	The Millards <jstcea4jesus@familymail.net>
To:	"Green Eggs and Ham"
Subject:	**Re: Where's Dulcie?**

Zelia, you are a bad girl! They probably stayed an extra night so they could go ring shopping, remember? So, are we all on for chatting tonight? I've got a great Evelyn story for you. It can't rival Dulcie's wedding story, but I think you'll like it anyway.

See you tonight!
Jocelyn

From:	VIM <vivalaveronica@marcelloportraits.com>
To:	Rosalyn Ebberly <prov31woman@home.com>
Subject:	**SAHM I Am**

Dear Rosalyn,
Connie put me back on the SAHM list after she told me about your "this town ain't big enough for the two of us" e-mail. I had no idea Mama and Daddy's attitude was such a big deal to you. You always act like it don't make no never-mind to you.

Contrary to your suspicions, I didn't quit my job or join the loop just to ruin your life. Your quality of life isn't high enough on my priority list to merit ditching my career for it, but you've always had a rather high opinion of your own importance.

You're my big sister, and for some crazy reason, I look up to you, admire you and want to be like you—goes along with being the little sister, I guess. I've always thought you were very unselfish and brave to stay home with your children, and it's paying off because they are turning out great. I guess I figured if it works for you, it would work for me, too. I love Frank's kids, and I want to give them the best of who I am, not the leftovers. That's why I'm staying home.

I joined your e-mail loop because you're always talking about how great it is, and I know I'm going to need the help and support y'all give each other. I'm not trying to take your place, but I would like to understand you better. So if I promise to be good and not pester you, could I pretty-please be part of your e-mail loop? I don't really want to be there unless you are, too. You know how *shy* I am… :) There ya go—what do you say, Sis?

Love,

Veronica

From:	Brenna L. <saywhat@writeme.com>
To:	"Green Eggs and Ham"
Subject:	Re: Where's Dulcie?

Rats! I was hoping she'd be home by now and able to chat with us, so I could tell you all together. I haven't even told Phyllis yet…but since Dulcie doesn't seem to be home yet, I'll have to do this by e-mail instead.

I am extremely pleased to announce that Darren and I have decided to…*adopt!* But not a traditional adoption. Darren really, really wants the experience of being with me through a pregnancy and delivery. So, after a TON of prayer and discussion and research, we've decided to adopt an embryo. There's this program called Snowflakes in California that facilitates adoptions of frozen embryos created during in vitro fertilization. They require a home-study just like Z's and all that, then let "genetic parents" choose us to adopt their embryos. It's a long process, and I've heard in vitro will be no picnic for me. The success rate can be quite low, too, which would mean more money for a second try. I have no idea where we'll get the money, but this is what we believe we're supposed to do. There are thousands and thousands of embryos, waiting for a chance to grow up. We didn't like the idea of adding to them by doing our own in vitro with a sperm donor, so this is perfect. And because it's set up like an adoption, we have an opportunity to know the genetic parents if we, and they, want. We started our home-study shortly after Easter, but Darren didn't feel comfortable telling anyone yet. But I just couldn't stand keeping it from my Green Eggs (and Ham) girls, so I convinced him to let me tell you, now that we're nearly done with the home-study.

Both of us are just bursting with excitement! It will be an adventure, and we know it might be difficult, but at the end of it, if the Lord wills, we will have a child together. I wanted all of you to be the first to know.

Love,
Brenna

From:	Zelia Muzuwa <zeemuzu@vivacious.com>
To:	"Green Eggs and Ham"
Subject:	Re: Where's Dulcie?

Okay, girls, this calls for a *celebration!* Our chat tonight is officially changed to a party! We're talking snacks, music, the whole bit. You with me? And maybe Dulcie will surprise us and show up after all. This is great news, Brenna. I'm so happy for you both.

Love,

Z

From:	Dulcie Huckleberry <dulcie@nebweb.net>
To:	"Green Eggs and Ham"
Subject:	**Where I Am**

Girls, I'm sorry to have disappeared on you for half a week! But we've been so busy, and the Internet room is quite expensive. So I won't be able to stay on for long. I just wanted to let you all know we're fine. Actually, we're much more than "fine." We're…in Cancún. :)

Love,

Dulcie

From:	Zelia Muzuwa <zeemuzu@vivacious.com>
To:	"Green Eggs and Ham"
Subject:	**Re: Where I Am**

Dulcie! DULCIE! Get your little self back online this instant and tell me WHAT IS GOING ON! CANCÚN? As in… Mexico?

From:	Dulcie Huckleberry <dulcie@nebweb.net>
To:	"Green Eggs and Ham"
Subject:	Re: Where I Am

<get your little self back online this instant and tell me WHAT IS GOING ON!>

I didn't leave, actually. I was waiting to see if I got any response from you all. Oh, and Tom is sitting next to me. He says to tell you you're sorta demanding, aren't you? :)

As far as what's going on, it's quite simple. See, at the reception at White Water on Saturday night, after the park had closed up, we got into a pretty big fight. Oh, Tom says I have to back up *before* the fight. Let's see… Okay, we left the kids at the hotel with Tom's cousin, which was nice, since it let us have some time to ourselves. After we ate supper under the pavilion, we went to put on our swimsuits. (No, I didn't take Jeanine up on her idea of "bridesmaid swimsuits"—I bought a new one myself.) You should have seen Tom's reaction to my suit! His eyes popped out and his face turned red.

Oh. Now he says I backed up *too* far. Picky, picky…

Fine, we'll pick up the story after we'd tried out all the water slides and the wave pool. Tom asked me the question I'd been dreading all weekend. Did "he" call?

"Who?" I asked. (Yes, yes, I knew who he was talking about—he wants me to make that clear.) The guy at church. The…HOT one.

"Oh," I replied. "That one. Actually, yes."

"And?" (There were about fifty question marks after the word when he said it, but I didn't want to put all those in an e-mail.)

I told him that I explained to poor Travis that he'd misunderstood me, that I was married, and happily so.

"You lied to him."

"Did not!"

"You're really happily married to me?"

Ouch. Well, since he mentioned it, hmm…not so much, actually. So anyway, we got into this big argument about why he left for Alaska, why he stayed away so much in KC and whether or not I wished I was free to go out with Travis.

The answers he gave were as follows: because I wanted him to, and because I didn't need him.

The answer I gave was the following: of *course* I didn't wish I was free to date Travis, I hardly even knew the guy, why would I trade in a committed, loving relationship for something so totally wrong, and the only reason it was tempting for even a moment was that I was lonely and missing Tom and tired of feeling like I was raising the kids on my own while he was away all the time, and I didn't understand why he would choose to be away when he had a family waiting for him who loved him and missed him.

(Tom wants to know why it is possible for a guy to answer two questions in a quarter of the space it takes for a woman to answer one. Well…duh! Right, girls?)

So anyway, BIG FIGHT. We started yelling at each other, and everybody was listening and staring. So Jeanine (arrayed in bridal swimsuit of cream, with seed pearls, sequins and satiny skirt) and Morris (in a black Speedo…eww) stormed over and ever-so-politely suggested we join them for the cake cutting.

Unfortunately, we didn't get the hint. All the way over, it was "You're too independent!" "Don't have a choice when you're always gone." "All you want from me is a paycheck every two weeks." "WHATEVER." (Tom says that was my weakest comeback of the evening, and I must agree. Maybe I'm losing my touch.)

So we got over to the cake table. Jeanine had donned a cream-colored pareo over the swimsuit, and Morris had tugged on some shorts, thankfully. While they cut their piece and fed each other, Tom and I carried on an under-our-breath argument:

"You think I'm incompetent."

"Do not."

"Do, too—you even told your friends you thought I was in the way."

"No, it's just that it had been so long since you were home all the time, I'd forgotten what it was like."

Morris cleared his throat, looking meaningfully at us. We smiled and continued muttering.

"What it was like? You mean how unbearable it was."

"How should I know if it was unbearable or not? It hardly ever happened!"

Jeanine said, "Are you two finished?"

"Yeah, Mom." Tom looked back at me. "All I'm saying is that I prefer to be where I feel appreciated and where I can make a valuable contribution."

"And all I'm saying is that it's hard to make a valuable contribution when you're *not around*."

He grabbed my arm. "You aren't listening to me, Dulcie."

"Oh yes, I am, Tom. I hear you loud and clear. You want to be involved in the family, but you're running away, *just like your dad*."

Well, I heard Jeanine give a little strangled yelp, and Tom's face got beet red. I tried to yank my arm away, but he held on too tight. The next time I pulled, he suddenly let go and I stumbled backward.

Right into the cake table. One table leg collapsed and I fell to the ground. I remember it almost like slow motion... the cake slid off the table. Onto my head! The top layer landed in my lap.

I got so mad, I picked up the cake in my lap and hurled it in Tom's face. *SPLAT!* The guy never even saw it coming 'cause he was still stunned from watching the table collapse. For one moment, the topper stuck out from his face like a carrot nose on a snowman. Then it, and a great glob of frosting, slid like an avalanche down his chin and landed on the outdoor turf carpet with an ominous *plop*. As he scooped the goop out of his eyes, it occurred to me at that point that I might not be long for this world. Nobody else moved. Masked with mush, Tom leaned over and grabbed a fistful of cake from behind me...

...and smeared it all over my hair and my face.

"You jerk!" I yelled at him. I got him in a headlock and pulled him down with me. We rolled backward into the debris that used to be my in-laws' wedding cake.

"You're the most self-sufficient, stubborn girl in the whole world!" he shouted as he stuffed cake down my swimsuit.

Jeanine finally found her voice. She shrieked at us to stop it *immediately*. But we were too far gone. All the months of frustration and irritation got taken out on that poor, unfortunate cake!

"And you want everything to be both ways! Valued at home, and yet absent all the time!"

"What's wrong with that?"

Frosting was everywhere now, and we were coated. "Don't you know you can't have your cake and eat it, too?" I yelled.

Suddenly, everyone started giggling. And then there was full-blown laughter. I couldn't figure out why, until Tom started chuckling, too. Then I realized what I'd said. I groaned and laid my head back in all the mush. Tom leaned over me, his face white with frosting.

"Yes, I can," he said, right before he kissed me.

The kiss was sweet and sticky and gooey, and we forgot about everyone else watching us and just kissed and kissed—until I heard my mother-in-law, resignation in her voice, say, "I give up. Let them eat cake!"

Fortunately, there were enough sheet cakes on a different table to feed the guests. I thought for sure Jeanine and Morris would be livid. But they said when you get to be their age, you realize that good entertainment is worth a few wedding cakes now and then. They also came over to us, after we'd showered off all the confection, and presented us with a packet.

"We were talking," Morris said.

Tom asked, "What's this?"

"Our honeymoon itinerary," Jeanine told us. "We want you to go instead."

Tom shoved it back at them. "No way. We aren't taking your honeymoon!"

I shook my head, too.

"You obviously have some issues you need to work out. We figured ten days in Cancún without the kids should do the trick." Morris refused to take back the packet.

"Yeah, well, where are they going to go?" I asked.

Jeanine smiled patiently. "With us, of course."

Tom sputters, "You just got married!"

"What better time to let the girls get to know their new grandpa?" Jeanine said.

Morris glanced from me to Tom and back at me. "Look, five years from now, if our marriage is in the mess yours is in right now, you can repay us the favor. Okay?"

They wouldn't let us talk them out of it. So we took the girls to stay with Grandma and Grandpa and then went home long enough on Sunday to grab our passports and suitable clothing. We got to Cancún on Monday afternoon and are staying in this fabulous beachfront suite, and having the time of our lives. We'll be home a week from today.

You know, at first, I thought Jeanine was crazy for marrying Morris. But seeing how he handled the wedding, and how sweet he was to me and Becky—even after our third-degree interrogation of him (which we're all laughing about now—no hard feelings whatsoever, thankfully)—and his kindness to me and Tom made me just love him. And he's great with Tom. He might turn out to be the good dad my husband always wanted.

And that, my friends, is "what's going on." Gotta go…

From:	Zelia Muzuwa <zeemuzu@vivacious.com>
To:	"Green Eggs and Ham"
Subject:	**NO STINKING FAIR!**

Hey! None of us have gotten a trip to Cancún for fighting with our husbands! Much less, for ruining our MIL's wedding cake! Man, I'm going to go kick some cabinets!

But, Dulcie, before I go, you never said—did you work everything out with Tom? Are you two going to be okay?

Z

From:	Rosalyn Ebberly <prov31woman@home.com>
To:	VIM <vivalaveronica@marcelloportraits.com>
Subject:	**Re: SAHM I Am**

<If I promise to be good and not pester you, could I pretty-please be part of your e-mail loop?>
Oh, Ronnie, y'all are so...*cute.* Okay, fine then. There ya go. (Did I say all that right?)
Rosalyn

"She looks well to the ways of her household, and does not eat the bread of idleness."
Proverbs 31:27 (NASB)

From:	Rosalyn Ebberly <prov31woman@home.com>
To:	SAHM I Am <sahmiam@loophole.com>
Subject:	**[SAHM I AM] I'm Back**

Dearest Loop Sisters (and one biological sister),

I had no idea when I decided to leave this group that it would rend such a hole in your hearts. So many of you have written, practically panic-stricken, at the thought of my departure. What a blessed encouragement to hear how my humble leadership and homey advice have impacted your lives. I'm especially indebted to my sister, Veronica Marcello, who recently joined SAHM I Am for the purpose of following in my footsteps. Her love and friendship is what finally convinced me of the importance of returning to you all.

I promised some people I would be more honest and transparent with you. That doesn't come easy for me, but I will try. So, for starters...I probably missed you more than you missed me. I like to think that you all need me, but the truth is, I need you just as much. Maybe more.

But that's enough vulnerability for one e-mail. A woman can only handle so much change at once, you know.

Love,

Rosalyn

> "She looks well to the ways of her household, and does not eat the bread of idleness."
> Proverbs 31:27 (NASB)

From:	Zelia Muzuwa <zeemuzu@vivacious.com>
To:	"Green Eggs and Ham"
Subject:	**Re: [SAHM I AM] I'm Back**

Well, I never thought I'd live to see the day... She was positively *almost* humble. Whaddya know about that? :)

From:	Dulcie Huckleberry <dulcie@nebweb.net>
To:	"Green Eggs and Ham"
Subject:	**Re: NO STINKING FAIR!**

<Did you work everything out with Tom? Are you two going to be okay?>

Oh yeah, sorta got distracted at that point, didn't I. Sorry to make you wait two days for the answer to that. Although, I thought it'd be fairly obvious. :)

Yes! We worked it out. It turns out, you think I have insecurity and self-image issues? Apparently nothing compared to those of my dear, dear hubby. I found out, while we lay out on the beach and talked and sipped virgin daiquiris, and watched the tide come in, that Tom's biggest fear has always been that he'll be a horrible dad, just like his father. He never had anyone teach him how to be a good dad. So he always felt intimidated by me, because he thinks I've got it all together. (Boy, do I have him fooled or what?) But he *is* good at computers. So he put all his effort into being a good programmer and making lots of money so he could feel like he was doing something right.

Anyway, once I understood where he was coming from, it was no problem to fix all our misunderstandings. He now knows I do want him to be home with us, and that I don't think he's in the way, that I was just blowing off steam to you girls when I wrote that e-mail. In fact, I told him that was my whole problem—I *need* him. I don't think I'd make a very good single mother at all. Having him gone all the time made me feel so lonely. He also knows that sometimes I say stupid things to people that I don't mean, thus the "romance novel" comment. And I now know he *wants* to be with me and the girls, too, and that he just needs a bit more encouragement about his abilities as a good dad and husband.

So, the long and short of it is, as soon as possible he is going to quit his job! Hurrah! No more KC and definitely *no more Alaska!* He talked to Morris, who knows of an opening for a programmer at a company his friend works at in Springfield. He still has to do all the interviewing, and if he gets the job, we will be moving. And if not, he might have to do the consulting job—in Omaha—a bit longer. But we'll figure that out when we come home from our dream vacation.

The rest of how our trip is going? Well, come on! We're at a romantic, exotic beachfront resort in Cancún, Mexico, with no kids! How do you *think* we're doing? You know, every couple should postpone their honeymoon until after they have kids. They'd appreciate it ever so much more.

Gotta run. We're heading out to some Mayan ruins today. And then, we have a moonlight date arranged on the beach. Did I ever tell you how exquisite Tom's backrubs are?
Love and hugs to everyone ('cause I'm overflowing and have plenty to spare),
Dulcie

From:	desperatemom@nebweb.net
To:	SAHM I Am <sahmiam@loophole.com>
Subject:	I'm New

Dear Mothers,
My best friend has been bugging me about joining this group, but I've been refusing because I don't like computers or e-mail. However, the events of the past twenty-four hours have changed my mind.

I decided to purchase a computer after my fiendish nineteen-month-old daughter watched me step out of my house in my pj's and robe this morning to grab the paper and deliberately locked the door behind me and stood making faces at me in the window. It didn't bother her that I am seven months pregnant with her little brother, and had to use the bathroom. I had to knock on neighbors' doors until I found someone home who would let me use the phone to call my husband. The neighbor, a middle-aged man, had a hard time not smirking at my pregnant, waddling, bathrobed predicament. Upon my husband's arrival and unlocking of our door, I entered the house and found said daughter had scattered an entire box of Cheerios throughout my kitchen and living room, including between the couch cushions and in my potted plants.

I decided to get e-mail when I found out my best friend, who was my last link to sanity, went crazy, destroyed her mother-in-law's wedding cake, had a food fight with her husband, and got a trip to Cancún as a reward.

I decided to join your e-mail loop when she told me she and her family are planning to move to Springfield, MO, where her husband's new stepfather found him a programming job and has offered to teach him all the things her husband had wanted to learn from his dad, but hadn't.

She says the friends she's made here have changed her life and helped her be a better woman and a better mother. I'm sure hoping you can do the same for me.

Sincerely,

Marianne Hausten

SAHM I Am
DISCUSSION QUESTIONS

1. With which one of the characters do you most strongly identify? Why? How does that make you feel?

2. The "Green Eggs and Ham" girls (Dulcie, Jocelyn, Phyllis, Brenna and Zelia) have close friendships, despite knowing each other only through the Internet. How do you think they developed that relationship? What are some cultural barriers we face today in forming close friendships? How can we overcome these barriers, and how important is it to do so?

3. Which character is the "voice" of the many expectations placed on women and men? What are some expectations you feel pressured to meet, and how do you feel about this? Where do these expectations come from and why do they exist? How reasonable are they? What do you think can be the result from trying to perform to these standards?

4. During the weekly discussion concerning what books the SAHM I Am loop members are reading, there is a lot of talk about nonfiction versus fiction and the relative merits of each. Compare the attitudes of Rosalyn and Connie on this subject with Phyllis's view of it. What does it mean for a book to "nourish the soul," and what books have you read that have accomplished that in your life? What role, if any, does entertainment play in this nourishing process?

5. During a discussion on what their lives were like before they had children, Phyllis makes this comment: "I love my children. I love my husband. But there are days when I feel like I am living their lives instead of my own. And I have a feeling that some morning, after they're grown or gone, I'm going to wake up and realize my life ended a long time ago, that Phyllis Lorimer died without anyone—including me—noticing." In what ways can you identify with this statement? How can we balance our own individuality and personhood with the demands of caring for our families or fulfilling other

responsibilities? Why is it so difficult to find time to maintain this balance? What happens if we neglect this balance and either live totally for ourselves or totally for other people?

6. What is the source of most of Dulcie and Tom's marital conflicts? If you were Becky (Tom's sister) or one of Dulcie's friends, what advice would you give them about their relationship with each other?

7. Dulcie's self-image is a constant source of stress for her. What aspects of your own self-image are a struggle for you? From where do our unrealistic expectations of ourselves come? What can we do about it? What does Dulcie mean when she says, "There's more to being content with myself than fitting into a certain clothing size"?

8. Think about the characters in this story who have been, or will be, touched by adoption in some form or another. Do you know people who are part of this "adoption triangle"— adoptee, adoptive parent or birth mother? What are some of their feelings about adoption? How are their experiences, or the ones of the characters in this book, different than the typical portrayal of adoption in the media or in books? What do you think about the following conversation between Brenna's husband, Darren, and their daughter, Madeline, regarding her new understanding of adoption?

"Well, I was thinking on the bus about it. And it's sort of like God, you know?"

"God? In what way, squirt?"

"Well, you know, like how God made us part of His family—when we're born again. That's what they say at church. So, are we adopted, Daddy? Are we?"

9. Brenna and Darren struggle with accepting Darren's infertility. Both male and female infertility can be devastating for a couple who desire a child. Why is

this? How do you think our culture (both secular and Christian) views people who are infertile? What should our response be toward someone in this position? How can we create a more accepting and supportive environment for people dealing with this problem?

10. Phyllis and Jonathan are deeply wounded by the church they were serving. In what ways do our churches most commonly wound people? Why does this happen when Christians are supposed to be known by their love? How can we be part of the solution in preventing such wounds from being inflicted? What is the most healthy way to respond when a Christian hurts you? How can we show love and concern for a person who has been hurt by the church?

A NOTE FROM THE AUTHOR

Our current notion of "stay-at-home mom" grew out of the Victorian era of the Industrial Revolution, when it became fashionable for middle-class and wealthy women to stay home while their husbands went off to work. Prior to this, most families, except the upper class, operated cottage industries from their homes, requiring both parents to work together to maintain the business as well as raise children. During the post-WWII years, women were encouraged to stay home in order to create job openings for the men returning from war. The Stay-At-Home Mother became the ideal for motherhood—the calm, gracious, well-groomed perfect housekeeper, always ready with milk and cookies, whose children were the epitome of good manners and obedience.

Is this reality for any of you? Yeah...me neither. Yet, it seems many of us are still trying to attain that myth of domestic perfection, and when we fail, we feel guilty. Let's face it—for a lot of us, being a SAHM is not the Utopia we are often taught to expect. Our tasks are myriad, tedious and repetitive, and the pay is often loneliness, frustration and a sense of failure. The rest of the non-SAHM world tends to view us as pathetic creatures who are wasting our talents and abilities on wiping noses, changing diapers and cleaning house. Honestly, some days, it feels like they're right!

Even though we know in our hearts that what we are doing has incredible value and that staying home with our kids is really and truly a special privilege and blessing, it's often hard to remember this in the middle of a child's temper tantrum or while cleaning up the globs of jelly on the kitchen floor. That's why I wrote this book. Somehow it's easier to handle the challenges of this life when we have someone give us a hug and say, "I totally understand." Consider my story that empathetic hug.

It's hard to be empathetic without being realistic, though. So, in this book, you'll notice that the characters tend to be pretty frank with each other and deal with issues that are as messy as a two-year-old eating spaghetti. I tried not to give easy answers or the typical Christian platitudes most of you are tired of hearing. In fact, my goal wasn't to give answers at all—they're not mine to give. But if you read this story and come away feeling encouraged, understood or having a better comprehension of what being a SAHM is really like, then I've done my job. And if you have a bit of fun in the process, all the better.

I want to give you some additional information regarding a few of the issues in the story. You or your friends may be dealing with these things, and it's nice to know where to find helpful resources. This is by no means a complete list, but it should get you started:

Embryo Adoption: Endorsed by Focus on the Family as an excellent way to provide frozen embryos a chance to be born and grow up, embryo adoption is an ethical alternative to many of the more controversial infertility treatments. The Snowflakes program at Nightlight Christian Adoptions has more information about this unique, beautiful way to build a family, www.snowflakes.org.

Motherhood: Christian Mommies, www.christian-mommies.com. Extensive site with lots of articles, a discussion board and other resources.

Infertility: Hannah's Prayer Ministries—Christian Support For Fertility Challenges, www.hannah.org. This online ministry includes support for both male and female infertility as well as miscarriage, the death of a child, etc.

International Adoption: RainbowKids, www.rainbowkids.com/index.chtml. This extensive Web site is a great starting place to begin researching international adoption and related issues.

Stay-At-Home Mothers: Hearts At Home, www.hearts-at-home.org. This Web site offers a magazine, conference info., bulletin boards and extensive links.

Women: Her Well-Being, e-mail discussion group, www.groups.yahoo.com/group/her-wellbeing. "A practical how-to list for Christian women, offering a listening ear, practical advice and a safe place to talk about 'women's stuff' and share our stories and concerns." Also, Christian Women Today, www.christianwomentoday.com, an extensive Web site with articles, discussion forums, advice columns and just about any other resources to help and encourage women in all stages of life.

E-mail loops like the one in the story can be found for most of these topics and just about any others through Yahoo Groups (www.groups.yahoo.com) and similar sites. You can do a search for your subject and peruse the list of available groups, then subscribe to the ones you are interested in. Some groups are more nurturing and considerate of people's feelings than others, so you might have to try several before finding one that is a good fit for you.

Visit my Web site, www.meredithefken.com, for more information about me, my upcoming books, additional articles and resources on some of these subjects and support for writers. I would love to hear from you and give you the opportunity to receive my newsletter, so please send me an e-mail at meredith@meredithefken.com or snail-mail me c/o Steeple Hill, 233 Broadway, Ste. 1001, New York, NY 10279.

Thank you again for choosing my book to read. May God richly bless you.

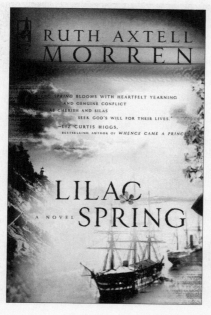

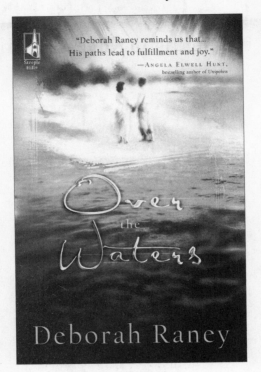

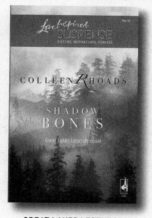

Love Inspired
SUSPENSE
RIVETING INSPIRATIONAL ROMANCE

Her Brother's Keeper

by **Valerie Hansen**

An ordained minister turned undercover investigator is on a mission to uncover the truth about a young woman's past. But can he do that without hurting the woman he's come to love?

Available at your favorite retail outlet.
Only from Steeple Hill Books!

www.SteepleHill.com

LISHBKTR